The Face at the Window

Kiran Manral worked as a journalist with *The Times of India* and *The Asian Age* before she quit full-time work to be a full-time mommy. She was among the top bloggers in India, before she moved on to writing fiction. Her earlier novels include *The Reluctant Detective, Once Upon A Crush* and *All Aboard*. She has also recently authored a book on parenting titled *Karmic Kids: The Story of Parenting Nobody Told You*. She lives in Mumbai with her family and struggles with a serious Nutella addiction.

AMARYLLIS

Copyright © 2016 by Kiran Manral

AMARYLLIS

An imprint of Manjul Publishing House Pvt. Ltd.
• 7/32, Ground Floor, Ansari Road, Daryaganj, New Delhi 110 002
Website: www.manjulindia.com

Kiran Manral asserts the moral right
to be identified as the author of this work

Registered Office:
10, Nishat Colony, Bhopal 462 003 - India

Distribution Centres:
Ahmedabad, Bengaluru, Bhopal, Kolkata, Chennai,
Hyderabad, Mumbai, New Delhi, Pune

ISBN: 978-93-81506-78-3

This edition first published in 2016

The Face at the Window

Kiran Manral

AMARYLLIS

AMARYLLIS

An imprint of Manjul Publishing House Pvt. Ltd.
• 7/32, Ground Floor, Ansari Road, Daryaganj, New Delhi 110 002
Website: www.manjulindia.com

Kiran Manral asserts the moral right
to be identified as the author of this work

Registered Office:
10, Nishat Colony, Bhopal 462 003 - India

Distribution Centres:
Ahmedabad, Bengaluru, Bhopal, Kolkata, Chennai,
Hyderabad, Mumbai, New Delhi, Pune

ISBN: 978-93-81506-78-3

This edition first published in 2016

'I can't go back to yesterday because
I was a different person then.'

– Lewis Carroll, *Alice in Wonderland*

To my mother, Shama Sheikh.
Because you never stopped believing I could.
Even when I thought I couldn't.

Chapter 1

THE MOST DIFFICULT thing to do after a life well lived is to sit down and type it all out. To start with, your fingers are old and gnarled. You can see the skin crinkled up like paper, the knobby knuckles, the veins standing up blue and aggressive, and you wonder, when did your hands change, when did they stop being young and firm and definite, when did the hesitancy creep in, when did the trembling begin. Your mind sieves through memories as thick as molasses and as bitterly sweet. The words trip on your tongue but hesitate to make their way to the page because you debate endlessly in your head about which of them you should put down in print, terrified of the permanency of the written word.

Memories are the kind of elusiveness that shift, change form, and remodel themselves by the second. It is a challenge to wrestle with them, to get them to agree to be analysed, to be put down in words and encapsulated in sentences, moulded into paragraphs. As long as they are shifting, morphing into different things as the moment suits them, they aren't bound by one person's recollection of how things were, of how they happened. These are my memories. And this was my life. And so I try to write this. I am already half way through what I am trying to put down. I have no idea who would want to read the story of my life. But I write it out, more for myself, than for anyone else who would care to read.

'Do you want some tea?' Nina asked, poking her head through the door. Nina was a good girl, my grand daughter. Almost sixteen and with her head already buzzing with secrets, hopes, ambitions and dreams that took her into a place I could not dare to intrude, not even when I tried to tell her that I had been a teenager too, once. And that I knew how confusing things were when one was neither child nor adult, in no man's land that came with its own constitution and rules that no adult or child can hope to ever understand. Of course, to her I was forever a senior citizen.

The only thing Nina had got from me were my eyes, the rest was all her mother, my daughter. Brilliant blue, which could go from twinkling to Arctic glacial in a second. I got them from my mother, I was told. I had never seen my mother in person, only heard about her. And her crisp blue eyes. My own were faded now. Like most of me. It was startling to look at myself in the mirror and see this stranger – wrinkled, crumpled, fragile, hair a shock of white neatly cropped to a crisp chin-length bob. That had been my standard look for the past many decades, I was not about to change it now. And now the hair was a wispy halo around my head. In a stiff wind, I looked like a dandelion head. A flat hair band sometimes gave me dignity, but it weighed me down, and I often went without it. Vanity, I had discovered, was the first affectation to be dispensed with as it got more difficult to live.

'Yes,' I replied. The smile coming unbidden to my face. 'I would love some, my darling. And I would love it if you sat with me while I had it.'

She smiled her half-smile and rushed down. She would return with a tray bearing a pot of tea, some biscuits, a mug of hot chocolate for herself and whatever she could manage to rustle up from the kitchen.

I lived in a cottage on the outskirts of a sprawling tea estate, ambitiously named Windermere, for the past ten years and some more – just me and Manikji, the wizened caretaker who lived in an anteroom with a wife, as wizened as him. They took care of me, and I of them. And when I died, they would continue being taken care of by me. I had ensured that in my will, a copy of which lay with my trusted solicitors, Dewan & Dewan. I trusted them, they had helped me sort out my affairs when I moved here, alone, retired and confused. I trusted them with the execution of my will, not that I had much to leave behind, but I would like to know that in the event I passed away, those who had cared for me would receive their dues.

I shuffled the papers I had typed out through the day and put a paper weight on them. It was one of those glass balls with snow flakes that swirled and twirled around an imposing, turreted castle. I watched as the flakes darted around from the movement, and then settled down, unwillingly, until the next time the paperweight was lifted. I lifted it once more and set it back, watching the swirling speckles within. There was a slight tremor to my hands now that I hadn't noticed a few months earlier, it felt like I was slowly relinquishing charge of my body to a force beyond me, a force called mortality. It was a fight between me and death, a battle to see who would win. In my head and heart I was still young, the body had not yet succumbed to the machinations of time, the heart was not weary, my soul was still restless, still looking for the meaning to it all. The restlessness defined me; the day I stopped searching would be the day I would lie down and die. I was sure of it. Avoiding dying meant to continue being restless, to continue questioning, searching. I had passed on my restlessness to Nina. She had it in her eyes, a searching that couldn't be defined, a searching that was destined to never be fulfilled. I wondered where her searching would take her, she of the bright blue eyes in the dusky face, the slim body with the quick movements that belied her youth and her anxiousness, her shyness that drew a veil over her, enfolding every gesture, every movement in a sort of hesitancy.

She knocked on the open door and entered without waiting for me to reply, bearing a tray laden with a teapot, a cup on a saucer, a mug with hot chocolate and a plate neatly arranged with some biscuits, a couple of sandwiches and two muffins. 'Here, Grams, you've been typing away since morning. In fact, you've been typing away most days I've been here. What is it you're working on?'

She craned her head to check out the typewritten sheets on the table as she passed it.

'All in good time, darling,' I replied. 'Now, could you please pour out some tea for me, my hands are rather cramped with hammering on the keyboard all day and cannot be trusted with a heavy pot. I might just drop it on the floor, smash it to smithereens and get yelled at by Bimla for having stained the wood. Bimla can be quite terrifying. I'm not even wearing my adult diaper at the moment.'

She squealed with laughter. 'Grams, how you exaggerate!' She poured me a cup, without sugar, just the way I liked it, not too strongly brewed, with a squeeze of lemon in it and no milk. Her hands were delicate and soft, hands that had never done any manual work all their life. My hands, at her age, had been calloused and rough from a childhood of scrubbing floors and washing vessels. I looked down at them unwittingly, liver-spotted, the blue veins standing out against the light skin, the fine hair that I no longer bothered defoliating, faded to a dull white, the texture of my skin now blotchy, rough and faintly scaly, a roughness that never ever went away. Even after I gave up doing household chores, my hands were always a give away to my deprived childhood, regardless of the fact that I never did much housework after I became a teacher at Datham Hall, a residential school for girls in a hill town not very far from the one I now lived in. My hands told the story of my life.

I looked at Nina, my grandchild, fondly. Born of my daughter, my only child. My only surviving child, to be more accurate. Millie. Named after my mother, the mother I never knew and had searched for at every stage of my life, Millicent. There was a fierce love that burned me when I first saw Nina, fresh out of her mother's womb, a love, I acknowledged sadly, that I had not felt in the least for her mother when she had been born. To me, the squawking bundle of flesh could not have been more beautiful as she already was, her tiny wrinkled fingers, her flailing limbs, her puzzled gaze, her tawny skin, so unlike mine and her mother's but so like her grandfather's. A grandfather I hadn't spoken to her about, a father her mother didn't know she had, a genetic inheritance that I had kept away from them, a secret that now fluttered within me, begging to be released.

'Nina,' I asked, 'Has there been any mail today? Did you check the box when you went down the lane earlier?'

'Just this,' she replied, handing across an innocuous white envelope while helping herself to a sandwich simultaneously. My name and address were typed on the front, and the post mark said New Delhi. It had no return address. I squinted down at it through my new progressive-lensed spectacles, turned it over in my hands, and slit it open with the brass engraved letter opener I had on my desk. A thick embossed sheet tumbled out, with a handwritten scrawl across its surface.

Dear Mrs McNally,
We have not had the pleasure of meeting ever but I wish to rectify it. I am very unwell and I do not have much time left. Do call me. I would be very honoured to hear from you. There is a lot I need to speak with you about. If you

do not wish to call, I shall understand.
Regards,
Garima

The paper was visibly expensive and handmade, printed with the
name and address of the sender. Garima Devi, a hark back to
another age where privy purses had replaced titles and the nobility
was struggling with the need to merge into a new India which was
a secular, democratic republic.

I placed it back on the table with a trembling hand, terrified to
take my rheumy eyes off it. Garima. I had never met her. The two
years I had been her husband's mistress had plagued me for the
rest of my life. Unknown to her, she had haunted me along with
an all-encompassing guilt that had stayed with me for over four
decades. Ghosts from the past have an uncanny habit of rushing at
you and swarming into your present when you least expect them.
I wondered how she had tracked me down, found my address.
Perhaps she had asked someone at Datham Hall, the school I had
taught at, the school her daughter was in when I met her husband
for the first time, the school I retired from decades later. They had
my postal address and telephone number in their records, in the
event that any of my ex-students wanted to get in touch with me.

'Who is it from?' asked Nina.

'An old friend from Datham Hall,' I replied with a calm I
did not feel. Garima. What did I have to say to her now, after
all these years, and what did she have to say to me? The person
who had connected us was gone. Forever. There was nothing that
connected us anymore. Or was there? I looked at the young girl
sitting opposite me, her brilliant blue eyes blazing into my own
faded blue. She connected us, I realised. I owed it to Nina and to
Millie to call Garima, I told myself for a brave moment before the
cowardice reared its head again. Would I shatter all that they had
constructed about themselves as their sense of self, would they hate

me for the lies I had fed them all these years? Would it be better if I just ignored the arrival of this letter, if I just slipped it into my drawer and shredded it later, when I was alone, when Nina skipped out for one of her random walks around the neighbourhood? I would ponder over what I needed to do with it later, when I had the room and my thoughts to myself. There was this, the notes I was typing furiously, notes that detailed the story I wanted them to know, a story I had moulded to my convenience, one that I planned to seal once I had done writing it and would have my lawyers hand over to Millie when I was dead.

It was strange to have a letter before me that churned my intestines into a terrified froth. I look forward to letters on a regular day. The postman cycles past every day, dropping off newspapers, magazines, letters and bills in the letter box at the gate post, but what I wait for are the letters. From friends, from my daughter in London, who now merely sends a card for my birthday or for Christmas and relies on the telephone for all communication, from old acquaintances in Calcutta, from the nuns at Datham Hall, from my ex-students, the teachers I taught with. There is a charm to letters and cards that emails and SMSes can't ever replicate, you cannot inhale them, drawing the fragrance of the place they have been mailed from, the feel of paper in your hand bearing the weight of the words contained within. You cannot rub your fingers over the paper and visualise the sender, seated at a table, writing, perhaps with a smile on their lips or a frown splitting the brow. You can't see the pressure of the pen on the reverse of the page and imagine the mood the person might have been in when he or she was writing it. Smiley face icons cannot hope to replace words thought out carefully in order to put a smile on the other person's face, the sharpness or the laxity of the handwriting telling stories about the frame of mind of the writer, the smudges on the sheets of paper telling their own stories, blotches where tears might have fallen, hastily scratched out words where another would have been more appropriate, stories that the writer of the letter might not have intended to communicate. I have letters wrapped up in a soft muslin cloth, letters that are unsigned, tied up with a ribbon I had once used to hold my soft, brown hair in place, and had been gently untied by the writer of those letters. Occasionally, I unwrap them and breathe them in, knowing that the molecules from the hand that wrote them might still be scattered on the surface of the paper, a hand that is long dead.

Would things have been different for me if the writer of those letters had not put a gun to his temple and pulled the trigger? Would I have ended up this eccentric old Anglo-Indian woman, alone in a cottage in the foothills of the Himalayas? Would there have been something else to my story, would I have ended up as more than just a forgotten footnote in the history of my own life? Most people in this small hill town assumed I was a widow; I did nothing to correct the assumptions. If you leave assumptions lying around unchallenged and uncorrected, it isn't long before they morph into facts. It was a convenient story, one that didn't need too much detail tacked onto it to embellish it, and had served me well. The people of this town had grown to accept me wandering around, my hat on my head, my eyes squinting against the bright sunlight, on a warm day, when the weather was kind to my knees. Masterni, they called me. Angrez Masterni. Others called me Mrs McNally. The good neighbours from the neighbouring cottages dropped in sometimes, perhaps once in a couple of weeks, waved when passing, or trotted across if I was seated in the verandah or in the garden to exchange a few words. 'Neighbouring' is a relative word. The nearest occupied cottage was a good ten minutes away. The cottage immediately behind mine, reached through a bend in the path that connected both our cottages to the main motorable road was a five-minute walk away, and was occupied by holiday-makers during season, and by those looking for a getaway during off-season, the ghost tourists who wanted their privacy and gave you yours. That was all the contact I had or needed with people.

Some of the other cottages down the road too had been converted into for-hire cottages for vacationers who came and went during peak season. The cottage behind mine had been rented out to a writer in residence for the past four months. He was a journalist, I was told, from Delhi. He was on a sabbatical to finish a book, as Bimla, the harbinger of all the neighbourhood gossip, relayed to me, but I had never actually exchanged a word with him. I had seen him walking past, long and lean-limbed, with hair an unruly mass of shoulder-length curls, and a confused, distant air that kept him preoccupied as he marched down the path that connected our cottages to the main road.

She had pointed him out to me one morning while I was sitting in the verandah with my morning tea. 'Bibijee, peechey waaley cottage mein yeh saab aaye hai.' I looked at him. He had heard Bimla's voice floating over the wind and had smiled at us. I nodded back with a smile and went back to the book I was reading. I saw him occasionally, his backpack slung awkwardly on his back, his stubble deepening in intensity into a full-grown beard, his hair spilling past his ears in curls that grew increasingly riotous, crawling over his collar, touching his shoulders as the months passed. Sometimes he smiled and nodded, but we had never exchanged words. I was not much for exchanging words with people I didn't know; I kept to myself, it was safer, drawing up the blanket of self-absorption around one, keeping one cocooned from whatever it was the other might bring, joy or sorrow.

The occasional call would come from Millie. When she remembered to call, that is. I had a difficult relationship with Millie; there was no love, but instead, a tenuous relationship that went beyond the animosity that had been the mainstay of our early years of getting to know each other. Me, with absolutely no maternal instinct towards her, and she with an ill-disguised tolerance towards me, which in retrospect was justified. Millie led a busy life in London; she was the head of fund-raising at WomenUnity, a UK-based charity that worked towards generating self-employment for women across Asia, Africa and South America. Nina, her daughter, was studying at a boarding school a few odd kilometres and a four-hour drive away from where I lived. Millie had pulled enough strings to get her admitted there, knowing I was barely a few hours away in case of an emergency. The school wasn't the one I had taught at, and the one Millie had spent a few years at, but then Millie didn't have fond memories of those years at Datham Hall.

I wouldn't blame her. Those years of her life had been perhaps the most difficult. Thankfully, they were a part of her past now. The present was better, there was purpose and comfort. And some love too. Nina and I knew that Millie shared a home in South London with a tall, straggly, light-haired man named James who worked as an investment analyst. He had seemed a pleasant if rather dry person with an occasional acerbic, witty remark that would make up for his sterile reaction to most things around him. He had what was almost a borderline fetish for clicking infinite pictures of everything – cracked walls, the wild flowers blooming along the gravel path, flowers that bloomed and died unnoticed, Bimla sitting in the verandah smoking her evening bidi, with her eyes glazed and distant, staring out into the blue sky like she was watching a motion picture play on a screen made of clouds. Sometimes I wondered if I had ever seen him without his DSLR in his hand, except perhaps when he was eating a meal or when he had his glass of Scotch on the rocks in his hand at the end of the day, reflecting amber in the light of the golden bulbs that I refused to replace with the fluorescent in the living room. James had visited me just once, with Millie, the year they went on a trip to Rajasthan. Millie loved the desert. She would go, every year, for a few days to a selection of properties in Rajasthan – palace hotels, wildlife sanctuary resorts, havelis converted into home-stays... she sampled them all. It was the call of the desert in her veins, the part of her she didn't know about and I'd had no courage, all these years, to tell her about.

Nina, down for a few days of a mid-term break, kept herself busy going through the books on the shelves in my study and walking around the paths on the estate in the evenings. Unlike other teens, she had no desire to go to the disco or shopping or hang out at malls and such which would have made staying in an isolated cottage in a hill town the kind of nightmare to send a regular child run screaming to the authorities about emotional torture. She loved this, the slow passing of the days. And when it was time for her to go back to school, I would hire a tourist vehicle and drop her back myself. But for the few days or so that she was with me I was happy. I was content.

My routine remains constant, I rise every morning sharp at six, force of habit from the years of living in a boarding school, regardless of whether it was summer or winter, no matter what the temperature outside. I would bathe, dress with care, put on my lipstick, bright red if you must know, sit down to breakfast and then get to my study to write or read. Occasionally, some kids from the worker's quarters down the road would come home and I would help them with their school work. This happened in the early evening, just before tea time. I had taught some of them before, at the education centre in the tea estate a little further down the road, for a few years before the effort of walking all the way got to me. I was a woman of routine, and I was lucky enough to have a place of my own to adhere to that routine.

'What are you writing about, Grams?' Nina asked again, clearing out the tea tray, scarfing down unfinished sandwiches with the confidence a young metabolism has of burning them off with minimal effort. It was delightful to see that Nina enjoyed her food – the articles about young girls starving themselves to a ridiculous size zero worried me.

'What am I writing about?' I repeated, sighing deeply enough to rustle some papers. 'The story of my life. It is saucy, racy and filled with drama enough to make a movie of it.' Her eyes widened. I laughed. 'Nothing quite so interesting, darling. I'm just sorting out my memories. Writing for myself. Trying to capture what I remember of what I've lived, trying to make sense of it all.'

Her brow furrowed, she looked at the papers with a quick glance. 'Can I read it?' she asked hesitantly. I shook my head.

'Not now. Perhaps when I'm done,' I said, keeping my empty cup back on the tray.

'Not many days left now, love. I've lived my life, and now, am waiting for the call to come. I hope your grandfather is still waiting for me up there, and hasn't found a new love interest.'

Her face crumpled a bit when I said that and she bounded up to hug me, 'Don't talk like that, Grams, nothing is ever going to happen to you.' I hugged her back.

'No, my love. Nothing is ever going to happen to me.' But I could feel a sudden clenching of my gut as I said that. I didn't believe those words. I could feel the skin falling away from my bones, the body shrivelling up, the life force slowly drawing up in me, like it was gathering its strength before a final break from the body. Death was circling me, miasmal and fetid. I could feel it around me, in the way the mornings seemed more like a surprise, like I had been granted a reprieve, an extension. I had stopped believing in God when I was around thirty. But sometimes, unbidden, snatches of the Lord's Prayer rose to my lips. Religion stays with you long after you have lost faith, buried somewhere in your subconscious, waiting to rise and take over your need to turn over your cares to a higher power who could bring forward resolution. For me it was the growing up in a convent that paradoxically turned me away from religion. I was born of sin, I was a spawn of immorality, I was born out of wedlock and being told that constantly was enough to warp one's self-image forever and make one reject the morality enforced on one through religion.

The nuns had no clue about my parentage – I was found wrapped snugly on the convent steps, I'm told, one dark night, with the wind chilly and fierce and the moon large and shining straight on the steps I was placed on. It reflected off my eyes as they stared wide and clear at the nun who answered the clanging bell that had been rung by an unseen hand. 'You didn't cry,' Sister Julianne always told me, 'You just kept staring at all of us with your big, blue eyes.' I don't cry even today, I just keep looking out into the world with my blue eyes, now just that bit rheumy and blurred, with the wire-framed spectacles a permanent fixture on the bridge of my nose.

It has been sixteen years since I retired as a teacher from Datham Hall. I've lived all those years out here, in this peaceful cottage on the hills, surrounded by green as far as the eye can see, and a crisp blue to the horizon on a clear day, the blue so crisp that the eyes hurt. The eyes, they hurt a lot now, bright lights make me wince. I just had a complete medical checkup at the local pathological laboratory and showed my doctor the reports.

'As strong as a horse,' Dr Sanyal had said, scanning the sheets of typed figures. 'Your sugar and cholesterol levels are under control. Your blood pressure is slightly elevated, I suggest we monitor it for a while before deciding whether to change your medication. Apart from that, you're in good shape for your age.' Yes, the knees ached a bit when I walked more than it was absolutely essential but I expected that.

The heart, it still beats stoically in my ribcage, but it knows its time is up. Strange how the repository of one's existence is one's heart, when all the heart does is pump the blood through the body. Not the soul that puts the life force into the body. The soul is intangible, it floats beyond oneself. It returns, pulled back by threads of loves, old and new, of the lives connected with one, of the belief that no, it isn't time yet. The heart would beat on until the moment it decided it had done quite enough beating for a lifetime. A miracle organ, the heart, constantly beating through sickness, through health, through wakefulness, through sleep, through sorrow so terrible you think it would stop then and there, and through joy so intense you wish it would stop right then to freeze that moment forever. It beats on, regardless. And when it finally does stop, so does the body. Switched off, like a machine, the engine that powered it shuddering to a halt. The life force swirling away into the ethers, wherever it was that life forces went after the body had perished. Right now I am alive. The heart is beating, the soul is still restless, the feeling that there is more to come niggles. What more though, I don't know.

So I hugged the child and sent her down to the kitchen to keep back the tray and the uneaten sandwiches and to tell Bimla that dinner would be plain stew and bread, unless Nina felt like having something more substantial and as usual, dinner was to be served at seven sharp. Keeping a routine gave me purpose. Else, it all whirled into one unformed whole where time weighed down on me, just an interminable waiting, waiting for it to get over, to move on to the next realm, the next phase of consciousness.

I sat back at my desk, tucking the letter I had received this day carefully into a drawer, hiding it beneath a sheaf of newspaper clippings. I put my fingers on the keys of my old, battered Olivetti portable, a typewriter that had travelled with me from Calcutta when I was in my early twenties and had been learning how to type and which had remained with me, steadfast in its devotion, till I reached the end of my days, now. The day had passed. And I wondered if I should switch to the computer as Millie kept exhorting me to, but we had power cuts, and the inverter wasn't always reliable. For now it was the trusted Olivetti, and the spool of typewriter ribbon that inked my fingers when I changed it.

The R key stuck as I typed, and every R in my manuscript was at an awkward crooked angle to the rest of the text. I liked that, it added some distinction to what seemed like rows on rows of regular words. I picked up where I had left off, banging away at the keys, unaware that the evening had dimmed into night and that someone had stepped into the room, unnoticed, and switched the lights on. It had to be Nina and not Bimla. Bimla avoided climbing the stairs if she could help it. Despite her mountain stock genes, she had knee joints that had been worn out from years of climbing steep trails. She announced herself coming up the stairs long before she entered the room, with the creaking of the stairs and her breath coming in audible gasps that penetrated wooden doors. Bimla too had grown old like I had, from the time she and her husband had joined my new household almost a decade and a half ago. They aged early, the hill women, the sun carved lines like maps into their thin, papery skin, the toil of their early years and the lack of an adequate diet bent their bones and wore out their knees.

Manikji and Bimla had been with me since the day I had taken up residence in the cottage on the recommendation of Colonel Dayal, the estate manager of the adjacent estate who had popped around to say hello, and helped me move the two trunks I had with me into the house. On learning I planned to live on my own, Colonel Dayal, Rtd, for that was what his card announced him as, kindly offered to help me find house-help, and produced Manikji and his wife Bimla at my doorstep by the end of the day. They needed somewhere to stay, and food. Manikji, due to a heart attack a few months ago, could no longer do the heavy labour needed at the estate. In his kind way, Colonel Dayal saw this as a way to benefit both of us. Manikji and Bimla were childless and didn't want to return to their village, where they had no land of their own and the family home was over run with his brothers and their children and grandchildren. This was a perfect solution. One that gave me support in a strange place, and put a roof over their head and food in their belly. In exchange for which they would manage the housework for me, do the cooking, with Manikji free to take some odd jobs around the place to earn a bit of extra income. It was an arrangement that remained unchanged since the day it was instituted. And now, after a decade and a half, the home was as much theirs as it was mine. I couldn't contemplate living without the couple to help me get through the day. Tiny as the cottage was, it took a great deal of work to keep it in running order, and I was quite finicky about dust and cobwebs and neatness. The terrified orphan raised in the convent was always lurking around within me, quick to wipe a surface clean before it got noticed, fearing the wrath of a disapproving finger run over a corner to check for dust.

My story had to be put down, as quickly as I could, before my fingers refused to type anymore. And like every story, it has a start and it will have an end. I don't have the end yet. I don't know how it will end yet. Me, sitting in this room, on this isolated road deep in the foothills of the Himalayas, on the fringes of a bustling tourist town, with the rain pouring down outside, a steel grey sheet, and the typewriter clicking under my fingers, the snowy wisps of smoke coming out from the chimneys of the little houses along the winding road, curling up towards the heavens and getting battered down by the incessant grey rain. My joints had begun aching again, a sure pointer to the dampness and chill that was setting itself into the air, in preparation for the winter to come, bringing with it the fog, the swirls of icy wind, the grey days when you looked out in front of you and saw nothing but miles of nothingness.

But there was time for winter yet. Right now, it was still the crispness of autumn setting in, cloaking the trees with a dappled, fiery blanket of red and gold. The leaves would shrivel up and fall, littering the pathways and open land. The leaves that survived autumn would freeze in winter and fall off, their life's purpose served. We had electrical heaters now and a wonderful hot blanket that kept me warm as much as it could through the knife-edged cold that cut through the skin and pierced the lungs, putting in pneumonia and bronchitis and the dry, racking cough that ate away the lungs so that year by year one crumpled into oneself like the shadow of the person one used to be.

Dare I call Garima? Dare I open the gates to the ghosts of a past I thought long buried? Or should I close the door behind me, and move on, without rippling the smooth flow of the lives I was leaving behind. More importantly, would I live out another winter? Would I complete my story?

Chapter 2

THERE WAS AN evil wind howling through the undulating hills that night, rattling the loose panes in the windows of the cottage, keeping me up all night. Unbidden, the Lord's prayer came to my lips, *Our Father who art in heaven, hallowed be thy name...* I said it moving my lips silently, as I had all those years ago, on my cold hard bed in the convent back in Calcutta. Praying didn't come easily to me anymore, I had to hack out the words from deep within myself, but it brought me solace. It warmed a part of the soul that I long thought had shrivelled up and died.

I grew up with prayer, it was difficult not to when one was growing up in a convent, surrounded by threats of hell and brimstone and the overwhelming guilt that one was inherently evil being drilled into our brains by the nuns. They might have been well-meaning in order to keep a bunch of unruly children in line, but ended up scarring us with a concept of a vindictive God one could never really love. I checked the alarm clock with the large digital numbers I kept at the table by my bedside, the one that had been given to me by a student whose father owned a watch showroom in

Delhi – Mona Sahni. I remembered every student by their complete name. I wondered where Mona Sahni was, if she still cocked her head and squinted her eyes when she was getting a dressing down. I wondered if she still had the lovely fringed lashes that framed her eyes like an Oriental fan. Some children you regret losing contact with, they stay back in your mind like unbidden guests, popping up when you least expect them.

Stormy nights always marked something momentous in my life, I thought. I wondered what tonight would bring. I remember a particularly stormy night when I was around fourteen. I had just got into my bed after the sparse dinner of broth, bread and kedgeree, my stomach still rumbling for more, pulled the thin covers over my face, terrified of the thunder and lightning smashing the skies together and dragging them apart, like a pair of growling monsters engaged in a battle unto death. I always slept like that, it kept the monsters away, the sleep monsters that crept into my head through my ears and took over my dreams. I had barely begun to drift off to sleep, when I felt a hand on my shoulder shaking me not too gently. 'Wake up, child, wake up.' Sister Julianne was looking down at me, her wimple firmly lodged on her scalp with not a strand of hair visible, seeming to all purposes like a steam ship, with her overflowing chin and stomach filling out her habit with the kind of insouciance that was ill-suited to one who had devoted herself to a life of deprivation and service to the lord. 'Come with me,' she said, stationing herself over my narrow bed, with the trunk under it bearing the handful of my worldly possessions. 'We have some visitors who want to meet you.'

The rains were lashing the convent. The wide grounds, carefully nurtured by the gardeners, were a hopscotch of muddy pools as far as the eye could see, the window panes were rattling in their frames with a fury that suggested demonic possession. It was an evil night. The thought of someone beyond the thick stone walls of the convent knowing about me and coming across in such horrible weather to meet me had me totally confused and disoriented. I got up, tucked the bedsheet back in neatly, by force of habit, slipped my feet into a pair of worn slippers I had hand stitched back to functionality many times over, and which were a size smaller than what would have been ideal for my feet, and followed Sister Julianne as she led me out of the dormitory where all us orphans and charity boarders lived together. I could see heads popping up in curiosity as we passed.

It wasn't the norm for any of us to be called out after lights-out at nine in the night. The convent didn't get visitors at night. The nuns woke up at five a.m. for the morning prayers and then school began at seven-thirty, with the day scholars and boarders mingling for those few hours that school was on. By lunch time, classes would end for the first batch of students and the primary students would come in for their classes which ended at five-thirty p.m. Post classes there was the cleaning of the classrooms, the kitchen duties, the evening prayers, the dinner to be served on the huge wooden dining table with the thirty-two chairs, the washing up to be done.

We went through the long corridors, past the doors to the living quarters of the nuns, past the common dining hall, all the while the questions thudding incessantly in my chest about who it was that had come to meet me. I didn't dare ask Sister Julianne; I had learnt well enough about speaking only when spoken to and not asking too many questions. The nuns had canes they used if they decided you were getting beyond what they considered appropriate behaviour and this included asking too many inconvenient questions, and I had been at the receiving end of more canings that I could care to remember, the palms and the back of my calves still bore scars that were a testimony to this. Some weeks there was hardly time for the old welts to soothe down before new ones were planted on them. The skin on the back of my calves was thickened over with the canings, the palms of my hands, were coarsened with work and raps from the wooden ruler by the class teachers.

'Hurry up, child,' she chided me. 'Don't drag your feet.'

The rain was still heavy outside as we turned into the cosy parlour that was used to receive visitors. The room was lit up with yellow bulbs shining in old glass lamps, cracked and slightly faded, dusty with the neglect of being far out of reach. There were two people sitting on the settee, their backs towards the door, a male and a female, beyond middle age by the salt and pepper in their hair. The male rose and turned to the door as we entered and the female inclined herself into a silhouette towards us.

'There she is,' the man said. Now that I could see his face, I realised he was old, his face lined with care and tanned to a careworn leather by the sun. He was dressed in a sharp grey suit, broad-shouldered and sharp-featured. You could see that he had been handsome in his youth, and still retained the lingering awareness of that handsomeness. The lady was fragile, beautiful, clear-skinned and gentle, her eyes big and searching, and filled with tears as she saw me enter. The old gentleman put his hand on her arm and patted her. She rose, her soft silk sari making a swishing sound as the fabric of the pleats rustled against each other, and carefully made her way towards me, her hands outstretched.

I looked at Sister Julianne. She smiled at me, and pushed me forward. 'These are your grandparents. They've come a long way to see you, from a tea estate from near Darjeeling, a place closer to Kalimpong they tell me.' My grandparents? Where were my parents? Who were my parents? Why had my grandparents come now, after all these years, when I was grown and ready to move out into the world? Why had they not rescued me when I was a child? I stumbled towards them, uncertain of how I was to greet these strangers who called themselves my grandparents, no instant love or bonding in my heart. I knew, even back then, that love did not spring naturally in the human breast; it lurked, hidden in the shadows, waiting to emerge and flood the heart when one was least aware of its presence and least likely to offer any resistance.

The lady wrapped her arms around me and stared at my face intensely, almost as if she was imprinting my face on her mind. I was already the same height as she was – I would eventually grow to be much taller than she was, over the next few years. The elderly gentleman patted my head delicately, with a strange hesitancy, as though he was terrified I would crumble to powder beneath his touch. Perhaps it was the hesitancy of unfamiliarity. 'Yes, she does have something of his features, but her complexion, that's all her mother,' he said with what seemed like a touch of regret. 'What little I can remember of her mother, that is, after all these years.'

'We're so sorry,' he added, now speaking directly to me. 'We didn't know of your existence, not until a month ago.' This felt like a story out of one of those books I had read in the library during the long days when school was out and basic duties were done and I had nothing to occupy myself with, except running away into different worlds, where I could imagine I was a lost princess and someday my family would find me. And so, it would seem, they had.

'Come, sit next to me, child,' said the lady. Her face was gentle, but wreathed with sadness. 'You must be wondering where we were all this while, and why have we suddenly come here out of nowhere.'

I had questions, many questions bubbling inside me. Mother Superior came into the room to introduce herself to my newfound grandparents, Raja Chaudhuri and Nirmala Devi, his wife. Their son, Rameshchandra Chaudhari, was my father. Was. He was no longer alive, they told me. He had died of a brain fever a few months ago and had on his deathbed confessed to his parents about his daughter being in a convent in Calcutta. A daughter he had conceived illegitimately with Millicent Jones, a stenographer at their Calcutta office. They had no idea what became of Millicent, my mother. 'She left the country after you were born,' my grandfather told me. 'She gave you to the nuns and went abroad, to create a new life for herself. My son never contacted her, he was too ashamed.'

At fourteen, I did not know what that shame was, a shame that came from not having the moral courage to own up to one's mistakes. At seventy-eight, I knew that shame only too well. I lived that shame every single day of my dying years.

I would piece together the relationship between my parents much later, through conversations with the staff at the Chaudharipore Estate's office in Calcutta, comprising a typist and a peon, and a manager who had seen my father grow from a stripling boy to a young man with a tea business to manage. He had a balanced head that unfortunately got swayed by a momentary dalliance begun in a moment of indiscretion, which would eventually become the one thing that would haunt him for the rest of his life. My father did get married to a suitable girl chosen for him by his parents and lived out a few years playing at being a householder, but the docile, young girl in a sari would remain just a momentary prop in his life, a prop who passed away during a long and painful labour, made worse because her husband showed interest in neither her well-being nor that of the child pushing weakly out of her. The baby got stuck in the birth canal and both mother and child died before the nearest doctor could cycle up from his home a few kilometres away from the estate. That was all I knew about my father's story, and I knew even less about my mother.

My grandmother would have been amazed that I ended up here, on the outskirts of a plantation, at the other end of the country, given that all I had wanted in the years I lived with her was to escape back to the city. Life turns and comes full circle, one returns to one's beginnings in some form or the other. For me it was this silent home, in the middle of nowhere, where the night sounds echoed in the stillness outside, like it had so many years ago at the estate in Chaudharipore, terrifying me, a city-bred girl, with its absolute isolation.

It was still raining here, outside my little cottage in this lonely stretch of road. A steady drip above my head alerted me to the fact that the roof could be leaking again and we might see a puddle on the landing in the morning. I picked up the bedside clock and pressed a button on the top to check the time. It lit up as if by magic and showed me that it was three-fifteen a.m. The witching hour. The dream demons had never quite left me, but now they seemed to have settled themselves comfortably in my brain, clearing out nooks and crannies where they made themselves at home and surfaced now and then to give me a dream that would have me spring up from a supine position, with my heart slamming into my ribcage and then thudding violently enough to cause a physical ache in my chest.

Thunder was rolling through the mountains, making the windows rattle in their loose panes and lightning jagged virulently, splitting the skies into an apocalyptic chiaroscuro of light and shade, of hope and despair, a mottled landscape of an alien world beyond the clouds where lives were not mortal and death was not final. A chill crawled up my spine. An unexpected sound made me sit up in bed, it sounded like a rap. I put my spectacles on and gingerly moved my legs out of the warm bed. I like to think I am spry for my age, but sometimes my joints let me down, they lock into painful rigidity and render me immobile for a while, until they finally concede to let me move again. Today was one of those days. I had to wait for the spikes of pain to slowly dissolve and the joints to flex before I could get my body to rise, for the knees to take the weight of the torso, now rapidly shrinking into slack skin over bone. Old age is cruel, the mind moves faster than the body does, one feels trapped inside an unresponsive bodysuit not of one's choosing, crumpled, creaky, a mockery of what one once was. I clutched the side table for support and wrapped the warm flannel robe kept on the chair by the bedside around me and belted it, noting absently to myself that the belt was taking up less space than it normally did, I was shrinking into myself. I heard it again, the rap at the window pane, or was it hailstones that made the sound? No, this was just one rap, sharp, clear, defined and insistent, not the shower of knocks one associated with the occasional rain of hail. I pulled the curtains to a side and looked out through the glass at the rain pelting down fiercely, making the dark outside a nowhere land of blackness. And then the rap again, inches from where I stood, startling me out of my skin.

'Who is it?' I asked, moving again to open the window. 'Kaun hai?'

I put my head out, the raindrops fell on my spectacles, obscuring my vision for the instant. There was no one to be seen. No one. Just the blackness of the night, obliterated by the sheet of rain falling grimly, blurring a view already obscured by the pitch blackness of the night and the cloying pervasiveness of the fog. I put my head back into the room, away from the water pouring outside, and closed the windows. Lightning flashed again and a face stared at me from the window, pressed against the sheet of glass. A face that seemed disturbingly familiar, but appeared uncertain of being welcomed. A face with glistening, red eyes that pierced right through me, she stood there... suspended in mid-air.

My window overlooked a drop. There was no way any person could have stood there. I gasped, a choked, clawing gasp, and stumbled backwards into the room unable to tear my eyes off her. My leg caught the edge of the rocking chair, and I fell hard and noisily onto the floor. I felt my ankle twist beneath me and a searing pain stabbed my ribs, making me scream out loud. The face at the window floated as I looked on, too terrified to take my eyes off her. I could hear her voice in my head, calling out my name in a sibilant tone, a voice that was not human, a voice I could hear but not with my ears. I opened my mouth to scream but no sound emerged. I could hear sounds of people stirring out of their beds, feet rushing along the passage, the click of a light switch, and hushed voices asking what had happened. An urgent knocking on the door. The hands from the red-eyed thing at the window reached in and closed around my neck. A high-pitched scream was the last thing I heard before the world went black on me. It was my own.

Chapter 3

I WAS FIFTEEN and back at my grandparent's tea estate, wandering through paths that were deserted, except for the insects crawling on them above the earth and the reptiles slithering beneath. Dusk fell around me, sudden and immediate, the sounds of the night began creeping up. I was stumbling across what I hoped was the direction home but was in fact taking me further into forest territory, where the mid-level tea shrubs gave way to taller trees, denser, casting shadows that moved as the wind charged through their leaves. The main bungalow had disappeared from view and I was moving through another direction, one I had not explored before, where the workers' cottages thinned out and the dense thicket of the forest began taking over the sloping, steep terrain. The gentle gurgle of the stream I was familiar with was harsher, threatening. The ground was damp and squelchy; my feet sank in with each step, unexpected rocks and stones piercing my thin-soled shoes.

Why had I drifted away from the path, why had I gone deeper into the estate than I should have, I didn't know. I could feel the prickly bramble in the undergrowth tearing at my skin, the thin

canvas shoes I had on were little protection against the sudden, sharp
stones that dotted the narrowing path. I needed to bathe in salt.
The thought of leeches attaching themselves to my skin made my
heart thud in my chest. I imagined the sharp bite of the creatures
as they sank their teeth into my skin, sucking out my blood until
they grew plump and slimy and drained me of all the blood in my
body, till my fingernails and lips turned blue and my eyes rolled
up in their sockets. I screamed in terror as the misty fog rose up
before me, wrapping me in it, much like a python would wrap itself
around its prey, crushing its ribs, asphyxiating it, before swallowing
it up whole. And there, in the thick of the dark forest, right in front
of me, she loomed, smiling, a sickly smile filled with evil promise,
her eyes red slits of fire, her arms outstretched in what was almost
a loving embrace and I ran straight into it... that face centimeters
away from mine, the stench of death and decomposition flooding
my nose, entering my lungs, choking me. Then blackness, deep,
long, interminable blackness.

'Grams, Grams!' Nina's voice, worried and on edge, woke me
out of what seemed to be a deep dream but I could still smell
decaying flesh on me. I opened my eyes to find myself in my
familiar bed in my bedroom with the cabbage-rose-printed curtains
with lace tattings edging them on the window, all as cheerful as
I remembered.

'Yes, yes, Nina,' I said faintly, the energy drained out of my voice,
as though I were hearing it from a distance. 'I'm okay, I'm okay.'

I looked around me, blinking hard, feeling my eyes dry and
painful from having been shut for so long that the light pouring in
from the open window hurt and I shut them again, opening them
gently, bit by bit until I could take in the glory of a bright day.
Everything around me was familiar, yet tinged with a fractional
unfamiliarity. A patina of strangeness hung over the entire room. The
room smelt exactly like a crisp morning should, the stench of decay
which had invaded my nostrils was slowly replaced by the smell of

autumn segueing into winter, tinged with the acridness of piles of leaves being burnt in some distant corner of the path mingled with the sharpness of a clear day outside. It had long stopped raining, I realised. The storm had spent its wrath, the sun had emerged and was shining down in a blaze of fury, determined to soak up as much dampness as it could from the glistening mountain slopes.

'What day is it today?' I asked.

'Saturday,' she replied, stroking my forehead with hands that were soft and gentle and unbearably maternal for a girl her age. 'It's eleven in the morning. You've been in and out of consciousness for a couple of days now. You were running a high fever, delirium Dr Sanyal said it was,' she said, her expression older than what should have been appropriate for her age, anxiety mixed with fear, an expression I had never seen before. I squeezed her hand firmly, realising that there was a weakness to my grip that hadn't been there before.

'You scared me, Grams.'

'Ah, my child,' I beckoned her nearer to hug her, with arms that strangely seemed to not want to move on their own volition, and felt like I was struggling against a buoyant force to manipulate them. 'Come,' I tried to inject some cheerfulness into my voice, 'Let me freshen up and have some food, I'm famished.'

She laughed in relief, checking my forehead to see if the fever had really left me. 'Grams, I thought we were going to lose you,' she said in a strangled voice. 'You were conscious but it was like you were somewhere else, in some other place, sometimes with your eyes wide open, and you weren't responding! It was really scary.'

I drew her close to me and hugged her. I was blessed to have a grandchild who cared so much about me. Most current-day teenagers wanted nothing to do with their grandparents, and considered them inconvenient appendages to their lives. 'I feel perfectly fine now. Whatever that fever was, it has left me.' A face swam into my mind's eye. I shut my eyes and tried to wish it away, the hollowed out cheeks, the pale skin, the red glinting eyes, spitting out fire at me from the abyss of flames it contained within it.

A sudden, vicious twinge in my ankle made me wince as I tried to sit up. 'What has happened to my ankle, Nina?' I asked, pulling at the covers, realising that I might not be able to have it bear my weight as I struggled to get to the bathroom, which was a little distance away from my bedroom, down through the corridor. The foot was swathed in a crepe bandage and looked scarily swollen.

'It looks worse than it is, Grams, don't look at it,' Nina said, helping me up and arranging the sheets fussily around my foot again. 'I need to bandage it again, I planned to do that once I'd sponged you.'

Thankfully, it just seemed like a nasty sprain, according to the doctor, she told me as we moved down the passageway to the bathroom. The doctor had called in a van with a portable X-ray machine from the newly established chrome-and-glass fronted diagnostic centre that had been inaugurated with much fanfare by the local politician currently in power. I wondered how much it had cost and what I owed the doctor. A retired teacher's pension did not run to such luxuries and I dreaded asking Millie for funds to cover these exigencies.

'At your age the bones won't heal, and that would lead to you being bed ridden and all the resultant complications that ensue.' I had been delirious, she told me. And I had called out names. I'd cried, she told me, in my sleep. 'Big gasping sobs. And you called out to Vijay. Who is Vijay?' she asked me, a small frown creasing her forehead, the floppy fringe she insisted on cutting herself, falling across it uncertainly, like the rest of her.

I shook my head and raised my brow, 'I can't remember. It could be Amitabh Bachchan. I used to be quite a fan of his movies.' I was not about to elaborate further, not right now. The letter tucked in the drawer of my desk upstairs, hidden beneath a pile of newspaper clippings about Datham Hall came back to my mind. And the face I had seen before I passed out that stormy night took over. An involuntary shudder ran down my spine, setting the fine hair on my arms on edge.

Nina reached across and pressed the bell she had insisted I got fitted next to the bed the last time she had visited me. Bimla came bustling into the room, exclaiming loudly and joyfully at seeing me sitting up and looking as healthy as I could after being semi-conscious for two days, thanking a pantheon of gods and promising bells at temples and a ten-rupee coconut at each, which was a generous bargain on her behalf given that I barely paid her enough to save.

'Dr Sanyal is due today around noon, but right now I'm going to help you get to that door and be waiting outside it.' Nina was a stubborn child, for fifteen. Rather like I was at her age.

'Did you tell your mother about my fall?' I knew, without waiting to hear her reply, that my daughter would not have had the time or the inclination to enquire about my well-being over the telephone. Nina nodded and said nothing.

I hadn't been a good mother to Millie. I had given her up when she was born. At that point, I had thought it was for the best. In retrospect, I realised I had just been cowardly. It was amazing how life came full circle, despite oneself, how all the patterns repeated themselves, condemned to live out some karmic dance of souls that never found resolution despite the changed circumstances. She was playing the same absent parent with Nina. But yes, with me around, Nina would have a grandmother to love her. Millie hadn't had either. No one, just an ever-changing retinue of foster homes. Was it any wonder she had grown up to be the detached, clinical person she was?

Bimla bustled in with a tray full of assorted biscuits and a pot of tea. Nina carefully poured out the tea and handed me a biscuit, from the pack that told me it was good for digestion. It felt strange to nibble, the mouth had an acrid taste to it from not having brushed or eaten in a few days. The acridity was infusing the biscuit with a strange flavour it surely did not possess. I needed to brush my teeth, thankfully most of which were still my own. I put the half-eaten biscuit back in the plate on the tray placed carefully by my side and made to get up. The foot yelled in staunch protest.

'Grams,' Nina said sternly, 'Stay put, please. What is it that you want to do?'

'I need to go to the bathroom, Nina,' I replied. 'And that is something I must do on my own.' I wondered, with a faint flush of embarrassment, whether I had wetted and soiled myself in the two days I was in and out of consciousness and if I had, who had cleaned me.

She had the grace to look a little embarrassed and helped me to my feet, where I tested the twisted ankle and winced a little as it protested. The body took its time to heal when one had reached my age. The knees protested loudly after having been immobile for two days; they refused to take the weight of my body and buckled under me. I grabbed the jamb of the door for support and tried to make it on my own. To my shock, I couldn't. Nina sprang to her feet and helped me to the tiny bathroom in the corridor. As I passed the window rapped by the creature that night, I looked out, feeling an unmentionable chill tap-dance up and down my spine. It was a scene I looked out on every morning, but today it seemed different, almost like one was looking at it through a filter that infused an element of strangeness to it.

A gentle autumnal sun was shining outside. To the left of the window, the green expanse of a well-cared-for lawn and a tiny patch of garden ended with a tidy gravel path which in turn led onto the little driveway for the occasional car leading onto the main road. Straight ahead was the open expanse of view to the grey and brown mountains streaked with white at their tips, where nothing could have stood, given there was nothing there to stand on, except a rolling gentle drop. The scene looked back at me, like it always did, with no trace of the pale-faced woman who hung in the sky above it that stormy night, floating to the window, pressing her face against it, looking at me with eyes that were long dead.

I sat on a stool in the bathroom, the high one I used for bathing, and splashed some water on my face; it was icy cool. The effort to move myself from the bed to the bathroom had exhausted me. My face, which was already shrinking into itself, seemed even more skeletal this morning, the skin hanging looser around my neck, soft folds that moved when I turned my head. The circles under my eyes were stained blue, angry, and I saw, on my neck, faint imprints of what could be finger marks, faded now, but real. I looked again, touched them. This was what was making my neck feel painful. I brushed my teeth and washed my face again, looking back at the stranger in the mirror who mocked me, for thinking I would look back at myself as I was, firm fleshed and beautiful, with my piercingly blue eyes not yet faded to an indeterminate shade of sludge grey blue. This was an old woman looking back at me, this couldn't be me. But it was, I knew, I had lived my life and I had nothing to show for it except this child waiting outside the bathroom door, having warned me to not lock the door, waiting to rush in should I call for help, should I fall.

It was also time for Nina to return to school the next day, her mid-term break was nearly up, I realised. I would have to go on that long drive to drop Nina back to the care of her house parent. I didn't dare send her unescorted or by train and bus. There was too much in the newspapers about the terrible things happening to young girls in the country and this hitherto calm and placid hill town had recently seen a tourist gang-raped by a bunch of locals who had offered to help her find a hotel.

I freshened up and limped out slowly, holding on to every solid support available at every step. This new frailness annoyed me. Nina had kept a dress out for me to change into and helped me into it without making a fuss over me or the leg, the way I liked it. I didn't dare get into trousers yet, though I had begun preferring trousers to dresses around the time I hit my forties, finding them much more convenient to move about in. I limped over to the small table and two chairs by the window where she had set up the tray and sat myself down gingerly, looking outside, wondering about what I had seen, what had brought that on. Nina moved a small stool so I could lift my bandaged leg and keep it propped up. She brought out the cane she had got me the previous year – the one I had resolutely avoided using and bunged behind the door – and set it against the chair, next to me. I frowned at it, trying hard to resign myself to the fact that I needed it.

'Nina, I need to drop you back to school tomorrow,' I sighed. I felt weak and drained and not up to long-winding, nausea-inducing car journeys on treacherous mountain roads.

'It's okay, Grams, I'll take a bus or a train or something. It's too long a ride for you to take right now, with your leg swollen and that fever just having left you.' She swiftly put her palm against my forehead to check if it had returned. Satisfied it hadn't, she handed me a fresh cup of tea, with a biscuit placed carefully in the saucer below.

I did not trust the world with my granddaughter yet. I had had no choice but to let my daughter fend for herself as I had. But now I had a choice. And my granddaughter would not have to.

As I watched from the window, looking towards the entrance of the pathway, a small red car drew up and stopped a little distance away from the house. A dapper man in a pale, indeterminately coloured half-sleeved shirt and khaki trousers, carrying an important-looking valise, got out of it and made his way towards the front porch in quick, long strides, up the steps with a litheness that belied years of mountain climbing.

'Dr Sanyal is here,' Nina exclaimed and fled towards the door of the room, stopping for a brief second to check herself in the reflection from my dressing-table mirror. Seconds later, the doorbell rang, with those resonating church chimes. It had seemed an ironical statement, given that I'd given up the faith when I was choosing the bell, but now it had started to grate on my nerves.

Bimla opened the door or perhaps Manikji did, and slow and firm footsteps followed by a sharp knock on the bedroom door announced Dr Sanyal. Dr Sandeep Sanyal was in his early thirties, an odd age for a doctor around these parts. Most of the young ones went out to Delhi or industrial towns around North India and stayed put there with lucrative residencies and practices and didn't bother about these one-horse-touristy hill towns scattered around the country.

Dr Sanyal was different. For one, he didn't really need the money. He came from a wealthy, landowning family in Bengal and the fact that he had studied in Calcutta formed an immediate bond between us. He had come to this town as a college student, he said, as a base point for a few treks, and decided he would settle down here eventually. He acquired his MBBS degree and shifted lock stock and barrel to this small town and set up practice in the Mall Road area, carefully picking his location so as not to encroach on any old established practices. He worked round the clock during tourist season, when the hotels were packed to the rafters with families and honeymooning couples, and had enough time during off-season to set off on treks that took him away for as long as a fortnight, during which his patients reluctantly went to old Dr Sharma in the Old Market, who saw them with cheer and good humour until Dr Sanyal returned. Which he would, skin burnt to a crisp, face carved into leaner planes, his eyes tinged with the sadness of having witnessed a surreal, desolate beauty and isolation that few of us are privileged to witness.

It had taken Dr Sanyal a few years to build up a dedicated base of patients, but I was willing to risk my health with a younger doctor. Old Dr Sharma was as doddering as he could get and his clinic was always crowded with patients hanging off the ceiling waiting for their turn, not to mention that he rarely made home visits these days. Dr Sanyal suited me fine; he loved to drive about town and I looked forward to his visits during which we spoke of the city we shared, of our memories of the city, interspersed with his current occasional trips back. It was being painted a particularly grotesque shade of blue, he told me, under the new regime, just voted in after years of rule by the Leftists. All the public buildings, the street dividers and the traffic boxes. He showed me the photographs on his iPad, the fantastic device that just lets you touch it instead of keying things in, with no keypad required. 'Such a horrible blue,' he shuddered and so did I as I saw the painters hard at work. 'They should have chosen a beautiful, elegant blue like your eyes.' I had laughed and patted him on his hand. Men who flirted were nice, even though one knew that the flirting was not from any sort of sexual interest but merely from an old-fashioned sense of chivalry that was so lacking in the current generation.

'So, we're up and about this morning are we, and looking as pretty as ever?' he said, his face serious but his eyes twinkling, as he swept into the room, filling it up with his presence. I noticed Nina colouring up a bit as she moved away to make space for him to sit next to me. He took my hand gently and smiled. He was a good man, this doctor, but a little too old for my granddaughter to have a crush on. Even though he wasn't married. 'No temperature.' He checked my breathing with his stethoscope. 'No signs of any congestion.' He raised my leg and gently unwrapped the bandage. A man with a gentle touch was rare.

'How is the leg, can you apply pressure on it?'

'Yes, I did go to the bathroom, not with ease, but it was quite tolerable,' I replied.

He bent to look at the sprain. 'It still looks a little ugly, I'd advise you to rest it a bit and to keep icing it a few times a day. There is no fracture, but if it doesn't heal well I would recommend further tests, an MRI perhaps to check if there is a ligament tear.' He handled the ankle again, gently. 'Ice, rest, elevation and a crepe bandage through the day should have you as good as rain in a couple of days. And the medicines I've prescribed should help with the pain.'

He looked at Nina who was lurking self-consciously at the foot of the bed while he was checking my ankle. 'This young girl here has been taking wonderful care of you while you were unwell,' he said, a smile on his face. 'She is quite wonderful.'

'That she is,' I replied, smiling. Nina's face turned a blazing red.

'What I cannot understand is how you fell into that sudden high fever which refused to break,' he said. 'The blood tests showed no infection, but we'll repeat them today. I've asked the lab to send in someone to take your blood samples, just in case something shows up. Anyway, except for that nasty business with your ankle, your vitals seem to be fine. You must rest that ankle a bit for a few days, no walking around except for essential bathroom visits.'

Nina decided to retrieve her tongue from the cat and say something. 'I have to get back to school tomorrow and Grams wants to come with me. Please tell her I am perfectly capable of making the trip on my own. I can just take the bus, and walk it from the bus stand when I reach.'

Dr Sanyal looked at her, amusement at her determination in his eyes. 'You, my young lady, are quite capable of making the trip on your own, but I think your grandmother would be quite worried to let you travel on your own over such deserted stretches of road, even if you choose to go by bus.'

Nina's face dropped a bit. 'In some countries I would be an adult. I'm almost sixteen you know. I'm not a kid anymore.' Her tone was sullen. She resented being spoken to like she was a child more than the vetoing of the suggestion that she be allowed to travel on her own. The look she gave him was heavy, veiled and there was nothing of the child I'd assumed her to still be in it.

'There is no option, I have to go drop her myself, I will not be at peace until I do so,' I replied.

He smiled. 'As your doctor I cannot give you permission to travel. You are still rather weak, you know. I need to do some more blood tests on you, I'm not ruling out an infection, that fever was not a regular one and I need to know what caused it. Plus, your foot is in no condition for you to sit through a four-hour car ride one way.'

Nina pouted in the corner of the room, checking her reflection in the glass of the window as he spoke, her face stormy and petulant, on the verge of outright defiance.

'Perhaps I could drop her to school. I do have folks I need to meet who live not very far away from where her school is. That is a trip I have been postponing for a while. I could drop Nina and be back tomorrow itself, it is barely a few hours away on a clear day.'

It sounded perfect. I could trust the good doctor, I knew. Some men you trust and I was endowed with a pretty good people-radar, I thought. I could see from the beaming smile on Nina's face that there was nothing she wanted more. I agreed and the time of leaving for her school was decided as seven in the morning of the next day. 'That sounds like a good idea, and I would be much obliged, Dr Sanyal,' I said. Within me a thread of doubt lingered as to whether this was the best decision under the circumstances, or whether I could have found an alternative. I did trust him, I did, to ensure Nina reached safe and sound. It troubled me to realise it was Nina I didn't quite trust. It was a momentary kernel of doubt I swept away. I was being ridiculous. She was a grown girl, she could handle all situations. Or she should learn to, I told myself. There was only so much she could be protected from.

I rang for Bimla to get us some more tea. I liked my tea with no milk, and Dr Sanyal, I knew preferred his strong and sweetened terribly with almost three heaped spoons of sugar.

'Grams, when I'm gone, please rest your foot and rest yourself. And take a break from that typing all day. It is tiring, even though you're sitting in one place.'

'Typing?' Dr Sanyal frowned.

'Yes, typing,' said Nina, 'She's writing the story of her life but won't let anyone read it.'

'That would be interesting, you know. I've always thought your grandmother would have a fascinating story. There is so much about her that is shrouded in mystery. Although,' he turned towards me, 'I would strongly recommend you take it easy for a few days and don't exert yourself too much. I would love to take a look at what you're writing though.'

'Just a school teacher's memories, doctor, nothing more,' I smiled. 'It is almost time for lunch. Dr Sanyal, would you care to join us for lunch? I'm sure Nina could do with some more youthful company than we relics can provide her.'

He declined graciously, nodding his close cropped head. He was a good-looking man, broad shouldered and manly in a way few modern-day men are. It was no wonder that Nina blushed wildly every time she caught his gaze. Ah, child, I wished I could tell her that it was completely alright to be attracted as long as she didn't fall in love with him.

Love, now that was dangerous. It plucks your heart out of your chest cavity and throws it into the skies where all you can do is watch it freefall towards the object of your love, and hope he or she would catch it. And very often your heart would land with a sordid, painful thud on the ground, or worse, a ditch, and lie there forlorn, neglected and pitiful until you found it, picked it up, glued the various parts back together and put it back into your chest where it would continue to beat on, stolidly, with only you knowing that there was a beat missing. A beat audible to no discerning ear, but your own, a slight sense of being out of tune with yourself, a heart that beat on reluctantly, for the sake of keeping up appearances, in the forlorn hope that some day it would get back in rhythm, that some day it would have something to beat for. And then, over the years of missing a beat, you would grow irretrievably out of beat with yourself, and end up discordant.

'That's settled then, I will be here early tomorrow morning to pick up Nina. I think you're doing alright now. But strange fever that was, it came on suddenly and didn't respond to any medication at all,' he mused as he moved out of the room. 'I wonder what brought it on.'

I knew what had brought it on, but I had no clue how to figure it out. Nina tripped out of the room to see Dr Sanyal off. I saw her standing on the patch of green grass outside, her stance open yet paradoxically uncertain, her back towards me, saying something to him that I knew was for his ears only, him casting a quick glance behind towards the window where I sat, knowing I would be there, watching, and laughing quickly, before getting into his car and waving at my window as he drove off. I furrowed my brow in worry. I hoped it was a crush, one that would run its natural course and wear off when she went back to school, back amongst boys her age. I hoped that boys closer to her own age might interest her more than a man twice her age would. I didn't know it then but I was so wrong. So terribly wrong.

Chapter 4

THE WEATHER STAYED clear the next morning, as Nina left for her boarding school. She had thrown her things together in the most ramshackle way possible and I'd barked at her to get it done again neatly in my best school-marm manner. She'd sulked for a bit and then given in, doing a rushed job but one that I couldn't find fault with. I remembered how we checked and surprise-checked the children at Datham Hall for neatness in the way they stacked their clothes. As the doctor's car rolled up on the narrow strip of road outside the cottage, the sun was just emerging from behind the mighty Himalayas in the distance, tinging their snow-tipped peaks a glorious pink. She bounded out, dragging her strolley behind her, her lips glossed up in a soft pink that wasn't as becoming as the natural hue they had, and a smidgeon of kohl in her eyes which converted her unexpectedly into a grown up, no longer a child, a child-woman perhaps. The school blazer and trousers she had on couldn't conceal that she was outgrowing them, both physically and otherwise.

I had already called her House Parent the previous evening and informed her that I would not be accompanying Nina on her trip back and that she should let me know the moment Nina reached the premises. Nina had a new mobile phone, a touchscreen she was surgically connected to all day. She insisted I switch to a newer model myself, one in which she could get me an internet connection and download WhatsApp. But I clung on, with a misplaced determination, to my old Nokia model, given to me by Millie when mobile phones first came to India many years ago. It was still functional and whenever it misbehaved, I sent Manikji with it to the mobile store in the marketplace where they put it right. 'Carry this with you when you go on your walks,' Millie had said. 'Just in case.' The 'just in case' lingered in the air between us like a premonition about to take seed. It took me a while to figure out the phone's functions but I eventually did. Millie had fed in the important numbers on speed dial. Her work number. Her home number. Her mobile number. The doctor's number. The number of the estate manager who lived down the road. Colonel Dayal, a sturdy, reliable sort who could be counted on to rush to one's help the instant he was called.

The handset was sturdy enough to knock out an intruder if so required in an emergency, but I hadn't had the opportunity to test that theory yet. The numbers on the keypad had been worn out over the years, but I didn't use it much anyway. The only reason I might consider changing it would be because it gave me a pain in the wrist if I had a conversation longer than ten minutes on it. But then who would I speak to for so long? Slowly, one by one, people had dropped out of my life, becoming busy with their own lives. Friends had aged and died, students had grown up, got married or divorced... keeping in touch was an effort. Solitude was easier, it asked for nothing from oneself but that one existed and one was content with one's existence.

Millie had not taken into consideration how vacuous the connectivity was in this remote outpost. I liked being remote and inaccessible. Despite my daughter's very vocal opinion about how it would be better if I sold the old, crumbling cottage with the never-ending, maintenance steadily eating into my already meagre and depleting resources and moved into one of the spanking new housing complexes coming up smack in the midst of town, I continued stubbornly to live here, magnificent in my desolation and solitude.

This was not just a cottage to me, this was home. Windermere. Ambitiously named perhaps for a cottage but the only real home I had known all my life. All the rest had been temporary residences, with the constant awareness that one would have to move out eventually, that one couldn't let oneself get too settled in each because one never knew where one would need to move out to. Windermere was where I hoped I would end my days... this was where I had decided to spend the rest of them. I had bought this home with the money I earned from a lifetime of squirreling away my precious salary, buying only what was absolutely necessary, sticking to essentials, doing without luxuries. I had been lucky enough to get it at a price that was, even for this remote a location, dirt cheap, something that had worried me initially but once I had seen it, never questioned the reason for the bargain it was because I had fallen so completely in love with it. The winding path, the wrought iron gate, the welcoming patio, the windows set beneath eaves, the climbing rose vine steadily working its way into the stone and mortar, the verandah that ran the length of the front, accessible from the living room and the dining room, the wooden planks that thumped underfoot... this was home, in all its faded glory.

I stopped Manikji from helping Nina with her strolley. It had wheels, she was young and strong, she needed to learn quickly that the world would not help her with anything. She would have to learn to carry her own stuff, fight her own battles, slay her own demons, be her own knight in shining armour. I was sad to see her go, but I was glad for the solitude I would reclaim.

I climbed up the stairs to my study after waving her and Dr Sanyal off, wincing at the spikes of pain shooting through my body each time I placed my right foot down on the floor. As far as studies went, this was exactly what studies were meant to be, crammed with books, shelves right up to the ceiling and a nice leather wingback chair in front of my work desk facing the window. I hadn't put these together, the shelves were already built and stocked with books by the previous owners, an old couple, I'm told they were. The house had changed many owners since it had been built, I was told by the old-timers. The owners I bought it from had used it as a summer home, till their only son emigrated to Australia, took up citizenship there and called his parents to join him, which necessitated the disposing of this cottage within a month, which is why I'd got it so cheap.

When I read books owned by strangers, I saw the inscriptions on the opening page, with names of people I had never met, but felt I knew intimately because I read the books they owned, books they had read through, marked passages in, put bookmarks in, pressed flowers in. There is a curious camaraderie that can seep through the ownership of books, a bond that transcends the print on the pages, the yellow patina that tinges the paper. One wonders how the person who had read the book before had responded to the lines that you now respond to, what had been on their mind when they underlined certain sentences, whether the sudden slosh of dissolved ink had been a teardrop splashing itself on the page unbidden or whether it had been a hasty movement of a hand encountering a glass of water kept at an injudicious distance from the reader.

I loved my work desk. Not that I had much work to be done at the desk before I began typing this out, painstakingly, with skills I had long forgotten, and fingers no longer supple and flexible enough to bang on typewriter keys ossified through disuse. I couldn't work without wincing and flexing joints that were swollen with the onset of arthritis that I kept at bay with painkillers whenever it threatened to overwhelm my day. From the window I could see past acres of sloping tea bushes from the tea estate that began down the road, right to where the pine forests took over and the mountains rose steeply, the sky cerulean where the white-tipped peaks in the far distance met them, fringing the eastern horizon like guardians of a forbidden realm.

Somewhere on the main roads in the midst of town, buses roared past with arriving and departing tourists, taxi drivers called out to people waiting at the bus-stand, hoping some would change their mind about taking a bus and opt for one of the many share-taxis that plied between fixed routes. Local guides tempted tourists alighting from buses with cheap, decent lodgings and full-day sightseeing tours. And then there were the residents, bustling about their day to day life, going to schools, colleges, temples, hospitals, living out their lives like they did every day, unmindful of the scenic beauty around them because this was what they lived with, it had become a blind spot to them. There was a serenity to the scene that made it even more beautiful than it was, a serenity born of the calm acceptance that this is how things were, would be and needed to be. The sun was a blaze of light, the day was startlingly bright, as bright as cloudless mornings are up in the mountains, with none of the shamefaced abashment that fog and clouds bring when they arrive.

I settled myself at my desk, before my typewriter. I could see my silver hair reflecting off the window pane as I typed. It shouldn't have come as a shock to me, considering I'd gone silver in my mid-sixties. In my mind's eye, my hair was still a soft brown and hung to my shoulders like a thick curtain, that, when parted, showed my deer-in-the-headlight blue eyes. The huge sheaf of papers seemed untouched from the last time I had seen it, but something seemed off, I knew it instinctively when I looked at it. It was too perfectly arranged, which is not the way I normally kept it, careless and distracted, as I finished typing out each page and then revising, scratching out, rewriting with pencil and then retyping the page. I put the niggling suspicion that someone had been reading through the sheets out of my head, inserted a paper into my trusted Olivetti and rolled it into position, looking back at the last sheet I had typed and finally figured out what it was that was wrong – my last sheet was half typed. It had been left in the typewriter when I'd last exited this room. Someone had taken it out from the typewriter and placed it at the bottom of the sheaf of papers. Someone had placed the papers in reading order. Someone, I didn't know who it could be, had been reading my manuscript.

I furrowed my brow in puzzlement. Bimla and Manikji were unlettered, and Nina wouldn't have dared touched the papers without my permission. No, I swatted the thought down in my head. She would not do that, I was sure of it. That was not the way I had raised this girl, and it was me who had raised her more than her mother. I pressed the bell, called Bimla up and instructed her to have tea and breakfast brought up to me on a tray rather than me needing to make the long trek down again, with the misbehaving ankle, even though I had a sturdy, beautifully carved wooden walking stick to support myself, something Nina had bought for me from a local exhibition much to my irritation. I didn't then, but now, barely a year later, I was glad to have it at hand. Only for a while though, the ankle would heal and I would not need it again for some years, I consoled myself. But a small, quiet part of me accepted that perhaps, I would never let it go now that I had realised how easy it was to lean on something rather than struggle to support oneself with knees that shook with every step.

'Did anyone enter my room while I was unwell, Bimla?' I asked, curious about who it could have been who had set my papers in order. 'Only me, Bibijee. I came in to dust the place.'

'Did you touch my papers on the desk?'

'Nahin jee,' she replied vehemently. 'I only dusted around them. I know how annoyed you get when your papers get disturbed.'

This was very curious indeed. But then the phone rang, and I had no further chance to dwell on the mysterious hand that had aligned my sheets of typewritten notes.

It was Millie. 'Mother, has Nina left? Her phone is unreachable.' She began without preamble. It was typical of my daughter to enquire about her daughter without even a cursory enquiry about my ankle or my well-being. A part of her brusqueness towards me always rankled, but we were no longer adversarial.

'Yes, she has. She should be reaching school within a few hours. You could call school and speak with her probably in a couple of hours, unless they get held up somewhere with a road block. But it is clear today, and no rains, so hopefully no risk of any landslides to block the roads. You might not get through to her for some parts of the route, there is patchy network on that stretch.'

'I wish you hadn't sent her off with that doctor. I mean, how well do you really know him?' The anxiety in her voice overpowered the normal reserve she had when speaking with me. I couldn't blame her, hers was a mistrust born from being pawed by too many foster fathers in a childhood where she had been more damaged than cared for. The only person to be blamed for it was me, and my selfishness. Or cowardice. Or self-preservation. Whatever you may choose to call it.

'Well enough,' I replied. 'I think he is a man who can be trusted to take good care of her and not take undue advantage of her at any point. I think you should trust my judgement, Millie.'

'Let's not even start about trusting your judgement, Mother, there's a lot I can say about that beginning from right when you put me in foster care and never bothered to check up on me ever,' she said, her voice cold and biting. 'Anyway, there's not much I can do about Nina from here, can I?' she said, her voice suddenly bitter and tired and weighed down with what was clearly maternal guilt, something I was all too familiar with, having been through the same a million times over.

There was an awkward silence as the words between us stopped. 'And how are you, Millie?' I asked, gently, unsure of what to speak to my only daughter about. We had no topics to discuss except that which revolved around Nina.

The line, surprisingly clear, sighed back at me. Or rather Millie sighed. 'I've been busy, Mother. Just really tied up with travel and organising ground-level promotions for various projects in South America and Africa. It has been very exhausting. I'm looking forward to my break in winter.' Another awkward pause. 'How are you, Mother, is your ankle better now? You gave Nina quite a scare, the poor child was hysterical when she called me. You must be more careful. Luckily this time she was around to care for you, what if this had happened when she had left and you were with no one but those two simpletons you have in the house.'

I laughed. 'Don't you worry about me, Millie. I can take good care of myself. I have been doing so since I was a child. And Bimla and Manikji may be simple, but they're quite devoted to me, I can trust them to take good care of me in case of any eventuality.'

'They're also robbing you blind, I'm sure they're pilfering stuff behind your back. Anyway, Mother, I will speak with you later.' Millie called me Mother. Not Ma. Not Mamma. Not Mom. But the very formal Mother. It was a stilted form of address between mother and child, but Millie and I never had any connection until she had grown to about the same age Nina was right now. I had no maternal feelings towards her, except perhaps a sense of guilt and an obligation to do right with her, given that I had done so much wrong by her.

Millie was a good-looking woman, even if she seemed to deliberately downplay her looks. She got her features from me, and the firm set of her jaw and the determined glare from her father. She had also inherited his eyes, an indeterminate hue between hazel and brown, eyes that had been burnished bronze by squinting into the desert sun. Millie hadn't inherited my eyes, but Nina had.

Millie kept herself simple, even spartan, with an occasional slick of a frosted-pink lipstick as her only concession to adornment. For evenings out, she preferred the starkness of a post-box red lipstick that flamed out from the pale palette of her skin. Perhaps the only thing she emulated from me. She preferred a severe blunt cut at exactly chin length through the seasons and would wear a small comb or a clip to keep it off her face. She dyed it a jet black, to contrast with her pale skin. The only jewellery she wore were a pair of solitaires in her ears and a simple diamond ring. She got that from me too, a lack of affection for ornamentation. It was so strange, the way little quirks percolated down through the generations, even if the emotional bond did not. She would eventually get this four-carat green Colombian emerald ring surrounded by diamonds that I wore on the third finger of my left hand when I would die, regardless of whether she cared to wear it or not. It had been placed on my finger by her father, and it was hers by right.

I sighed and straightened my leg from the little footstool I'd placed it on in order to elevate it a bit but only ended up in discomfort. I steepled my fingers and rested my chin on them, looking out of the window without registering what I was seeing. When I was Nina's age I had stepped out of convent life for the first time ever. The boarding school might be Nina's equivalent of convent life, sequestered and protected and yet with a violent and ugly ecosystem all its own. For me, emerging from the convent was my emergence into a cocoon even more tightly woven than life at the convent. I was the only young person in the large rambling bungalow at Chaudharipore and dimly aware of the fact that I was not a legitimate heir, not loved unconditionally, and only brought back because I was the sole link the Chaudharis had to their deceased son.

Memories are fragile, you try to grab them and they skitter away in various directions. Trying to gather them together to write them out is difficult, they resist, get clouded and escape as wisps of smoke. Nothing seems as crystal clear as it once was, a milky film of opacity envelopes everything. Odd details stand out in one's mind, not a continuum. A fragrance, an odour, the smell of toast burning perhaps or the whiff of jasmine, a shade of pink, a flower pressed between the pages of a book, brings on a sharp burst of memories that drown you with their immediacy. I could remember the colour of the dress I had been wearing when I left school after the final matriculation exams, a brilliant blue, as cerulean as my eyes, picked out in defiance of the nuns who advocated colours that were muted and didn't draw attention to oneself. I couldn't remember packing up and getting ready to move out of the convent at all nor any details about the long journey, which involved changing two trains, taking a ferry, a train that zig-zagged at points in order to climb the steep gradient of the mountains, and then a final stretch by car, but I could remember, down to the minutest stroke, the faded framed print of the painting of the Blessed Virgin that hung on a peeling wall in my room in the boarding quarters. These days I could barely remember what I'd had for breakfast the previous morning, but I could remember the cold porridge and acrid smell of burnt toast from the thousand breakfasts eaten at the convent. My mind was slipping away, slowly and steadily, memories of the immediate sieved out through my brain, and only those from the past remained.

I could remember the feeling of sudden and absolute panic that hit me as I left the convent, the only home I had known for fifteen years. In a sense, going to the tea estate owned by my grandfather was the first time I was stepping out into the world outside the gates of the convent. Panic coiled, serpent like, in my chest and threatened to stifle my beating heart, which was thudding so hard I was sure it was audible to everyone around me when Mother Superior showed me the letter, with my grandfather's firm sloping handwriting on the envelope and on the sheet of thick, white, embossed writing paper within.

'My estate manager will be down in Calcutta on the 15th of this month, and will escort her to us. I will give him a signed letter from me to you to assure you of his trustworthiness.'

Mother Superior looked at me kindly. 'I'm sorry, but we have to let you go to your grandparents. I am sure this is for the best. Unless you wish to continue living here and devote your life to Christ.' I shook my head to indicate a negative. I did not see myself living out a life of renunciation like the nuns. In a sudden display of unseemly emotion, her eyes filled up. She stood up from her desk and hugged me. 'We will miss you, child.'

I cried into my pillow that night, huge gasping sobs that had my room mate bung a pillow at me to get me to shut up and let her sleep. I had spent fifteen years in the convent, it was the only life I knew, the unhurried graciousness, the sense of melancholy that hung over it... but I had had enough, I wanted to step out, to see the world beyond the high walls that enclosed us. I was not cut out for a life of renunciation and withdrawal into prayer and piety, for the sterile claustrophobia that such an existence would bring.

The manager, Barua, when he arrived to escort me to Chaudharipore, was a dour, middle-aged man with a permanently disapproving expression, multiple chins and an accent I couldn't quite comprehend. Our conversation was limited and stilted. We spent the two days travelling together with functional conversation, an acutely wary politeness on his part, an uneasiness on mine. We passed through railway stations with tin roof sheds, ate meals at railway canteens and freshened up in rest-rooms, took a ferry across the river Ganges, where coolies waited in a swarm of red on the opposite bank to grab passengers and their trunks. We changed to another overnight train to Siliguri. The first-class refreshment room where we breakfasted, at Siliguri railway station, stayed in my fading memories, my first ever experience of being served by waiters in white uniforms and white head caps. We passed through flat land, then through miles and miles of curving mountain road dappled with mist and deciduous trees that slowly began making way for coniferous trees. The trees loomed menacingly along the sides of the track to little bridges suspended between drops that made me dizzy to look down, where the air changed from humid to crisp and dry, and the houses began clinging precariously to the sides of the road, which snaked round and round. We disembarked from the train to climb into a jeep sent to receive us, with Kaji Daju at the wheel. I never knew him as anything else for all the years that I lived there – he was a fixture on the premises, driving my grandfather around on the days my grandfather didn't feel like taking the wheel, or when my grandmother wanted to go into town to visit the gymkhana or when I wanted to visit the gymkhana library, much better stocked with books for a young girl, compared to the desolate philosophical tomes that comprised the better part of my grandfather's collection. Our luggage was loaded into the back of the jeep, and we drove through miles of curving road, further and further into the sky, on roads that hugged the edge of the mountains.

The tea estate came upon us as we turned a steep bend in the road after a few hours of driving through increasingly steep topography. All of a sudden, like it was hiding itself, lurking in wait, like a child playing a prank, to catch us unawares, the dazzle of green expanse of tea bushes hit the eye. The thick blanket of clouds parted at that very moment, letting streams of late afternoon sunlight drift down on acres and acres of a rolling, rounded hillside dotted with green shrubs. 'There it is, Chaudharipore,' said Barua, extending his hand to the right of me, his voice tinged with a faint sense of ownership and pride. I turned to the car window to his right and saw a huge gate spanning the road open up as we rolled up to it. Hillocks rose gently on either side of the gate, the road was a dead-end. As the car entered through the gates, two uniformed men manning it gently closed it behind us. A sense of panic gripped me – I was now truly and completely out of the convent and on my own.

I would spend five years at Chaudharipore, before I moved on again. What was it about life being a river constantly in flux, taking you to places against your will, smashing you against rocks, throwing you off gorges, before finally slowing down sedately to merge you with the all-encompassing, all-forgiving sea.

Chapter 5

BARELY HAD I begun to wonder if I should call up school or Nina to check whether she had reached when the rains returned to the hills. Bimla came in asking if I would like my supper brought up to the study, her face agonised by the effort of having to climb up to this warren perched right on top of the house.

The rain, cloudy grey, drizzled down unceasingly on the well-manicured little patch of lawn outside the cottage with flower beds of roses, gladioli, carnations, marigolds, lilies, chrysanthemums, a riot of yellows, pinks, reds and whites that spilled over, uncontained in their glory, despite the neat borders that Hari Singh, the gardener, took great pride in nurturing. 'That would be nice, Bimla,' I smiled at her.

'Memsaab,' she asked hesitantly. 'Has Babyjee reached? Koi phone aa gaya?'

I shook my head and picked up the telephone receiver, intending to call. My memory was not as good as it used to be, I couldn't remember Dr Sanyal's or Nina's number off the top of my head and looked around for the small phone diary somewhere on the desk, when my mobile phone rang. The ring of the mobile never failed to make me jump out of my skin. It was from the House Parent at school, a matter-of-fact matronly lady from Amritsar, Mrs Walia, who spoke in measured tones and only the essential, but still managed to convey that your child was in safe hands and would be cared for, even in your absence.

'Ma'am,' she said, crisply, 'Nina has reached safe and sound. Would you like to speak with her?'

'Yes, please, if you could be so kind as to hand her the phone,' I replied.

'Sure,' she said.

There was a brief static-free silence before Nina's voice floated through the handset. She sounded like she had been laughing just before she took the receiver. 'Grams... I've reached in one piece. I bet you were worried out of your mind. How's your leg? I hope you're not walking around too much and resting it well. Dr Sanyal drives crazily, a couple of times I thought we're going to tumble off the road and burst into flames.' The sentences tumbled out of her with the careless lack of restraint that characterises youth. 'Are you still feverish, Grams?'

'I am perfectly alright, Nina, the same as I was when you left this morning,' I said, laughing. This chit of a girl was mothering me around in a curious role reversal.

'Take your medicines, don't walk around too much, get Dr Sanyal to come in to tie your bandage for you if you can't do it yourself, Bimla is goddawful at doing it,' she said. I imagined Nina's face reddening a bit as she mentioned Dr Sanyal. 'Okay, Grams, I am off to meet my friends now, call me soon.'

I informed Bimla that Nina had been safely deposited at her school, and I would like to get to bed a little early myself. The day was still bright as I had my supper at my usual time, seven-thirty, and took myself directly to bed. The house was hushed and silent, except for Bimla clearing up the kitchen with some muted clanking of the vessels in the old stone sink and grumbling about the water that ran sputtering and erratic or dried up completely if Manikji had forgotten to switch the wheezing pump on in the course of the day. There were a few lights left on to illuminate the passageway and the stairs and they cast a dim light under the door as I switched the bedside lamp off and pulled the covers over myself, turning my back towards the window.

Ever since that night, I slept with my back to the window. I dreaded my eyes opening in the middle of the night to find a face I didn't want to see watching me from the other side of the glass pane. I needed the lights in the passage on, in the event I felt like taking a trip to the bathroom in the middle of the night, which I inevitably would, a couple of times at the very least. Old age takes its toll on your bladder, it presses on your subconscious until you dream of meandering through dark, dank labyrinths not of your own choosing, through an unfamiliar home with infinite doors and none of them opening into a cloakroom, while the uncomfortable pressure presses down upon you, the chill seeping into your bones, till you wake with a start, switch the night lamp on, slip your feet into your warm towelled slippers and shuffle along, slowly, carefully down the passage to the attached bathroom. It was at these times, in the middle of cold, wintry nights, that you thought back to an earlier phase in life when you could go to sleep at night and wake up directly in the morning, without needing to get out of the warm confines of the bed at any point to visit the bathroom.

The night was windy, the rain pelted down, occasional cracks of thunder splitting the eardrums and the lightning preceding it lighting up the sky outside the window with ghostly shadows that sang siren songs. It looked stormy again. I looked out of the window from the bed, the same window that had had that pale face looking in at me that night. It showed the steady dripping of rainwater running down from a gutter in the roof and pitch black darkness outside, a moonless night, perhaps, or if there was a moon, it had taken shelter behind the barricade of storm clouds. A loose shutter somewhere within the house kept flapping itself noisily in a repetitive motion, grating upon my feeble attempts to get into deep sleep. I pressed the bell for Bimla, and asked her to check which shutter it was, and to fasten it before it was ripped off its hinges by the relentless howling wind. My limited resources weren't stretchable enough to take on more repairs of the cottage than were absolutely necessary, and I hesitated to ask Millie for funds whenever I ran short. Bimla shuffled off, called for Manikji and between the two of them they stomped noisily through the house, their steps resounding on the wooden floorboards, checking every window for the errant one. The flapping stopped abruptly, there was a disturbing quiet in the house. Or as much quiet as these old houses can have, before something wakes them up again in the dead of the night, a shift in the wind, a change in the weather, a sense of disquiet with the tree brushing its leaves against the roof, like a lover's lingering touch, even after the goodbyes have been said and the gaze has been turned away.

These old houses aren't ever completely quiet. They sigh and moan and hiss. They have a life of their own; they let the wind in through minor crevices, like an infiltrator into a fort, where it then proceeds to swirl around hissing, spreading its tentacles to corners where it would scoot out dust bunnies lurking undisturbed. It will rattle ornaments placed on mantelpieces, pounce on you as an unexpected chill draught running an icy finger up your spine and then running that same icy finger down again. And there was the dampness, the eternal dampness, seeping through the walls, dripping from the roof, even after one has got the local handy man to climb up and apply sealant to all the spots. I could feel the dampness seeping in again through the walls, as the rain hammered down on the roof and the lightning split the sky into jagged streaks of silver, black and blue and purple, followed promptly by the urgent growling of the thunder that complained after it, in the whining, aggrieved tone an ageing relative might have when compelled to follow a group of fleet-footed youngsters on an excursion.

The doorbell rang, it was uncharacteristically late for it to ring. It was an apologetic ring, but one, given the loud church bell chimes I'd chosen, that resounded through the cottage. A quick look at the alarm clock, with its big bright digitized numbers, told me it was one in the morning. I gingerly levered myself out of bed and tried to look out to the main pathway to check if I could see anything, a vehicle perhaps. No. The driveway was empty, pelted down with the unceasing rain. If this rain didn't ease up, I thought, we would see flash floods again in the hills, and days of supplies being cut off. Who could it be, at this hour, in this desolation?

I pulled on my dressing gown, tied the belt, with hands clumsy and clammy with fear, the gnarled knots in them protesting the sudden haste. My joints weren't cooperating, the recovering ankle grumbling at the hurried movements with sharp stabs of pain that made me wince. The bell rang again, more insistent now, shriller, a call for help. I could hear heavy, flat footsteps plodding down the passageway; Bimla was probably making her way out of her room next to the kitchen and moving slowly towards the front door. I stepped out into the little foyer, looking at her look through the glass panes at the side of the door and switch the porch light on to get a clearer look at whoever it was on the other side of the thick, carved wood door. Manikji had followed her and stood behind her warily with a heavy iron kitchen ladle in his hand – a cautiousness which had not occurred to me would be necessary when doorbells rang at unearthly hours.

'It is that writer saab from the cottage behind,' she said. 'He's completely drenched. Shall I open the door?' I nodded at her to do so. I moved carefully towards the door, wincing as each step reminded me that my body no longer recovered as swiftly as it used to. He stepped in from the pelting rain, stooping down a bit so his head didn't hit the top of the doorway, looking older than he did from the distance, with the light from the bulb hitting him full in the face, revealing skin that had begun to unravel in delicate skeins from the corners of his eyes and the grooves carved in by laughter and the sun running from the edge of his lip to the side of his rather defined nose. He stood there awkwardly, dripping wet from head to toe, completely ruining the rug in the passageway. Bimla, too polite to make him stand back, looked at the rug and then at me with a pleading gaze.

'I'm terribly sorry,' he said, 'about disturbing you so late in the night.' His voice sounded shaken and terrified, at odds for a man his size. He took a deep, laboured breath, scrunched his eyes shut and then opened them again, almost as if he had something to say and decided against it.

'Please do come in,' I replied. A man who apologises for disturbing one's sleep must always be forgiven.

He extended a wet, dripping hand, realised it was not in a condition to be shaken, withdrew it and wiped it against his track pants, which were dripping wet and didn't absorb any of the water being wiped off on it.

'I'm Sumit Kamat. I have been staying in the cottage behind you.'

He glanced out again at the thunder and lightning putting up a rather spiffy show for anyone who might care to watch. Cottage Four in the line-up of cottages sprinkled on this desolate road on the outskirts of town. Or Ivy Green as it had been lovingly named by the owners.

'Of course, I know you,' I replied. 'We've never spoken, but we've waved and smiled at each other. What brings you out in such terrible weather at this time of the night?'

'I've had a bit of a disaster in the cottage, the ceiling seems to have fallen in, the entire place is flooded,' he said, sounding more amused than worried, 'And this is just awful weather to spend getting wet all night. I just needed a dry spot to spend the night.

I wondered if I could impose on you and sit out in your rather welcoming verandah.'

I noticed then he had a windcheater on, and was holding a laptop carefully under it. There was an uncertainty in his manner, an edginess that came from more than merely being out of home on a rainy night. 'You couldn't spend the night on the verandah, it would be rather uncomfortable. We have a perfectly good guest room which isn't in use at the moment. You could have a good night's rest there.' Bimla, following the gist of the conversation, looked at me askance.

He looked trustworthy, tall, lean in the fashionable way it seems to be lean these days, with a couple of days worth of stubble on his chin, his appearance the casual dishevelled look of one who couldn't be bothered with how he presented himself to the world. His clothes were what he might have worn to go to sleep, track pants, a faded T-shirt under the windcheater and flip-flops or what people of my generation called Hawaii chappals. His features were sharp, his eyes alert, and it didn't look like he'd been roused from sleep by a crash over his head, strangely enough. His skin was so light it could be Caucasian, and I just noticed that his eyes were a haunted, indeterminate greyish-greenish brown in the flickering light of the incandescent lamp in this dimly lit hallway. Millie's eyes were the same colour.

'That is very kind of you, ma'am. I will be gone first thing in the morning, as soon as it clears up.'

'My pleasure,' I replied. 'You are most welcome to stay the night here. I will have Bimla open the guest bedroom for you.'

He pulled off the dripping windcheater and left it awkwardly on the little bench outside on the porch, before stepping back in. I asked Bimla to open the spare bedroom on the first level; it was rarely used except when we had more than one guest, but had been aired out just a couple of days ago, so it should be in perfect condition to welcome an unexpected guest.

Bimla, following my instructions, went up to the guest room, opened it with an air of being much put upon and announced grumpily that the room was ready to be occupied, wherein he thanked us profusely for the kindness and moved up the stairs, taking them two at a time, like a jungle cat on the prowl, rushing through the undergrowth, swiftly, silently, moving faster than the prey it was stalking.

Bimla ambled down the stairs heavily, shaking her head, grumbling under her breath about the rain and the wind and people who woke up decent, god-fearing human beings at ungodly hours and made old women with arthritic joints rush around getting beds readied for them.

'Stop grumbling, Bimla,' I said in Hindi. 'The poor boy can't be staying out in such a storm. You're earning blessings from him and his family. If he was out in the storm, he would catch pneumonia and die at our doorstep. And then his ghost would haunt us all our lives.' She cast one baleful eye at me and disappeared into the back of the house to her living quarters.

Manikji ambled down the stairs having assured the saabji that if he needed anything, he just needed to press the buzzer placed beside the head of the bed. I wondered if the heater in the guest room was working well. The stormy weather had brought in a chill, and I could feel a slight shiver in my bones. I moved into my bedroom and closed the door, wondering about this young man, who he was, and why he needed to come out to an isolated cottage in the mountains in order to write his book. But I wasn't even sure if that was the reason why he was here all these months. All I knew was pure hearsay, gleaned from the whisperings of Manikji and Bimla who were on chatty terms with the housekeeper who worked in Ivy Green.

The guest bedroom was directly above mine. I could hear his footsteps moving around in the room, the flush of the attached bathroom being used, the unmistakable sounds of water being splashed repeatedly on a face. The man was restless, very restless. He was pacing around the room much in the manner of a caged animal, for well on fifteen to twenty minutes. It was almost two in the morning, I heard the sounds of a window being opened above me. The rain continued to hammer down and the cottage groaned in the most horrendous manner, like the ground beneath it was shuddering and trying to throw it off. The sound of an incessant drip from within the cottage caught my attention. If he had left the tap running upstairs, it would leak through the floorboards and drip into the corner of my room. A burst of wind had the roof shuddering. Maybe, I worried, I should get this roof seen to professionally; the old wooden beams holding up the roof had been reinforced with iron girders some years ago, and the sheets redone, but I wouldn't like to be found dead under the weight of it all, if it decided to collapse on me one night.

Sleep, when it came finally, was sudden and black and when I awoke at my usual time in the morning, the rain had let up and the air outside was crisp and crackling. I bathed quickly, and had Bimla bring my morning tea to the verandah. The winter chill had not set in and it was still possible to sit in the open without fear of catching a cold. October was a pleasant month. The weather was always the most pleasant in the morning, like nature had just stretched itself languorously and barely opened its sleepy eyes. It was a suspended state of animation, the morning. Birds were chirping in the trees in a frenzy, probably discussing the damage the storm had caused to their nests. Hari Singh was already in the garden, pottering around, pulling out errant weeds with a ferocity that belied his normal placidness. He nodded deferentially to me and ambled over, his bow legs making his gait awkward and shuffling, almost like he would topple over if he decided to go any faster.

'Masterniji,' he started, 'Kal raat bahut toofan aaya tha. They say lightning split Chaar Number, just sliced it into half.'

I involuntarily turned in the direction of Ivy Green, or Chaar Number as he called it, even though I knew I couldn't see it directly from this part of the house. Bimla came out on the verandah, wiping her hands on the ubiquitous apron she always wore over her faded salwar kameez with the large floral print that she seemed to prefer.

'The saab has woken up,' she informed me quietly, the disapproval on her face louder than any words she could utter.

'Could you ask him if he'd care to join me here for a cup of tea? We will have breakfast in the dining room today, in an hour,' I replied. I was curious to know more about this man from Delhi, who had been living next door for the past four months and never crossed my path. Not that I had stepped out all that much in the past few months. My trips into town too were few and far between these days. I couldn't seem to be able to bring myself to make the effort to travel into the main part of town. I had even delegated the buying of groceries, a task that I once enjoyed, to Manikji so as to not have to make the weekly trips. And Devidayal Singh, the proprietor of Singh's Grocery Store, was kind enough to send the bulk of my requirements via his delivery boy on a mere phone call, an absolute luxury given the distances and my lack of transport.

'Good morning,' said a sudden masculine voice at my elbow. The writer resident of the hapless lightning-struck cottage was standing awkwardly, waiting to be asked to sit down. Such manners were rare in the current generation. This signified either good upbringing or a good school or both. Or maybe the school teacher I had been for over thirty years was still lurking within me, despite all my attempts to soften myself up a bit over the past few years.

'Please join me.' I indicated the cane chair placed opposite the one I was sitting on. He lowered himself into the chair gingerly, testing whether it would take his weight. The chair held and he settled back comfortably, looking around at the early morning birds raising quite a din in the trees fringing the lawns.

'I hope you slept comfortably last night?' I asked him, noticing the dark circles under his eyes. His face had the slight emaciation that comes from being one of those who have no concept of meals at a fixed time and are more likely to eat when they remember to.

'The room was very comfortable, thank you, and it was very kind of you to allow me to stay the night, without knowing me at all,' he replied. Bimla brought in a fresh pot of tea with two cups on a tray, placing it on the table between us and taking away my used cup.

'I was delighted to be of help, you know one doesn't get too many visitors here, and if it hadn't been for the storm and the roof, we might have never got to know each other,' I replied, pouring out the tea into the cups. 'How much sugar?' I asked automatically, hand poised over the sugar bowl.

'None,' he replied. 'Thank you.'

He sipped his tea slowly and looked around. 'This is beautiful, isn't it? I've been here for a few months and I still have to get used to the peace and quiet in the mornings. You are lucky to be living here.'

'That I am. Where are you from?' I asked him, examining him closely. I tried not to be too obvious about it. He seemed confused at the question.

'Where am I from? That's an interesting question. I could say I'm from no particular place. The ancestors from my paternal side were from up North who moved down South and settled in Konkan, Goa and Karnataka. My mother is from Rajasthan.' That explained his unusually light colouring and eyes. 'My father was in the foreign service so I spent most of my childhood in boarding schools whenever he was posted in some remote outpost, or with my maternal grandmother in Rajasthan. My father is retired, and my parents now live in Delhi. I studied in the US for five years, and returned a few years ago. And since then I have been all over

India trying to figure out where I should live and what I should do with my life.'

That was a long answer for what would seem like a simple question. 'And what made you come here, a remote cottage in the middle of nowhere, a young man like you? Surely, this is no age to cut yourself off from civilisation?'

He laughed wryly. 'I thought I would drop off the surface of the earth, just hide myself away here and do what I wanted to do, but unfortunately civilisation won't leave me alone here too.'

I raised an eyebrow, waiting for him to elaborate. He shook his head dismissively. 'I have a tendency to get dramatic. Ignore that. I had actually come here to finish work on a book I am writing. I've taken a six-month sabbatical from my day job to get this book completed. It is almost done and I should be leaving soon. But seeing as I might not have a place to stay now, I might leave sooner than anticipated.'

It is a strange profession, this business of being a writer. You sit at your desk and hammer away at your typewriter or your keyboard all that your mind can construct into some form of sentences and words. You need to get away from the routine of regular living in order to do so, to sink deep within yourself, to let the words from your subconscious float out to the surface of your mind, from where you can pick them up and transfer them, through your fingers onto a paper, a computer screen, a medium through which they are imprisoned for eternity. It is a meditative process, one that needs you to exist in a kind of inner quietude. A quietude that can, in some, be brought about only through external quietude.

We sat in a companionable silence for a while, feeling the warmth of the morning sun touch our skins in the soft, gently apologetic caress only the morning sun after a damp night can give. It is strange, with some people there is no compunction to fill up the silences with a forced conversation. Sumit Kamat was already one of those people for me. He finished his cup of tea and set it down. 'And I must take your leave, I need to go back to the cottage and check if my clothes and things are salvageable.'

'Please have some breakfast with me,' I said, keen to not be inhospitable and send off a guest unfed. 'You might not find anything edible in your house.'

He looked confused and ran his fingers through the beard on his chin. 'I really wouldn't want to be a bother.'

'It's no bother at all,' I said and hauled myself slowly to my feet, ignoring the twinge in the ankle and the newly emergent stabs of pain in my knees, moving hesitantly towards the main door, regretting not bringing along the walking stick I thought I could dispense with.

'Can I help you, ma'am?' He sprang to his feet and took my arm, gently taking me across the awkward steps and up again onto the porch into the main house.

'Thank you, and do call me Mrs McNally. Or you could call me Masterniji, that's what everyone around here calls me.'

He smiled, 'Masterniji it is, then.'

Sitting at the table, with a hastily put together spread of marmalade, pancakes, cornflakes and scrambled eggs with toast, along with a bowl of fruit, he continued talking about the previous night.

'It was really very strange last night, the wind was howling like it had a voice, and it was raining so heavily. I haven't seen that kind of merciless rain ever in all the time I've been here. My housekeeper had also left for the day. She doesn't live in the cottage, just comes in twice a day to do the chores and make meals for me.' He stopped, buttered a piece of toast, took a generous bite from it and chewed it for a moment while contemplating something blankly in the distance beyond my head before turning his gaze back to me.

'The next thing I knew there was this incredible flash, followed by this loud clap of thunder and the rain was coming down on me, with some bits of the roof as well. My first instinct was to just get out in case it collapsed, so I just grabbed the laptop I was working on and came running out to find some safe place to pass the night.'

'That sounds really scary, you were lucky not to be injured.'

'Anyway,' he said, rubbing a hand across his eyes, 'Masterniji, thank you so much for the breakfast. I think I will go back to the cottage and collect my things. It won't be in a habitable condition yet and I need to go hunting for a place for at least two months more if I stay back here. I had a six-month break planned here. And I don't feel like returning to Delhi yet.'

Chapter 6

AN HOUR OR so after lunch, I climbed stoically to my study and sat at my desk, willing my fingers to type and my brain to churn out the words. Writing, which had once been something that came mechanically to me, was now taking longer and longer, and not just because the fingers refused to cooperate. The mind seemed dulled by something, I put it down to being unwell and the medicines lingering in the system. There seemed to be a blanket of fog clouding my mind. I could perceptibly feel my reflexes slowing down, there was an insidious switching off of the cells and synapses in my body, a delay in the response time between thought and action, between question and response, between awareness and reaction.

From the window, a soft breeze brought in the scent of the tiny roses laden on the vine creeping along the front door, making the vine a chiaroscuro of green and pink that framed the door and much of the porch. Somewhere in the distance, the birds were singing, intent on setting right all that was wrong in our world, and those who clocked their days according to the exacting schedule of office and work were settling to their afternoon cup of tea. I needed some tea too, I decided and wandered down in search of it. The leg was behaving itself, and only deciding to spring a sudden piercing pain upon me if I thoughtlessly decided to go too fast. The knees seemed to have reserved their outcries of pain for the early mornings and late nights; during the day they functioned as they were meant to, without calling unseemly attention to themselves.

'Bimla,' I called, as I descended the stairs, noticing that I now needed to hold onto the railings and the wall in order to balance myself as I walked down. I resented the infirmity I seemed to be slipping into. 'Chai, please.'

I decided to sit a bit in the verandah and read a book I had discarded a few days before I fell ill. I hadn't done much reading in a while. Bimla came around fifteen minutes later, with tea on a tray and placed it carefully on the centre table, poured a cup out for me and asked me what dinner was to be. She also informed me that we had a new rat menace in the kitchen and the trap had failed to control it, because despite her setting the trap out every night, the kitchen was in a complete state every morning with things strewn all over. I assured her I would call the pest control services, and made a mental note to myself to find the papers from within the drawer of my writing desk, where I kept all the servicing contracts and warranty cards for the various appliances in the house... we were overdue for a servicing on the water purifier, I remembered.

'Strange though,' she said. 'It doesn't eat anything at all. The first rat that I have seen that doesn't eat but just overturns stuff.'

It had been many days since I had taken a walk down the path that led to the other cottages on the road. Until a couple of years ago, I was a regular morning and evening fixture on the narrow paths around the cottages, until the weather became too chilly to walk. And I walked the short distance into the tea estate, where the couple of rooms that functioned as an educational centre for the children of the estate workers had me as a volunteer. While they had generously offered me a paid position in the school run for the workers, I'd declined it. A paid position meant a commitment, I could commit to nothing now, except the endless waiting for my days to play out. My visits to the educational centre too had stopped when the winter of the previous year had inflamed my joints so terribly that even a few steps outside the house had become agony. I never got around to going back to the educational centre. Sometimes the kids would skip up to the house on their way to the centre, press their noses against the windows, or ring the bell hesitantly to hand me a bunch of wild flowers, or some pine cones, or a basket of vegetables from their kitchen gardens. Some sat with me and studied in the verandah, some told me stories about monsters they had fought in the kachcha lane leading to the crematorium ground by the side of the river flowing past the outskirts of town, and yet others kept me posted about the births and deaths in the local population.

They came as they pleased. Some visited a couple of times a week. Some came every other day. Kurnal came by, muddy and battle-scarred from epic wars waged with the other students in the centre, or through sliding down the steep section of the path, or wet from wading through the stream at the other end of the estate and trying to catch fish barehanded. Sometimes he brought a fish with him, at others a shell or a pebble, with interesting coloured veins glinting though the surface. I had a box for the things Kurnal brought me and he would show his latest offering to me when he arrived before taking himself to the lobby and putting it in the box himself. Today he had brought me a twig shaped like a reindeer's antlers.

'Isn't that rather lovely,' I told him. 'But it is too big for the box.' He grinned uncertainly, shuffling his bare feet on the hallway rug, having removed his slippers courteously outside the main door. 'Let's prop it against this table, there, it looks quite interesting, doesn't it?' He nodded.

He came out and settled down on the verandah in front of me, with his notebook and pencil box. 'Masterniji, peechey khudai chal rahi hai,' he informed me gravely, wiping the snot leaking from his nose with the cuff of his sleeve, which strongly needed detergent and a brush, as did Kurnal himself.

I knew about the digging at the back of the cottages, new water pipelines were being laid out. It had been a long process and had only just reached our cottages and didn't seem to be in any state of completion even though it had been a couple of weeks since the crew began work. Not surprising, I mused, considering their steady work comprised more chai breaks than actual digging.

I asked him if it wasn't time for him to be returning home now that the sun was low on the western horizon, half-hidden behind the gentle slopes of the estate. Kurnal, all of eleven, spent his day running wild on the estate, tending to his goats, Golu and Molu. They had now been tied to the gate leading up to the cottage where they were placidly eating up Hari Singh's carefully planted rose bushes, a discovery which would no doubt lead to much irate bellowing from the vocal chords of my head gardener in the morning. I needed to keep my migraine medicine on standby. Along with a glass of water.

'Kurnal, why don't you tie your goats on the outside of the gate?' I suggested gently. He gave me a wide open look that questioned how I ever became a teacher if I lacked the elementary common sense to figure this out.

'Aagey road hai, gaadiyan aati hai.' I decided the flower bed could bear to be divested of some of its foliage rather than the goats ending up as road-kill, never mind that sometimes an entire day went without a single car passing this way.

The sun had dipped a bit since I stepped on the verandah, and deep shadows were now being cast on the emerald grass. A sudden dread pierced my heart, dread for what, I did not know yet. The scene seemed as regular as it could be. But yet there was this sudden patina of eerie anticipation that seemed to make it just that bit surreal, just that bit removed from the regularity of the everyday. Everything was hushed, coiled, waiting, for something to spring from the dark shadows under the distant looming coniferous trees. I instructed Kurnal to leave when he was done with the comprehension paragraph and leave his notebook behind for me to check. The mist was rolling in on the edge of the mountains, slowly and steadily, a grey pallor hanging in the distance, ready to sweep up everything in its path.

'Finis karkey jaao?' he asked incredulously, not believing his luck, given that on other days I mercilessly pushed him to read through a few pages of a book aloud to correct his diction before the comprehension was tackled.

I went to the hallway and sat on the little chair, putting on my walking shoes and picking up the lovely wooden cane I'd kept there. Accepting that I needed the support of the cane was a life-changing moment for me. I told myself that it was just temporary, because of the current fragile state of the ankle, and that once the ankle was completely healed, I wouldn't need it. But, in the space between what I was prepared to acknowledge and reality was the sense of immense gladness for the support it offered me.

I walked out of the front door, closing it behind me, informing Bimla loudly from the passageway itself that I was stepping out for a walk. Her 'Ji, Bibijee,' hung indifferently in the air behind me as some sort of benediction. The early evening air was crisp and clean like it always was, a crispness, a cleanness I only missed when it was not present. Nonetheless, there was a faint tinge of acridity in it, like a laboratory experiment had just been conducted in the skies, and sulphur and oxides and other combustible chemicals were still floating in the ethers ready to ignite. I turned the pathway and drew closer to Ivy Green to find it looking slightly lopsided, but that was only because half its roof had been taken off. Workers were hurriedly clearing up the debris with the help of wheelbarrows while a young man in a white shirt and grey trousers stood around directing them in a manner so officious he could only be a supervisor. He seemed familiar yet unknown. My self-imposed reclusion had made me a stranger to most faces in these parts, though they all seemed to know me and smiled politely as I passed on my occasional ambles around the place. I seemed to be the resident crazy white-skinned person, the one to be smiled at from a distance, to be given a wide berth.

'Excuse me, good evening,' I addressed his back.

He turned around with a start. 'Masterniji, good evening. How are you now? I had heard you were unwell.'

Nothing was secret in this place. It could only be Bimla gossiping with the other locals or Manikji chatting with his pals at the local tea shack who could have spread this information. Not that my being unwell was a matter of top-level secrecy, but it was a trifle disconcerting to have a complete stranger enquire politely about my health. 'Are you in charge of the repairs of this cottage?' I decided to be direct about my questions.

'Ramesh Dobriyal at your service, Masterniji, I am Colonel Dayal's assistant,' he replied jauntily. Colonel Dayal also managed the properties of some of the non-resident owners of the cottages around, Ivy Green one of them. I had spotted Mr Dobriyal around often enough, I realised, zipping down the road on his trusty two-wheeler, with the silencer occasionally needing to be seen to when it began informing everyone in a two-kilometre radius of his approach. His face was always camouflaged by his helmet, which is why I hadn't recognised him.

'A pleasure to meet you, Mr Dobriyal,' I replied. 'Thank you, I am, as you can see, completely well now, it was just a bit of a fall and an ankle sprain that had got me down.'

He clucked sympathetically. 'You must be careful, Masterniji, bones don't heal easily after a certain age.'

My bones must be chalk given the nutrition I'd received in my early years, but that could wait for another conversation. 'I will be careful henceforth, thank you. What's the damage like?'

He frowned, with the ignorance of someone who knows only what has been told to him. 'I really don't know, Masterniji, I just got here, but parts of the roof have to be replaced and there is leakage on the first and ground floors. The wooden flooring has been damaged but...'

The 'but' trailed off in the wind, hanging ominously between the two of us. I walked off the pathway, onto the grass and looked at the damaged roof. He followed and continued, 'First insurance claims and all that need to be sorted out before we can begin repair work; for that the owners need to visit and file claims.'

Obviously, Sumit was not going to be able to continue his residency here, given the condition of the premises. 'What about that young man who had rented it, where is he going to stay now?'

'Sumit Kamat?' he asked, his face creasing into a frown yet again. 'He's trying to find another place to stay. The lodge down the road is full up and it is already evening. He might have to go into town proper and find a room in one of the hotels.'

I moved heavily towards a stone bench set by the pathway and sat on it. It had been days since the fall and the leg was still troubling me. I looked at my wristwatch, it was almost five-thirty p.m. Time to start heading back, it would get dark soon, and by the looks of the sky, damp and rainy too. I was a little uncertain about walking around in the dark. I stood up determinedly, ignoring the sharp insistent twinge in the ankle, heckling me angrily. The sky was already filling up with small, angry clouds. I would do well to get back indoors before it began raining, even a light shower these days could have me catch a chill.

'I should be getting back now, do tell Mr Kamat that he is welcome to stay with me until he finds accommodation, and to not hesitate to drop by.'

Dobriyal smiled politely, 'Shall I send someone with you, Masterniji, or will you be able to manage on your own?' Noticing perhaps the slight uncertainty I had while putting my foot on the ground, the sudden tremor of my hand that bore on the walking stick with more pressure than I would have liked to display.

'No.' I waved him off, with barely concealed irritation. 'I am fine, I will manage.' The suddenness of my own fragility was surprising me.

He looked at me closely. 'You know, Masterniji, you remind me of someone whose photograph I saw once in the burra bungala in the estate, but there is no name on those photographs....'

This came as a shock to me. I had lived here for over a decade and a half now, and this was the first time that someone mentioned a potential doppelganger. I felt rather short-changed. 'That's interesting,' I said. 'Do you think I could see the photographs?' I asked him, turning back, waiting for his answer, feeling the twinge in the ankle intensify; the veins at the back of my legs begin to burn and the knees begin their sputtering of protest at standing longer than they had bargained for.

He looked at me, my walking cane and the long path into the estate from the gates across the main path. 'It is a long walk inside. Don't worry. I'll request the manager and bring the album across to your home tomorrow. Of course, those photographs are of someone much younger than you are, a lady in her twenties, but something about her....'

Who could it be that reminded this young man of me, I wondered. I hadn't come here until I had retired. It would be interesting to see those photographs he mentioned.

'Thank you, Mr Dobriyal, that would be most kind of you,' I replied.

I turned around and walked back towards my cottage. It wasn't a long walk, ten minutes maximum with a leg in fine form, twenty minutes for a leg that was acting up, through some curving paths, which occasionally dipped steeply. The evening was settling in nicely now, like any self-respecting autumnal evening should, with the twilight fading steadily from the skies in a blaze of pinks and purples, the sun having dropped abruptly into the abyss that would be the other side of the earth, where families would now stir, morning would break, and hopes would rise and flutter on the windowsill of a new day. The distant mountains were now imposing grey shadows with the snow on their peaks glinting ominously pink and blue and it would be a matter of an hour before they were swallowed up by the pitch darkness that would sweep in and hush the birds, now skittering as they flew back to their nests. A cold breeze began blowing up from the east, cutting into my skin. I hadn't thought of wearing a sweater when I stepped out, and the thick shirt and trousers I had on were not warm enough. I tried to hurry my pace; as drops began to splat on the path and on my scalp, I moved as briskly as I could.

Before long the rain was pelting down quite steadily and I hurried, getting drenched to the bone. Bimla came hurrying down the path with an umbrella as she saw me turn the corner. 'Doctor Saab aaye hai.' I noticed the small red car parked a little way off, and went in, shaking off the rain from the umbrella and me. He had told me he would drop by after shutting the clinic on Monday to check on me and my ankle.

Dr Sanyal had made himself comfortable in the drawing room and was busy on his iPad. He rose as he saw me enter the room. 'This is exactly not what a patient of mine who has just emerged from a spate of high fever should be doing,' he said, shaking his head as he took in my wet and bedraggled state.

'Couldn't escape the rain, Dr Sanyal,' I replied, laughing at the censure in his tone. 'What a pleasant surprise to see you. Please give me a moment, I will change out of these wet clothes and join you in some time. My days of wet clothing as attractive second skin are long past. Thank you so much for dropping Nina, I'm sure she was most delighted for your company.'

Something of a slight shadow crossed his face, a mixture of tenderness and pain and regret and some other emotions that made me catch my breath for the split second they were given free rein to play on his visage.

'I hope she wasn't too bored by my ramblings,' he replied. 'I think I saw her eyes glaze over when I discussed some of my patients and my trekking experiences. Had her drop off into deep sleep, which thankfully relieved her from paying attention politely for the rest of the trip.'

Manikji entered the room, bearing an electricity bill. 'Bibijee, they delivered this today.' We were on an electricity conservation effort, terrified by the spiralling bill each month, but it seemed to have little or no impact on the meter reading. I vowed to keep a watch out for the meter reading chap the next time he arrived and insist he show me what he wrote down. Manikji also swore to track him down and make him confess on his ancestor's remains that he was not putting down imaginary figures that pleased his fancy. We had actually been very careful about our use of electricity. The only thing I was not careful about was my pre-dinner gin and tonic.

I withdrew from the drawing room, and went into my bedroom when the rain intensified to storm proportions. It began lashing at the roof, and a bolt of lightning flashed in the distance, followed by the low, enraged rumble of thunder like some underground dragon rising from slumber and grumbling at being disturbed from repose.

I changed out of my wet clothes, towelled my head dry, ran a brush quickly through my hair to avoid looking like a dandelion and stepped back out into the drawing room to find Dr Sanyal joined by a bedraggled Sumit. 'We have company! Good evening, Sumit, though, I must say, it doesn't seem to be very good an evening out there.'

'Yes, it seems to be another of those wretched storms,' Sumit said, rising as I entered. 'I just stopped to thank you for taking me in last night. I'll be off now, I need to get back to the main town and check into a hotel I've reserved a room in. It's going to be terribly expensive though for a long stay.' His voice seemed a little uncertain as he glanced out of the window at the angry rain, daring anyone sane to step out and face its fury.

'Oh, I can drop you on my way back, if you want,' Dr Sanyal interjected.

I had only just registered the neat suitcase which had been behind the umbrella and coat-stand in the hallway.

'Oh, feel free to stay here for as long as you want to, Sumit,' I said. 'I could do with some company, and it is quite ridiculous for you to go hunting for a room at this odd hour.' Sumit demurred and picked up his suitcase, a neat black soft one with the mandatory handle that converted it into a strolley. I instructed Bimla to open the guest bedroom again and while Sumit settled in, Dr Sanyal got his stethoscope out, checked my ankle, checked my vitals and pronounced me on the mend.

'I had better be going,' Dr Sanyal said. 'It seems to be getting worse outside. I had just dropped by to check on you since I was driving past. A little boy from one of the families renting out the bungalow is down with a bad attack of food poisoning, I was called in to take a look at him.'

He looked out; the rain had become a curtain of grey. These rainstorms up in the mountains were sudden, grim and disappeared as swiftly as they came most times. The only thing to do with them, as with everything in life, was to wait them out. The worst would pass and the water would run down swiftly, leaving the scent of dampness as the only reminder of the wrath of the sky. I gave it half an hour at the maximum. Post that, I was sure it would clear up.

'I don't think going in this rain is such a good idea, Doctor,' I said. The roads were narrow and winding and often unlit, it could be dangerous. Rain loosened the earth, boulders and mud fell, blocked roads, and if one was unfortunate enough to be in a car when a boulder decided to make its way down, it could be quite fatal. 'Why don't you wait until the storm passes, and have dinner here with us and tell us all those amusing stories about other irascible patients like me? Especially the one about that Brigadier with the snappish dog who bit him in a rather tender part of his anatomy when he stepped on his tail by mistake...'

He laughed a bit and looked out again. The bravest of hearts would quail at stepping out in such a storm and Dr Sanyal had no one at home waiting for him to return, except a wizened housekeeper-cook who spent her evenings in a stupor smoking what were surely potent bidis filled with the illegal, hand-rolled stuff from the weed that soothed.

'I think I will take you up on that offer for dinner, Mrs McNally. I am just that bit hungry, and could do with some solid nutrition. Whatever has been cooked at home for dinner can't be too appetizing given my cook's record.'

I asked them both to help themselves to whatever they wished for from the humble bar I stocked in one corner of the drawing room and moved to the kitchen to see what fare we had at hand. Bimla had made a passable soup, some standard vegetarian fare, a yellow daal spiced with cumin seeds, chillies, and coriander, rice tempered with spices and okra as a side dish. There were some cutlets in the freezer I had her defrost and fry, and roll out some additional rotis. She had also attempted an unsuccessful bread pudding, which I asked her to serve, sliced neatly, and topped with some caramel syrup to disguise the patchiness of the pudding which hadn't browned evenly. We were a little low on vegetables and Manikji would be sent into town on his cycle tomorrow to stock up, if the weather cleared up enough for him to cycle down with no risk of sliding down a steep road and breaking a limb or two. The exercise would do him good, over the years he had gone from a scrawny forty-something-year-old to a rotund mid-fifties man who seemed like he should avoid going in the immediate vicinity of any sharp object for fear of bursting.

The storm had picked up outside and the wind was sighing around the house, as though it was readying to sweep us up and cart us off to Kansas. The temperature seemed to have dipped discernibly and an unseasonal chill had crept into the air. I had Manikji switch on the heater in the living room and got myself a cardigan to keep the chill off my bones. A snifter of brandy was called for, and I returned to the living room to find the two men in deep conversation, a curious comfort between them that seemed strange given they had just met. They turned towards me and rose politely as I entered, with Dr Sanyal insisting I sit on the comfortable armchair near the heater he had hitherto been occupying. Knowing my routine, as he did after all these years, he mixed me a gin and tonic, handing it to me without ceremony, although I would have preferred some brandy to combat the chill that was turning my bones into icicles. We moved to the dining room, the meal was simple and filling, just like food should be – nourishing the body, satiating the hunger and not taxing the brain too much in the eating of it. We finished the meal with the pudding and felt we were well within the state of being what the Buddha in his infinite wisdom termed nirvana. A sated stomach is probably the easiest gateway to bliss; it is the hungry stomachs that turn to rioting and violence.

The storm outside hadn't abated a whit and the wind still continued to sigh outside the window panes, rattling them threateningly, declaring intent of war. And, out of the darkness raining outside, a piercing shriek shattered the sounds of nature and had us all freeze in our places. After a long moment, when time seemed to stand still, I managed to get the blood flowing in my veins again and rushed to the window as quickly as I could without the cane to assist me, trying to figure out what had caused the scream. Nothing was visible in the darkness and the sheet of rain. And then came a second scream, a howl of terrible anguish, rending the sky apart, tearing the cosmos, piercing my ears and penetrating my very marrow. It was unearthly, a scream that couldn't have emerged from a human throat, a scream that came from a being that had seen the deepest depths of hell.

Chapter 7

PERHAPS I HAD imagined the screams. But no, everyone in the house was on their feet and at the windows, looking for the source of the screams.

'What on earth was that?' I asked all those around, gathered at two separate windows, Bimla and Manikji having arrived from the kitchen and the backroom to press their noses against the window panes, looking at the darkness without.

'Yeh daayan ki cheekh hain,' Bimla said, her voice dripping with a fear that could not be contained. Her body was shivering. She began reciting the Hanuman Chaalisa loudly. Manikji, suspiciously rosy-cheeked and unbalanced enough to make me make a mental note to check the contents of the alcohol bottles stocked in the bar cabinet, was bobbing his head, which indicated the definite presence of alcohol in his bloodstream.

'Don't be silly,' I told her in Hindi. 'It is a woman's voice. Someone is in trouble. The scream came from behind the cottage and not too far away.'

Dr Sanyal was the first to move; he was quick on his feet and athletic, it came from him doing his hour-long runs uphill before he hit the clinic and his treks into the savagery of the mountains. Sumit, a little less quick on the reflexes, perhaps the result of a life spent sitting in one place and typing things out, followed him into the rain outside.

Bimla and Manikji emerged from the kitchen and stood with me on the porch, getting lashed in the rain while the two men ran off into the dark storm, without bothering to grab umbrellas or raincoats or windcheaters.

I went back to the window and looked outside. I could see nothing. We waited for around twenty minutes, but it seemed longer in that dark limbo between moments ticking by in uneasy silence. Finally Bimla hurried back in from the porch, saying Dr Sanyal and Sumit were coming back with something or someone, and they soon entered, carrying a young girl between them. Her clothes were drenched, her face was lifeless. I recognised her, she lived in a hovel behind the four cottages and worked in some of them when it was tourist season, doing the basic cleaning and cooking. Basanti, her name was, if I remembered rightly. She would occasionally come to the back door and chat a bit with Bimla during the afternoons, fetch her some vegetables from the market, sell her some milk from her cow and offer to do some odd jobs around the house in return for some food.

I directed them to the small ante room, which had a little couch for the occasional visitor, and they gently put her down on it. Dr Sanyal took his bag from the living room and began checking her. She was barely conscious, in shock and hardly responding to anything the doctor asked her. Bimla got her a drink of water and sponged the dirt off her face, and asked her some questions in the native dialect, which I still couldn't understand when spoken fluently despite living in these parts for so many years.

'She doesn't know what happened, she says,' Bimla conveyed

to us, buoyed with her importance at being translator-in-chief, given that Basanti was in too much of a shock to communicate in Hindi, a language she was familiar with in regular times. 'She was at home and asleep, her father hadn't come back home yet.' At this point Bimla turned to me and reminded me in a loud aside that the father in question was Jogya, also known as the local drunk, who often had to be half-dragged, half-carried back home by able-bodied men, keen to ingratiate themselves with Basanti. Often, his stint at the local bootleg joint was sponsored by these men, who tried to convince him to browbeat Basanti into marrying one of them. Basanti dissuaded them all. The local gossip went that she had given her heart to Gopal, the postmaster's son who had moved to Delhi a couple of years ago in search of better opportunities, and who had given her his word that he would return for her.

'She suddenly woke up to find herself in the pit they've been digging to lay the new pipes,' Bimla continued.

'We found her semi-conscious,' said Sumit.

'She needs stitches,' Dr Sanyal said. 'She has a deep gash on her arm and what seems like animal claw markings all over her limbs.'

'How strange,' I replied. 'Did a wild animal drag her off then, intending to make a meal of her? There have been no wild animal sightings here, no hyenas, no leopards, not for years.'

Dr Sanyal nodded. 'That's the only explanation I can think of right now.' He applied some antiseptic to the wounds and removed from his bag the needle and suturing thread for stitching the ugly gashes on her arms.

The girl sat up and drew her sodden dupatta around herself with a strange dignity that did away with the incongruity of her bedraggled and muddied condition. As I moved out of the room, she stared at me strangely, her eyes red, burning, her face an expression of mingled malevolence and hatred that sent shivers down my spine. I had seen that expression before, on the face at my window. For a second, her face was the same face I'd seen that night. Spectral, drained of colour, almost blue-toned in its ghastliness. I must have imagined it, for when I looked back at her, her expression was neutral and placid again, her face clear and yet confused, not the twisted mask I'd imagined I'd seen a second ago. I tried hard to calm the sense of dread, of the unexpected running up and down my spine of its chilly fingers as I emerged into the passageway where Sumit stood, still drenched from the rain which had thankfully slackened.

'Heaven knows when this storm will settle down,' I said, going back into the drawing room.

'This is the most curious thing I've ever come across,' said Dr Sanyal, emerging from the room, having dressed her wounds and administered a tetanus shot, just in case the scratches were inflicted by a sharp instrument. 'The gashes on her body, and she claims to have no memory of how this happened.'

'Could she have been sedated by someone who wanted to kidnap her, and then changed their mind? Or is it something worse?' I asked hesitantly, wondering if the girl had been violated sexually.

'No, she seems to be okay, apart from the disorientation and the cuts on her limbs. What we need to find out is how those were inflicted on her.'

I could sniff blood, anger and hatred in the air. Whatever it was, the miasmal presence hovered over the room, waiting, watching, casting a shadow of gloom over everything, despite the lights blazing in every room. I would not get much sleep that night, I knew, my heart was beating faster than it should and a cold fist was clenching and unclenching my intestines, twisting them. A growing dryness in my mouth made me uncomfortable. I went in and looked at her arms and legs. Bimla had stepped out to the kitchen to get Basanti some more water to drink. The slashes visible on her limbs had been disinfected and the deeper ones bandaged, but they were still bleeding, drop by drop, all over the couch and on the floor. Basanti was staring down at the blood dribbling down from the bandages with an expression that was indecipherable. As

I walked in she looked up at me, smiling. Her face was no longer that of the guileless Basanti I had seen walking around the paths near the cottage, but the face at the window, the face that was haunting me, my dreams.

Her lips didn't move but my name echoed in my head, it was being called out in the same spectral voice the face at the window had used, the same spectral voice that chased me in my dreams, that I ran from through thorny undergrowth, through squelching muck, through leeches sticking to my legs, sucking me dry of all the blood in my veins. I fled the room, as quickly as I could manage with my reluctant knees, shaking uncontrollably.

'Did you see her face?' I asked Bimla, who was returning with a glass of water in her hand.

'What happened to her face?' Bimla replied, peeping into the ante-room and holding the door open just enough for me to peep within. The Basanti I knew looked back at me, the face back to what I remembered her as – open, guileless, child-like. I shivered involuntarily.

'Can you drop her back home if she is well enough to walk?' I asked Bimla, who looked at me curiously. It wasn't like me to hurry someone who had been injured out of the house, but she had learnt over the years not to question me.

The rain tapered a bit as Bimla and Manikji escorted Basanti back to her shanty, with two umbrellas between them. As she stepped out of the house, she turned around and looked back at us, her eyes narrowed, hissing, and I could almost hear her speak, in a language I did not comprehend, but paradoxically could understand because nothing was spoken aloud, it was perhaps all just in my mind. The chilly finger running down my spine had now grown into a hydra phalanx of snaking arms and was crushing my ribs in a bone-breaking deathly embrace. No one else seemed to have noticed or heard it. A part of me understood it to be a warning, a message and a challenge I needed to accept. I hugged myself, rubbing my arms to keep the chill from freezing my bones, noting how the flesh had fallen away from the bones, and all I could feel were the bones, covered by a thin, soft parchment of skin. Bones. I had shrivelled into skin and bones.

Dr Sanyal drove off home as the rain subsided, while Sumit said his goodnights and disappeared into the room he had previously occupied. I felt a little safer with a younger person on the premises, but nonetheless, I slept fitfully, dreaming of women floating in the sky, smashing the glass windowpane, reaching in with pale, ghostly hands and grasping my throat with a grip of steel that left me choking, the breath being squeezed out of my windpipe, slowly, deliberately, painfully.

I woke with a start and switched my bedside lamp on. It was three in the morning. Again. I sat up in bed and took a few deep sips from the glass of chilled water kept on my nightstand. My neck felt sore. I rose and switched on the light and looked around. The room was as it was when I had gone to sleep. The bladder announced its need to empty itself and I carefully began the long trek down the room, into the passage, across it, to the bathroom on the landing. There was an eerie, stultifying silence outside. This part of the world was always sepulchral and silent to begin with and while night times were even quieter, there was something tangibly different about this silence that I couldn't quite put my finger on. It lurked. It waited patiently. Almost like it was biding its time before it sprang upon us, a malevolent presence. I looked at myself in the mirror above the wash basin and splashed some water on my face. There were discernable finger marks on my throat. Distinct finger marks, red, raw, as if someone or something had tried to strangle me and then stopped, abruptly. I touched the marks and winced, they were real. I could still feel the pressure around my throat, the vice-like grip that had almost cut off the oxygen supply to my lungs and brain. Shivers born of a visceral fear racked my body as I made my terrified way back to bed, wondering if I should call on some god to protect me, but I knew no gods who would come to my rescue at such short notice, not after I had abandoned them.

When you get to my age, it is not death that scares you; in fact, part of you exults at the thought of its arrival. You anticipate death, much like a woman might anticipate the arrival of a lover, with the kind of nervous tension that dissolves her anxiety, the anticipation of his arrival more delicious than his actual arrival. You wonder how it would be... would it be a calm and gentle transition to the next realm of consciousness, similar to drifting off into a deep sleep or whether it would be a violent jerking out of the soul from the physical carapace and a brutal casting down through corridors of darkness filled with pestilent ghouls from a wrathful afterlife. You wonder, you wait, and you try to prepare yourself for it in the best way you can. But, I believe nothing can prepare you for death. Death, like being born, is something you have to experience alone. And having experienced it, be condemned to be unable to bring that understanding to your next experience of it. It is the fear of the unknown that scared me, not the dying itself. It was a fear that suddenly rushed back at me, a fear of what was around me, a presence that only I seemed to sense, that was visible only to me, that haunted my dreams and had now, stepped out of my dreams into my wakefulness.

I lay back in my bed, touching what felt like welts on my neck gingerly, and drew the blankets over me, feeling a chill seep into my bones, almost as if the temperature in the room had suddenly dropped to below freezing point. I let the bedside table night lamp stay on. I had no courage to plunge the room into darkness again, a little light made me feel safer from whatever or whoever was invading my dreams. I opened the drawer next to the bed, and fumbled for the Bible and a rosary I had placed there, a promise to the Mother Superior at Datham Hall, who had insisted I never stay completely without the presence of the divine in my life, no matter what I insisted my beliefs were. 'Don't believe in a god, don't pray, don't go for Mass, don't go for confession, but promise me this, you will always have the word of God with you, wherever you go.' I hadn't had the heart to refuse her.

I clutched the black clothbound book and found the words of the Lord's Prayer come to my lips unbidden. '*Our Father who art in heaven, hallowed be thy name, thy kingdom come, thy will be done...*' I recited aloud. I said the Hail Mary next. I wrapped the delicate beaded rosary around my wrist and said what I hadn't in decades, the words flowing from my lips from the reservoir of the thousands said through my childhood. I felt comforted, drawing a strange strength from the familiar prayers, realising I had forgotten nothing, even after all these decades the words tripped off my lips with ease.

The room was still uncharacteristically chilly for this time of the year. I turned the thermostat on the bed-warmer a little higher. Bed-warmers were better than hot water bottles. In my days as a teacher at Datham Hall, we had hot water bottles to keep us from freezing to death in our beds. And log stoves in a few lucky rooms, which kept the room cosy, but woke one up freezing when the fire died down in the middle of the night. And we also had thick layers of blankets, which weighed one down so well that emerging out in the chilly mornings needed willpower of steel. Bed-warmers and thermostat-controlled blankets, kindly gifted to me by Millie, were a blessing I couldn't dream of surviving a winter without. Of course, given the erratic power supply, the hot water bottles and log fires were still a part of our winter arsenal against the cold. As was glycerine and petroleum jelly, and coconut oil to keep our skin from flaking off in a shower and scattering itself as we passed or from keeping the hair on our head from rising with the static as we pulled on our thermals. I could feel waves of sleep wash up against my ears, when I heard my name being hissed again, a whisper so sibilant that it scratched against my eardrums. No one called me by my name anymore. I had become Mrs McNally over forty years ago to everyone. I'd become Masterniji a decade and a half ago. I'd forgotten I was once Julia Chaudhari. I'd almost forgotten I was once called only Julia. Julia, the girl with no surname.

The fine hair on my arms stood on end; I opened my eyes very slowly and noticed a slight shadow in my rocking chair opposite the bed, which now seemed to be rocking itself, gently, deliberately, rhythmically, like it would, if it were manipulated by a physical force. As I looked on, the shadow solidified into the outline of a woman, a woman who was slightly built and sunken faced. The only discernible features in her face were her eyes, the irises red and piercing. I gasped in horror, sat up in bed, my hand reaching out to press the bell that would summon Bimla and Manikji, without taking my eyes off the chair. There was no one there. The chair was now vacant but still rocking, with the emptiness of being suddenly vacated by a palpable presence. Surely, I was hallucinating. I grabbed the rosary and began praying with all the broken prayers I could bring to mind, shutting my eyes tight. Sleep eluded me. My heart was thudding in the most disturbing manner, my stomach was coiled up in knots. I was too terrified to get out of bed and too terrified to stay in. The echo of that sibilant voice hissing my name still resounded in my brain, twisting around synapses and neurons, with the buzz of a high-voltage current passing through the flabby folds.

When I finally dared open my eyes, it was morning. The room was still dark but a muted sun brightened the world beyond. And the rocking chair, by the window, was ominously still, a terrifying reminder that something not from this world had been sitting in it the previous night, with its red eyes fixated on me, leaching out my energy, draining my body of the will to live. And written in the mist fogging the window from the outside, was my name, scribbled in an erratic scrawl, over and over again. Julia. Julia. Julia.

Chapter 8

THE EVENTS OF the previous night seemed to be hanging over the crisp mountain air like a malevolent curse. The birds too seemed hesitant to fill the air with song. Sunlight straggled into the room, hazy through the misty clouds that floated across the lawns, stabbing through the thin lace curtains and casting faint shadows on the bed. I loved waking up with the first rays of sunlight on my face, the winter months had me toss and turn restlessly, waiting for the errant ray of sun to come in. And the sun came late in the winter, sometimes for days on end one didn't see it.

I had always been an early riser but these days I barely slept, a few hours at the most. It was like the body didn't need restorative sleep anymore. I pulled on my robe and went to look out the window. The world outside was the blinding flash of neon green that inevitably came about after intense rain. I looked at myself in the mirror above the polished-wood dressing table; there were faint marks on my neck, discernible marks. I hadn't been dreaming. The imprints were still painful to the touch. The rocking chair was empty, still. Surely I had been imagining what I saw the previous night. The faint rays of the morning sun had done away with the mist on the window, along with my name written in a sloping script. Drops trickled down the window panes apologetically now, erasing all evidence.

I switched on the tiny television in my room. The local cable television channels showed some girls doing a traditional harvest festival dance, their cheeks flushed pink with the exertion, their inexpertly applied makeup detracting from rather than enhancing their natural loveliness. The scrolling text below spoke of an exhibition cum sale at a school hall over the weekend, the inauguration of a new bank branch and ATM, the visit of a high-profile politician for a campaign rally in advance of the forthcoming elections, everything seemed to be on par for the course. I rang the bell for Bimla.

'Chai, Bibijee.' She came in with freshly brewed tea, just the way I loved it.

I sat sipping my first cup of the day as the old rumbling geyser heated the precious water stored to lukewarm for me to bathe in. A rap at the open door and Sumit poked his head in, his curls looking all shaggy and slept in. 'May I come in?'

'Please do,' I replied, sitting straighter in my chair next to the window, aware that I was perhaps not at my most presentable. I ineffectively ran a hand over my hair to smooth it down, knowing that it did not matter anymore, but vanity is perhaps one of the last things to go when one has been an attractive woman for a major portion of one's life and has been painfully aware of the power it could wield.

'Good morning,' he said. 'I heard you were up. I'm planning to go into town to find me some accommodation. I can't keep imposing on your kindness. By the way, did you feel anything weird last night?'

I looked at him, 'Weird? In what sense?'

He ran a shaky hand over his eyes. 'I woke up in the dead of the night thanks to a sudden clap of thunder and I swear there was someone or something in my room, beside the window. It was dark and I couldn't see too clearly. I switched the bedside light on and there was no one there. It completely creeped me out.'

I felt the chill go through me, like it had last night, and felt the finger imprints on my neck blaze with a heat that was odd, unwarranted, in the chilly morning air.

'It could have been a rat, we normally don't have them, but it could have come in through a grate,' I ventured, hesitantly. 'I wouldn't worry about it too much if I were you. These old houses have a life of their own and make the strangest sounds, especially when it is windy and raining.'

'I hope so,' he said.

I closed my eyes for one long moment thinking of the fingers around my neck, squeezing insistently, feeling the pressure on the voice box, realising that I couldn't have made a sound even if I tried because the pressure was too great. The shadow in the rocking chair, its red eyes blazing into mine, was still fresh in my mind. 'It wasn't a rat for sure. It was something quite different,' he insisted.

I shook my head, surely I was imagining things. I needed to speak with Dr Sanyal about these things, the face I had been seeing, Basanti, these marks on my neck. It didn't make sense. I decided to ignore his statement, or I would send myself into a vortex of panic from which there was no escape. 'I needed to send Manikji down to the store to get some groceries and vegetables too, we're almost out of provisions and I needed him to get some of my banking work done as well. Perhaps you could go together, although you are welcome to stay here for as long as you might need to.'

He smiled and went out of the room, politely demurring about imposing on me, and stating he would bathe quickly and be ready to leave within the hour if Manikji would be ready by then. I instructed Bimla to have a quick breakfast waiting for him and gave Manikji carefully detailed instruction on the groceries and vegetables he was to procure as well as the bank withdrawals he was to make.

The outside seemed calm enough, no evidence of the evil storm of the previous night. The newspapers of course, had not arrived. We received the newspapers rather late, and I inevitably ended up reading them from the afternoon into the evening, when the shadows stretched on the grass, when the laziness of the day coagulated into a long-suppressed yawn, waiting for the day to end and evening to fall, so it could curl up by the fireplace and soak in the warmth of the logs that crackled and burnt, and shoot occasional embers past the grate onto the floor.

It wasn't fireplace weather yet though, I still needed to get the chimney cleaned up and ready for the winter. Kurnal would help in gathering logs and kindling for the fire, which Bimla would store in the little storeroom just next to the kitchen where we kept most of the provisions. And freezing evenings and nights, when the snow fell thick and hard, would be spent huddled around the fireplace, talking, or reading a book, till I began dozing in my chair. Bimla and Manikji usually woke me up gently and I would then take myself to my room.

I wondered how Basanti was. The thought of her eyes boring into mine and the gashes on her limbs made me shudder despite myself. I resolved to ask Bimla to pay her a visit. Or was I being ridiculous, had I been imagining things? I would decide later, I thought. I would visit her and confirm for myself that I had been imagining the pinpricks of red in her eyes that had slashed me like laser beams, as well as the voice in my head that seemed to come from her before she went back to being the confused young girl.

I hadn't written for a few days. I was nearing the middle of my story. Stories are monsters, even if they are your own, they lurk near cave entrances of the mind, trying to pull you in so that they can devour you in a single gulp and burp up your essence, so you can never quite emerge without having lost a bit of yourself in it.

If the knees stopped behaving like they were warring factions with the rest of the body, I would take a nice long walk to the cluster of shanties behind the main road, where Basanti lived and see how she was. If the weather was calm, if there was no rain, if my ankle felt up to it, if I felt brave enough... There were many ifs. I would deal with those ifs later.

Bathed, dressed, I went out into the front verandah to look at my flowers blooming and get my dose of daily gossip from Hari Singh. He salaamed jauntily as I settled myself in the cane chair, and angled myself to get a good view of the mountains up front, and the soft clouds, drifting in, shading the autumn morning sunlight into a muted palette of dappled washed gold, and diluted cerulean. I had carefully wrapped a stole around my neck, to hide the bruises from curious gazes, bruises I couldn't explain, bruises that made it difficult for me to swallow food without wincing.

'Memsaab,' he said, ambling up scythe in hand, muddy from a herculean effort at potting some bulbs before the winter set in. 'I heard the Doctor Saab and Writer Babu found Jogya's daughter Basanti unconscious in the pit being dug for the water pipes last night?'

'Yes,' I replied, aware that Manikji and Bimla must have shared the information with him, given he stayed on the other extreme of the estate boundary.

'I think you would be interested in looking at the pit where they say she was found.'

I rose hurriedly, moved carefully down the few stairs that connected the verandah to the lawns and followed him to the rear of the house, where the path curved further, leading to the outhouses occupied by the old retainers. The ground was soggy from last night's rain and I wished I had worn better shoes; the dampness was soaking through the thin canvas shoes and the woollen socks I had hurriedly pulled on this morning. I was wearing thermal inners today, for the first time this season, and despite that could still feel the morning chill announcing that winter was just around the corner. It felt too early to have moved into thermals, but I wasn't willing to risk catching a cold, which normally extended into an ugly bout of pneumonia that would wrack my body hollow with chest-ripping coughing bouts all through the winter.

Hari Singh lived in the workers' quarters, and wasn't part of the regular labour that worked on the estate, or in the factory where the packing and bottling of the produce from the fruit orchards that employed most of the locals in these parts took place. His wife, his daughters and his sons did. He worked only in the gardens around the cottages and the burra bungalow. His passion was carefully nursing flower-beds, trimming hedges into impeccable evenness, planning a burst of contrasting colour, so gloriously uncoordinated that they razed the retina with their brilliance when in full bloom in the spring.

Hari Singh and I walked towards the main road, towards a little bend. He stopped beside some shrubbery and pointed without saying a word. I looked in the direction his fingers indicated and saw dark patches on the ground. 'Blood,' he said matter of factly. Some twigs were snapped awkwardly like something had been dropped on them from a height, and torn fragments of cloth were stuck to them – bits of Basanti's dupatta from last night. A dupatta that had been ripped to shreds, which I remembered seeing her trying to cover herself with in a moment of modesty. 'Julia,' I heard her voice hissing again, in my head, 'Julia.' I shivered despite the morning sun beaming down at us. A little ahead was the pit that the workers were digging for the new water pipeline and pump-house via which the cottages on this stretch would be supplied water. 'They didn't find her in the pit, did they?'

He shook his head to indicate an uncertain maybe. 'She says she was looking in, under the cover of darkness, when she knew there was no one around to see her, for things she could pull out and sell in the market, when she fell in or got sucked into the pit.

After that, she can't remember what happened or why she screamed, nor anything until she came back to consciousness in your home.'

I contemplated this information in silence, staring at the blood that still stained the ground, despite the rain that had battered the hills the previous night.

He lowered his voice even further. 'Her father has asked for the local witch doctor to come exorcise her. He thinks she is possessed.' We walked back contemplating this bit of information in a few minutes of silence, while I tried to piece together the events of the previous night in my head.

'Possessed? By what or whom?' I said. 'Let me go see her, I'll go there after breakfast.'

'No,' he replied, his face scrunching itself into a question mark, 'Memsaab, don't go there alone, I will accompany you. It is not safe.'

Bimla ambled out and joined the conversation, lowering herself on to the steps with a heavy thump. 'I thought there was something strange with her yesterday. Her eyes looked like that of an animal, red. I thought at first it was because of the lights going on and off in the house with the power outage, but I'm sure I saw her eyes flickering. Like the string of Diwali lights. But then when we took her home, she was fine.'

I rebuked her gently, 'Bimla, you probably imagined it. Don't say these things out aloud. She's a young girl, this could scar her for life, this talk.' Talk spread swiftly in these parts on wings that it did not merit, and additional inaccurate details tacked on for good measure.

'Ji, Bibijee, but everybody is talking about her since morning. It isn't just me. How many people can you ask to not talk about it?' she replied, her lips curled downwards and her face thundercloud stormy. She went back into the house from the back entrance via the kitchen, telling me that breakfast was served and the young Writer Babu was waiting for me to begin. I followed her, holding onto the cane grimly.

'I hope I find place in one of the lodges in town, it won't be the same as staying here though,' Sumit said, narrowing his eyes, squinting into the distance in the disconcerting manner he had of not looking at one sometimes while speaking. 'I will miss this sense of isolation, perhaps I could ask around for a home stay on some other estate.'

'You do know you're perfectly welcome to stay here. There is a room available, there is food available and I will try to keep out of your hair as much as possible. And I would welcome the company, I truly would. You might want to consider it,' I offered gently.

I had grown a little fond of this boy, he with his unkempt hair and tawny brown eyes. They reminded me of someone I had known, born of the desert, his features sharper, more aquiline than Sumit's, the nobility he was descended from evident in his profile and bearing. Ranvijay. A parent of one of the students at Datham Hall where I was a teacher. Millie had got his eyes. And his temper. And nothing else. Not even his name.

I sighed, feeling the emptiness of regret coursing through my lungs. Another time. I would think of Ranvijay later, when I could bear the stab of the memory, slicing itself into my heart and twisting its blade to cut through all the layers of unthinking I had plastered it up with.

Sumit smiled down at me with his honey-coloured eyes, the eyes which had their irises expand to black holes one could sink into. 'I would love to, but you have to let me pay you for my boarding and lodging,' he said. 'I insist.'

'We'll discuss that later,' I replied, patting his hand. I felt strangely drawn to this boy I barely knew. 'For now, go into town, check around the lodges, and if you don't find anything worth staying at, come back here anytime, knowing there's always a room for you here.'

He nodded and went off with Manikji; he walking jauntily a little ahead, while Manikji rode with great dignity on his trusty, rusting cycle, one which had been in service for over eight years now and was in urgent need of being replaced. I watched them disappear down the curving road, from my vantage point in the front verandah, with a sense of unease. The newly developed tremor in my hands worried me. Or was it a new-found fear that was making my hands shake involuntarily? A fear that had entered my soul when I first saw that face at the window, a sudden dissolving of my body into a dusty, brittle construct that felt on the verge of shattering into a million fragments. I squinted my eyes to spot a solitary figure coming up the path, walking in the careful way that someone who is not quite fond of walking but must do does. Dobriyal. He had parked his scooter on the main road, rather than risk bringing it onto the gravelly path, now slowly getting mossy with the constant rain and mist. He waved happily at me as he neared. I acknowledged the wave with a nod and a smile.

'Masterniji, good morning,' he pressed a rather old, falling-to-pieces album into my hand, 'Here. I brought this across first thing in the morning for you to look at, otherwise I would surely forget in the course of the day.'

'That is indeed very kind of you, Mr Dobriyal,' I replied, touched that he had taken time out to get this to me. 'If you just go through the photographs,' he said, 'You will find the pictures I was talking about flagged with a piece of paper. I shall come back in a day or two to collect it.'

He radiated calmness, like a little Buddha, compounded by his smiling, chubby face and his tiny eyes set deep into his face like two black pebbles.

'Of course,' I replied. 'You can drop by anytime you want today to collect it. Thank you so much for having taken the effort to get this to me. Would you like to have some tea?' I enquired politely, but he declined with a swift shake of his head, making his beginning-to-go-jowly cheeks shake independently on his face.

'No, thank you, Masterniji, I really have to be going now. Goodbye.'

He took himself off again in a measured gait towards the curve in the path that led to the main gate of the estate, his young shoulders weighed down with a great, unseen pressure that seemed to curve them down towards the earth. His white shirt, blue pullover and black pants made him look more schoolboy than grown man from a distance. I set the album down on the coffee table and looked at its cover. It was handsomely bound in leather of an indeterminate hue, which could have been brown or tan when it was originally made. And it was old. Very old, probably older than I was. It seemed to be falling apart and had been carefully cello-taped and glued together, with a plastic cover holding it in one piece. The pages were carefully laminated, to prevent further wear and tear, yet the smell of the years came through its pages, a sulphurous, decaying, acrid smell. The paper was so old, it felt like it would turn to dust in my hand. The black card paper pages were carefully stuck with photographs, edged with gilded corners, starting with sepia and then segueing into a black-and-white world of unfamiliar faces, posed carefully. It was a heavy album, my wrist hurt from holding it up. I would go through them at leisure, I decided, and kept it on the side table in the living room as I went back into the house.

I went to see Basanti along with Hari Singh a little after breakfast. The screams were audible as we approached the slate-and-shingle roofed stone-and-wood hovel. A goat tied to the outer enclosure outside the hovel bleated sadly as we passed it on our way in. The dry twigs gathered for kindling in the dark, grey winter months, were piled up against one side of the hovel, tied together carefully in little bundles, displaying the thrifty housekeeping of those who made do with little.

Hari Singh poked his head into the doorway first, a single sheet of salvaged wood from an old renovation of the cottages, tied to the hinge with wire and rope. Basanti was thrashing around on the rickety cot lined with worn blankets and salvaged sheets. Her father, rheumy-eyed and puzzled, sat next to her and stroked her hair gently. Her face was drawn, the faint bloom of pink across her high cheekbones had disappeared overnight, her cheeks were hollow, her eyes had sunk into their sockets and darted around like caged animals, bloodshot and unfocussed. When she saw me she sat up, suddenly calm, staring at me with her head angled down and her eyes focused on me with such ferocity! The voice came to me again, calling my name, the voice feathery and insistent, filling my head. 'Julia... Julia...' It drilled into my cranium, so that I put fingers in my ears to shut it out. Hari Singh stared at us, perplexed. Then she went limp and began mewling like a little kitten, almost as if she was hurting within, with some untold agony. She then closed her eyes and dropped off into what seemed to be a deep, drugged sleep.

'She's been like this since last night – sometimes she's normal, at others she's screaming,' Jogya said, breaking down as he spoke. 'Masterniji, help me.' My limbs began trembling involuntarily.

'Did you hear that?' I asked Hari Singh, as I clutched the door of the hovel for support. 'Her voice?' He looked around in puzzlement. Jogya looked around too, echoing his expression.

'What voice, Masterniji? I can't hear anything.'

I clutched my head and reeled out of the tiny, dank room, staggering on my unwilling ankle out of the immediate presence of that girl, her voice still in my head.

I called Dr Sanyal and explained to him that perhaps Basanti needed further medical care and that her father insisted she had been possessed. The cuts and bruises on her body could be self inflicted, he said. 'This could be hysteria, it could be attention-seeking, there could be a multitude of reasons,' he said. 'Do you think she'd benefit by a medical examination, would you like me to come around and have a look at her again?' he asked. I replied that I would be obliged if he could.

'I'll try in the evening, after I shut the clinic for the day. I'm sure it is just some sort of hysteria, we might have to get her assessed by a mental health expert. I could book an appointment at the Civil Hospital with the visiting specialist for her if I think it is needed,' he said.

'That would be kind of you,' I murmured faintly.

I should have mentioned the voices in my head calling out my name whenever she looked at me with her blood-red irises. But I didn't. I wondered if I should mention the marks on my neck or the shadow I thought I saw in my armchair the previous night, and decided against it. Or the narrowed red slits of eyes that Basanti looked back at me with as Bimla and Manikji helped her back home, the gaze that snapped my spine into two and which went back to regular in an instant, almost as if I imagined it.

I could feel my hands begin to shake, my mouth begin to dry up. I wondered when it would get over, and what it would take for it to get over. For some reason, I believed this was something I had to deal with myself. And I had no clue whether I would survive what had just begun. When I returned home, Sumit came back with Manikji, asking if he could rent out the guest bedroom, and insisted on negotiating a fee that would keep me very well stocked in supplies for the next couple of months. And I completely forgot to go through the photo album Mr Dobriyal had brought across to me. It lay, forgotten, on the table where I had set it down, bearing within it a face, which when I gazed upon it, would change everything I thought I knew about myself irretrievably.

Chapter 9

THE NEXT FEW days passed without anything noticeable occurring to mark their passing. They segued into each other with the kind of inevitability that monotony brings. It was a welcome monotony, one that was undisturbed by apparitions lurking outside windows or dragging me through deep dank forests or pits filled with reptiles.

Hari Singh and Bimla had already drawn their conclusions and decided that Basanti had been possessed by a dark spirit. Bimla had gone across to tell Jogya he should take Basanti to the Kali mandir at the other end of town, where the tall coniferous trees grew and protectively guarded the tiny stone temple with its ancient stone idol, where the priest would perform a havan and rid her of the spirit that had taken possession of her. Alternatively, Hari Singh offered to call the local oracle to their hovel for an exorcism. 'The oracle will demand alcohol and a goat to be sacrificed apart from money,' Bimla told me. 'Jogya can't afford that, Manikji and Hari Singh will help him take Basanti to the temple. There, he will just have to offer the priest some money and a coconut, and hopefully, the spirit will leave her.'

Something had triggered it off, these strange occurrences, though I couldn't pinpoint what it was. Apparitions manifesting themselves at my window in the middle of stormy nights, knocking, insisting, asking to be let into the house. Sleeping women being flung into pits in the midst of stormy nights, their bodies marked with cuts, whether self-inflicted, or inflicted by a strange, unseen force. The very real feeling of being throttled in my sleep with an invisible iron grip that didn't relent, leaving behind raw welts on my neck. I touched them under the scarf I judiciously wrapped around my neck. They had faded to a soft bruised purple now, but were still clearly visible against my skin, speckled though it now was with age spots and crepey with the loss of collagen and subcutaneous fat.

It was just after lunch that Bimla brought up the album I had forgotten on the coffee table downstairs all those days ago. 'Bibijee,' she said, carrying it into the study with a terror that came from handling anything unfamiliar, 'Yeh aap neechey chhod gaye the.' Mr Dobriyal hadn't come to collect it. And I had forgotten all about it.

I requested her to keep it down on the small table next to the window, with the two chairs, where I always liked to have my afternoon tea when I was in the study. I opened the album, and the musty smell of forgotten memories drifted up from the page to my nostrils. Posed photographs. Clicked with the strange formality that the camera bestowed on people of that era, where clicking a photograph was a matter of getting dressed up and sitting formally, arranging oneself for the lens, knowing that such opportunities were few and far between. There were rows of faces – white-skinned ladies sitting in a row, wearing dresses, hats perched delicately on their heads, legs crossed in a gentle manner, obviously from another era. Standing behind them in a row were men, their sola topees jammed uncompromisingly on their heads, their stern faces etched with lines carved out by long hours in the sun, unsoftened by the hint of a smile. I looked through all the photographs unhurriedly, wondering which one it was that Mr Dobriyal felt bore a resemblance to me. I came to a page, with a scrap torn hastily from a newspaper put in as a place mark – on it was a photograph of a woman in a flared-out, knee-length dress, cinched at the waist with a thin belt, hair cut in a sharp chin-length bob that was probably the fashion of the time, her frame unhealthily thin. And what had me gasping for breath as I looked on at her was the fact that it was her, the face at the window, the presence in my dreams.

She made an appearance in another group photograph, also marked by a newspaper, where she stood at the edge of the group, visibly detached from the group, her expression sullen, staring into the camera with a maelstrom of pent-up rage pouring through those long dead eyes, striking me with a force that had me slump back into the chair. I didn't know her name, but the face was unmistakable. A face that didn't have a name but a face that I knew intimately, a face that called out my name. A name I hadn't heard anyone call me, except the nuns in Kolkata, when I was very young. 'Julia...' I could hear her voice hissing at me through the dead pages of the album.

I sat frozen, my eyes on the photograph, unable to turn the page, unable to go back, unable to shut the album. There was a gentle knock at the door, and it opened softly. Sumit popped his head in. 'Busy?' he asked apologetically. The man was very attractive, in a quiet soft way. Perhaps it was a good thing that Nina was no longer here; she would have definitely fallen off the deep end.

'Come right in, Sumit,' I replied, with some difficulty. The face in the photograph had taken my voice away. 'Look at this photograph, does this lady seem familiar?'

I turned the album towards him as he lowered himself into the chair. He looked at the picture. 'Now that you mention it, she does. I can't place her though... is it a picture of you?' There was a resemblance that I could not see, but which Dobriyal and now Sumit discerned. I looked at the photograph again and tried to think of myself at the same age when this photograph was clicked.

Was there a resemblance, in the jut of the jaw and the tilt of the head and the oval contours of the face, the arch of the brows, the sharpness of the nose? Perhaps there was, perhaps there wasn't. I couldn't tell. If I closed my eyes, the image of myself that flashed into my mind was the one that greeted me every morning when I woke and dragged myself to the bathroom, the one reflected in the fading, lined mirror over the old sink – the thinning white hair, the wrinkles dragging my cheeks into striations, riverbeds of tears dried, a lattice of cobwebs beneath the eyes, the blue of the eyes faded to a diluted version of the brilliant reflects of the mountain sky they once were. Sometimes I looked at myself and wondered who this stranger was, then I would look down at myself and remember, it was me, stuck in a bodysuit that didn't belong to me anymore.

'Did you know that one genetic mutation around ten thousand years ago caused blue eyes,' Dr Sanyal had told me once. 'Before that every homo sapiens had brown eyes. One particular gene responsible for colour in our eyes was switched off in this common ancestor and that's how you have blue eyes.'

I wondered if the lady in the photographs had blue eyes. The photographs were sepia and revealed nothing. I knew, within my cold bones, that she would have had the same eyes as mine. Arctic. Blue. Frozen blue. Like the radioactive iridescence of the stalagmites in subterranean caves. Sharp. Dangerous. Beautiful. Sinister.

The slight shiver that ran through me had nothing to do with the soft breeze coming through the window.

'Who is she?' Sumit asked, reading the caption, written in a neat, dead, calligraphic hand below the photograph. 'What is this album? Where did you get it from?'

I explained the circumstances and how Dobriyal had insisted I see the album.

Sumit flicked through all the photographs, with the kind of speed that does not sacrifice detail in its scrutiny.

'No, nothing, just these two photographs of her,' I replied, my voice sounding weary and scared even to me.

'Mr Dobriyal seemed to think I resemble this lady and thought I should see it in case I turn out to be related to her in some way.'

Sumit looked at the photograph again. 'I must agree with him. I would have thought this was you from when you were young, if it wasn't dated....' and looked at me. 'Maybe it would be worth finding out more about her. There is a distinct similarity. Would you have any photographs of yourself when you were around her age. It seems to be around the mid-twenties.'

I pulled out a heavy brocade-print-covered album from a drawer bursting with the photographs and clippings I had gathered over the years and filed away carefully. There was always a certain self-consciousness in showing someone an album of one's photographs, an inevitable feeling of putting oneself up to be judged for the clothes one wore, the hairstyles one sported, the gawkiness of one's youth and the slow shuffle of the years hunching the shoulders, hollowing the cheeks, changing one from vibrant and vital to a shadow of one's former self. It served to have physical proof that one had existed, had done all the things one remembered one had, despite memories being traitors, shifting and morphing like coils of smoke from an incense stick, before slipping away into the crevices of the mind, from where they refused to be coaxed out no matter how much one tried to get them to emerge. Sticking pictures into a photo album filled in the details of one's life, details that slipped from the continuum of memory – that dress you were wearing, that haircut you'd just got, the necklace you'd worn especially for the occasion, the reason you were squinting was that the sun was getting in your eye and there wasn't enough time for you to move to the other side of the garden where you could look into the camera fearlessly, the child at the edge of the class photograph who was looking anywhere but at the camera because he was distracted by a bird's call. He could have been the most lovable of all the children you taught in that batch, and had stayed in your mind long after the scholars and the perfectly behaved ones had passed out because he made you long for one more stab at reliving your childhood again in more regular circumstances, not the cloistered confines of the convent, where everything was so regimented that you shivered with fear should you go a step against the prescribed regulations. I had no photographs of my childhood.

Sumit turned the pages carefully, and paused at one photograph. It was a black and white print of me standing by a window at Datham Hall, the boarding school I'd taught at for over twenty-five years, taken when I'd barely joined. The sunlight was streaming in from through the high-arched glass window behind me, in broken rays that skimmed over the top of my head, placing a cirrus halo behind me, making me gleam in an almost other-worldly manner. I was wearing a pale shirt of an indeterminate shade between beige and lemon with a slim, straight skirt that ended at my knee, it was a navy woollen-blend fabric I remember, and I'd purchased the material at the local suitings and shirtings shop, that's what they were called back then, in the small hill station town where Datham Hall was located.

Those were the days when the legs were firm and long, and the surface was uncrossed with angry gnarled bunches of blue and pulsating red veins. This was the skirt I was wearing when I walked straight into Ranvijay, who was turning hurriedly into a corridor, me with my head bowed, lost in the study notes of the class I was to take on map work, a class I was late for because I had spent too much time dawdling at a window, looking out at the fresh blossoms converting the trees fringing the grounds into dappled powder pink and green. This was the skirt he peeled off a couple of months later in frenzied lovemaking that resulted in what was perhaps simultaneously the happiest and the most painful phase of my life. And this was the skirt I tried on a month after I had had Millie to check whether I was back to my original waist size, hoping that my few months of unannounced, unconventional leave of absence would not be noticed by the rest of the staff at Datham Hall, realising that I wasn't fooling anyone. The changes were not obvious and thankfully we were in weather that allowed one to wear layers, but the signs were obvious to those with eyes sharp enough to see – the slight thickening of the waist, the overhang of the stomach post-delivery, despite my efforts at keeping it tightly bound, the swollen, unsuckled breasts from which I expressed the milk until they dried up in the absence of the tiny hungry mouth. Photographs were alive with tangible memories, memories that snaked around you and tore you, gasping and screaming through the ride all over again. I took a deep breath, folded my hands in my lap to stop the tremors and looked at my photographs again, and then looked at the photographs in the album Dobriyal had handed to me.

'She could be you,' he said. 'I would have thought they're the same person, in different times.' And he added. 'Are you sure you aren't related? This could be your mother if I didn't know that you came from Calcutta.'

We turned back to the album that lay open in front of us. Photographs of me, carefully gathered together from different points in my life.

I might have been around twenty-three in the next photograph Sumit paused at. 'Look at this one,' he said, laying the two photographs side by side. 'There's too much of a resemblance. Do you know who she was?'

I had no clue, I confessed, this was the first time I was seeing her photographs, though this wasn't the first time I was seeing her. But I dared not tell him that, I dared not mention the night she rapped at my window with her long-dead knuckle, asking to be let in, the night she sat in my rocking chair, watching me with dead eyes, the night I stayed awake and terrified until the darkness disappeared into the flush of the morning sun. I was unsure about speaking of what I had seen and what I was experiencing with anyone, I couldn't explain it to myself. Would people understand or would they inch away from me wondering if I needed to be institutionalised? I shook my head and looked back at my photograph on the table before me, looking at an image of me with a face still plumped out with youth. The photographs were a lifetime away, and the stance I held was intrinsically arrogant, coming from an awareness of one's beauty, with my lips full and firm, and my shoulders straight and un-stooped by time and weather and dried-up pain.

In the photograph, I was seated at a dining table, at Mrs Dutta's home. Mrs Dutta lived in a house below mine when I lived alone in Calcutta after returning from my five years in Chaudharipore. She had no children and had adopted me in all but name. My hair was cut into a lopsided fringe, one that was quite the rage in those days, what with a Hindi film heroine, she of the broad forehead and elfin face making the fringe a style named after her. My smile was wide and accepting of the person clicking me, my arms were skinny but not as skinny as they were right now, and the round-necked dress I had on was completely unflattering to my reed-thin self. The photograph had been clicked at one of the bridge evenings Mrs Dutta hosted and she had insisted on me coming down to make it a bridge four, since one of the ladies who was to join them had taken ill. I had served the lemonade and the tea and the dainty chutney sandwiches, which had been covered with a damp muslin cloth and kept in the refrigerator to prevent them drying out, and the wafers and the slices of plum and walnut cake that Mrs Dutta had baked the previous day. And after the cards were laid down and the last of the ladies had said their goodbyes, before disappearing into their chauffeured cars, Mrs Dutta and I had continued the party with a gin and tonic each, my very first experience of alcohol. And this was clicked when I was laughing at some joke, my intestines swishing with the then novel experience of the gin inside them. I had spent three years in Calcutta when this was clicked, three years on my own. I was to spend a couple of years more before I would move to Datham Hall where I would spend the rest of my adult life, before retiring to Windermere.

It was a tough life in Calcutta, living alone. Not to mention that I was tired of being looked upon as a scarlet woman by the neighbourhood, simply because I lived alone. It was only Mrs Dutta, rotund, jolly Mrs Dutta, who took me into her care, much like an eagle would take a sparrow's hatchling, and ensured I survived those early years alone in Calcutta. Like a mother would.

I had tried to find my mother. I went to where her family used to live, getting the address from Mr Ganguly, the manager at my grandfather's Calcutta office. I went to the house, it was locked and uninhabited. The residents, I was told by helpful neighbours, had all emigrated. They gave me an address for Millicent Jones's brother in England. I returned home to my single room with a kitchen, down the lane from the convent I grew up at, and looked at the address over and over again. Finally, I worked up the courage to write a polite letter, enclosing a picture of myself I got clicked at the local photo studio, asking for him to forward it to Millicent. Or to be kind enough to give me her address so I could correspond directly with her. It never occurred to me that my mother would be anything but glad to find me. I got a reply giving me an address in the UK to address future correspondence to. I wrote to it. And when the reply finally came, many months after I had cast out that first missive into the sea of postal routes and deliveries, it was curt and dismissive. 'I'm sorry,' the letter said. 'But you are surely mistaken. I had a child, yes, before I left India. But the child died within a week at the convent I had left her at. I was informed of this by the nuns I had left her with. I am very sure you couldn't be my daughter. I wish you all the best in your search for your mother.'

I had no mother. Or my mother refused to acknowledge me, whatever her reasons. I was adrift again. And I never asked the nuns for confirmation whether her letter was the truth or a way of disassociating herself from me. The photograph we were now looking at was taken a couple of years after I had received that letter from London, when I had decided that it was time I took charge of my life again, regardless of who my parents were, or whether my mother didn't want to acknowledge I existed.

'If you hadn't told me your mother was from Calcutta,' said Sumit, looking at my photograph, 'I would have sworn the lady in that album was your mother. Or that you had time-travelled between the photographs.'

When Mr Dobriyal came back for the album at the end of the week, I asked him if he knew who the lady in the photographs was. 'No idea, madam, will have to check the records. The photographs aren't labelled.'

Chapter 10

BY THE BEGINNING of November, it had become perceptibly
chilly. Winter was round the corner, with its sheets of snow,
unending grey pallor and the biting cold that pierced the bones,
numbed the mind and jammed the joints up. The tourist season
approached and happy families descended on the small town, in the
hotels and in the home stays around, with their children bundled
in warm clothes and the honeymooning couples distinguished by
the inability to stay physically unattached from each other, even
when climbing the non-steep paths.

I'd visited Basanti twice in the past few weeks, a horror drawing
me despite myself to see her. Each time I'd found her shrinking into
her skin. Her healthy, youthful face pulling in into itself, shrinking
into hollows, her skin feverish to the touch, her behaviour calm
and resigned on both occasions, before the episodes came upon her.
'Masterniji,' she rasped, clutching my hand when I visited her the
second time, stepping carefully past the goat droppings which had
accumulated because she obviously had not been able to maintain
the little room and the little open shed outside the home where they

were tied. 'I am going to die. This thing inside me, it won't let me live.' And then the grip on my hand tightened to a vice and refused to let go, and a voice called my name, hissed it out so that only I could hear it in my head. And I struggled, breaking my hand free with the little strength I possessed, looked into the red pinpricks of her eyes, screamed and rushed out of her hovel, as fast as my shaking legs and my cane would let me. I was terrified of going to visit her, yet I couldn't keep away, she drew me like a magnet.

Then there was that night, the night I saw Basanti walking barefoot, down the path towards the house, late at night. I rushed out as fast as I could, noting the glazed expression on her face, and the awkward stilted movements of her limbs. I called out to Bimla and Manikji to come and help me. Basanti stared at me with unseeing eyes as I asked her what she was doing out so late in the night, and then replied in perfect English, 'I've come to take you with me,' before falling into a dead faint.

'I can't understand what is happening to her,' Dr Sanyal confessed. 'There is nothing I can point out as causing an illness, she just seems to be wasting away.' He drew some vials of blood and sent the samples to a lab for testing. The only discernable results of those tests were that she was severely anaemic, so anaemic in fact that she needed blood transfusions immediately. He rushed her to the civil hospital from where she recovered sufficiently within a few days of blood transfusions for her father to take her home. There were no strange incidents in the hospital, but the moment she entered home, Bimla told me, she was back again to the moaning, ranting, shrieking creature that had so terrified me.

After a week of Basanti returning home, Bimla informed me that her father had brought in the local jhar-phunk-wala for an exorcism and even agreed to have one of their two goats killed for the ritual, despite Hari Singh carrying a stern warning from me not to have the ritual done. The next day, he brought back news that the witchdoctor had in fact beaten Basanti black and blue and tortured her with branded hot irons, and she was barely breathing. 'But the ghost is gone,' he announced, chirpily. I pulled on my walking shoes and sweater, grabbed my cane and raced as quickly as I could to Basanti's home. The humble house was looking distraught, as if something vital had left it. Inside, on the narrow bunk, Basanti was breathing heavily, blue black circles under her eyes, her lips moving constantly in some sort of chant I could not decipher. Bimla, who had run after me, gasped when she saw what the girl had been reduced to and promptly began haranguing the father for allowing the exorcist to torture her.

I'd called Dr Sanyal and got her taken to the hospital. The cuts on her arms had healed into ugly, raised scars. When I asked her if she remembered how she had got them, she shook her head from side to side, with great difficulty, in a manner that suggested she had difficulty manipulating her own body. 'I remember nothing of that night. Only of falling down into the pit while trying to take the pipes out and the next thing I remember is the Doctor Saab and Writer Babu bringing me to your house.'

Basanti passed away in the hospital two days after she was admitted there. Her father was shattered. 'All her vital organs collapsed. It seemed like her body decided to shut itself down... most inexplicable, there was no clinical indication of why this happened,' Dr Sanyal told me when he called to inform about her demise. Jogya was heartbroken; his daughter was the only person who cared for him in his miserable life.

The days after her death passed without incident. I wondered if the apparition had decided to go back to whatever dimension it had slumbered in before it had manifested itself at my window. No faces stared in from my window, no phantom hands gripped my throat in the dark of night. The ankle, sadly, continued to twinge occasionally, a reminder of the night I heard that rapping at the window. That night seemed a long way off. I wondered if it had really happened, the rapping at the window, the face that stared in, the hands gripping my throat and all the events that took place after that.

Kurnal would stop by the cottage almost every other day, tie his goats to the gate, wave at me shyly from the distance before coming to the porch, scuffing his feet on the rough coir mat placed at the entrance to catch the mud and grass, before coming in. I looked forward to his visits; he was a cheerful young lad, midway between childhood and teenage angst.

'And what will we study today?' I would ask him, as he settled himself on the step next to my chair, with his dog-eared book and stubby pencil, one he would sharpen efficiently with the pocket knife he always carried with him. 'History,' he would say, with much enthusiasm, it being a favourite subject with him, listening to exploits of the kings and emperors of yore, of bloodthirsty battles and invasions and the not-so-exciting-to-him story of our independence from the British. This would inevitably set him round to the track of asking me about my parents, who in the story I'd told him, were British missionaries who had died of cholera in Calcutta when I was an infant. It was a story I'd repeated to few of the neighbours – it sat well with the orphan with no family background and gave me some legitimacy, something I craved all my life. But then, I had woven so many stories around myself that sometimes I forgot who the real me was and what were the stories around me that I had constructed. The lines blurred, I kept forgetting the details, the dates occasionally didn't match up. The young widow. The daughter of British missionaries. The orphan brought up in a convent. The illegitimate product of a summer dalliance between a tea plantation owner's son and an Anglo-Indian typist. I tried to keep the skeins of the real and the fictional separate, though they often intermingled. I now kept them unravelled, by not talking about myself at all, anymore.

Occasionally, Manikji and Bimla would go off for almost the entire day to visit the temple of a local deity and visit assorted relatives in the vicinity of the temple. The day Manikji and Bimla went off to the temple, Kurnal stayed with me till they returned. He spent the day skipping around the garden, occasionally coming in to check whether I was still in functional order or had keeled over and passed away.

'I'm fine,' I would tell him, with a smile, every time he poked his head round the study door to check on me. When the door opened again, in the fading evening hour, I looked up to find no one there, just a shadow. A woman-sized shadow faded before my eyes before I could blink. I clutched at the arms of my chair. 'Kurnal, Kurnal….' I yelled, realising my voice, once strong enough to silence a class of forty into pin-drop silence, was now shaky and shrill.

'Yes, Masterniji,' he called back, from the ground floor, clambering up the stairs at top speed, making a din equivalent to an army of cavalrymen riding in to take possession of a fort that had fallen to their assault. 'Kya hua?'

'Is there anyone else in the house right now, apart from you, me and Sumit babu?' I asked. I could hear Sumit downstairs in his room, where he had been holed up since the morning, having emerged only for breakfast.

'Nahin, madamjee, koi nahin. I will allow no one inside without your permission,' he replied, his expression fierce and his cheeks chapped into a furious pink already. 'I'm sitting at the door itself.'

I told him to go eat whatever he felt like from the kitchen refrigerator. He bounded off, with the glee of childhood that sees treats in even ordinary things like bread, butter and jam. I looked again at the door which was now clear of any shadow. I closed my eyes. Something in my head. It had to be something in my head. Had I been hallucinating again? It had been over a month since the last incident.

'Everything okay?' Sumit's voice made me open my eyes. He'd heard me calling out to Kurnal.

'Yes, all good. I just thought I saw someone near the stairs outside the door. Obviously, I've begun hallucinating in my old age without needing to smoke some of the A-grade stuff being grown on a few of the slopes on the other side.'

He laughed. 'Well then, catch you later, I'm just stepping out for a bit, will be back by dinner time.' He bounded down the stairs back to his room. Bimla and Manikji returned soon after and Kurnal whispered worriedly to them as they entered. Bimla staggered up on her bad knee to check on me, and finding me apparently in great spirits, went down again, muttering under her breath about giving Kurnal the hiding of his life for having worried her for no reason.

Sumit's erstwhile cottage on hire had been repaired and made fit for residence but he'd passed on the offer in favour of continuing to live here. We'd fallen into a pleasant camaraderie. He bashing away at his laptop in his room, emerging for breakfast, lunch and dinner, and maybe evening tea and conversation. Or taking off occasionally to the main town, to the nearby artist's village which saw occasional theatrical performances by travelling theatre troupes, or the occasional author visit to conduct a workshop or simply read from their work. He would be gone for the day, wandering around the place with his backpack, clicking infinite photographs. He would come back later, download, edit and upload the pictures on his blog. He maintained that blog assiduously, chronicling life in this small hill town with a rare attention that few had paid it.

He had taken his fascination with the town further and decided to investigate the lady in the album Mr Dobriyal had given me. Sumit had the internet at his disposal and the strong legs to traipse around the estate and town and ask all the old-timers if they remembered her and what had happened to her. He didn't get any leads. Most of those who would have been alive at the time the photographs were clicked had passed away.

I didn't see *her* for many days after that evening. She wasn't pressing her nose against the windows, not sitting in my armchair as an etheric outline as I slept, watching over me much the way the eagle watches over the confused mouse from the skies, not pressing her skeletal fingers around my throat. I began to think I had imagined her, that my brain was conjuring up images of her from an unlocked corner. Perhaps I had seen a photograph sometime when I had visited the lodge, perhaps it was on a wall like many of the old photographs were, perhaps her face had stuck in my head.

Nina called to say she wanted to come home for the long Diwali fortnight. I thought it would be better for her to take up one of the many offers her friends extended of spending the holidays with them, but she insisted, wailed and wept earnestly into the phone when I said so, and it ended up in me caving in and organising Kishan, a local tourist taxi driver, and Manikji to go pick her up. I hadn't really recovered from that fall in my room. Over the past couple of months, the sense of disintegrating was getting stronger and stronger. I felt like I was falling away into nothingness, some place beyond where molecules from my body were slowly emigrating to, waiting for me to join them. A long road journey was not something I could handle anymore.

I knew that in a couple of years Nina might not want to spend her time with an old lady, that the bright lights of the city would lure her away from me, that she would get into college and discover boys and dating, and staying for weeks on end in an isolated cottage in a one-horse hill town would be the last thing she would want to do in her spare time. Her visits would dwindle, her phone calls would taper off to the occasional guilt call. Or perhaps I would pass away before it came to that.

Nina's room was being aired out, the curtains changed and the dust bunnies scuttled out under my supervision by Bimla. I wouldn't see Nina again for a long time. Her winter break would be spent with her mother. All I had to look forward to was the long, dreary, snow-covered winter, alone. Already, the afternoon sun outside had become dull and listless, like it was waiting for the pall of winter to descend on the pines on the hills, the clouds bearing snow to circle the mountains and blot out all light, the sky to go navy and deep just before the snow fell down, light as cotton, whispery like feathers, all-enveloping like a promise before clear sunlight would be seen again. Right now the clouds were still with us, soft and omnipresent. I was just through with the afternoon tea and was trying to ensure the room was attended to before the next day. Nina would be here anytime post-lunch, if she left early in the morning as had been decided. She would be sixteen in January. Time, it flew.

Sumit came bounding up the narrow stairs with the long strides I had so gotten used to. 'The lady in the photographs...' He paused for a moment. 'I believe I've found out who she is... rather, was.'

'How did you find out?' I asked. 'Who is she?'

He drew up a stool close to my desk. 'Someone who came here to live for a while, no one knows who she was or where she came from. No one knows her name. I was told of an old man who was a child around the time those photographs were clicked... his mother had worked as a maid in this cottage. I tracked him down and spoke with him. He's living in one of those new houses near the edge of town and barely gets out, but this much of his memory is still intact, mercifully.'

'What did he say, what did he remember about her?'

The investigative reporter in Sumit had him pull out a camcorder and notepad. He was rather meticulous about his notes and documentation. Because it was a quality I lacked, I admired it in others. I was a scattered observer, I recorded in my head, and my memory had begun to play tricks on me and wasn't the most accurate. 'I don't want to watch,' I said, 'Just give me the details.'

The knees had begun what was now becoming their daily protest post-lunch at being compelled to do anything more than momentary standing, and I flexed them a bit, wincing as I felt the cartilage protest within and the joints spasm. I could feel the popping within.

He switched the camcorder on. A man, frail, wizened, sat on his haunches outside a door to a small house, puffing away on a beedi. A shaky voice played back in the tinny way voices do when they have been detached from the body and captured in little recording machines. Morning sounds of birds chirping, and female voices barking instructions peppered the background. And the reedy voice from the camcorder spoke on.

'She was an Angrez. The rumours were that she had been a governess to a child from a wealthy family, but she fell astray. Missybaba was pretty. More than pretty, she had a sort of gentleness about her that anyone who came in touch with her would grow to love. She was like a flower, pale and pretty. Initially, she would come out, meet with the other residents of the estate. But that soon stopped. She would sit in the house all day and not step out, and then she stopped coming out of her room when it got obvious that she was expecting a child...'

The man on the camcorder continued, after a long puff at a bidi, which was almost burnt to his fingertips.

'No one was allowed to meet her. The daktar saab was called in often to see her. One day, she just disappeared, and those taking care of her packed their bags and went away. I was a small boy, I only remember what my mother told me... They say she killed herself after the baby was taken away from her. No one ever spoke of her again. Some people say they see her sometimes, walking around the estate, looking into windows. Poor soul, who knows what sorrows she had.'

I had never seen her walking around, looking into windows, in all the years I had lived here. Until recently. And the apparition I'd seen was anything but the gentle soul this wizened man was describing. This was a vitriolic soul, steeped in anger, intent on violence.

The temperature of the room was suddenly chilly. Sumit looked out of the window with unfocused eyes that were clearly not registering the stretch of rolling green estate in front of him.

'I wonder what happened to her, where she disappeared, whether it was really a suicide as the rumours go or whether she slipped away from town unnoticed and if she did so, what made her go away. Anyway,' he said. 'I've hit a dead end, I have no more leads at the moment.' He rose from the chair, 'But yes, Dobriyal was right. You do resemble her. In some way. I don't quite know how, given that she's obviously much younger in those photographs, but in you one can see what she would have looked like if she had lived and grown old.'

I looked at myself, reflected in the glass panes across the room – slight, white-haired, with a face wrinkled comfortably into lines that drew maps across what had once been clear and unlined, grooves that reflected a million smiles and lattices under my eyes where a million tears had carved out pathways through the skin. Yes, I could have been her, she could have been me. Somewhere between the two of us, the boundaries dissolved and I had lived her life out here, where she had once lived and left, or perhaps, not quite left.

Chapter 11

I SAW THE tourist taxi pulling up the driveway the next afternoon, and made my way carefully down from my study to hug Nina as she dashed in through the front door, bringing with her a bustle of manic energy that was the gift of adolescence. 'Grams, how are you?'

I assured her I was fine, not mentioning the odd pains that had started up in my stomach, the limbs that felt they no longer had any coordination at random moments, and the sudden sense of disorientation, dizziness that struck me without warning, the feeling that my mind was already setting off on a trip and leaving me behind. Bimla bustled up to take the duffel bag Nina was carrying and put it in her room. She was here for a few days, after which she would be going with a group of friends on a trekking trip.

Her eyes looked around like she had half-expected someone else to be there too, and when Sumit stumbled into the lobby through the doorway of his room she smiled shyly.

'Nina, this is Sumit, a writer. He will be staying here for a while until he finishes writing his book. Sumit, this is Nina, my granddaughter.'

They nodded and smiled politely at each other, and Sumit disappeared back into his room. Nina whirled me into the drawing room where she collapsed onto the sofa. 'Manikji was barfing all the way,' she laughed. 'Why do you send the poor man when you know he can't take the road trip? I was terrified he would pack up and die on me and I would be left holding onto his corpse on the long ride home.'

I laughed too. 'He will survive, and don't you worry about him. It is me who will pack up and die on you if I have to do these long road trips again.'

She frowned, her eyes, as blue as mine, set in dusky, olive skin, clouded over perceptibly. 'Stop it, Grams, you're going to hit a century, you know that. Look at you, absolutely no issues with blood pressure or diabetes or cholesterol. Your eyes are perfect, you walk faster than I can. Except for that white hair, no one will say you are over fifty.'

I laughed softly. 'All a matter of perspective one would say. Anyway, how have things been at school and why hasn't there been an email or a call from you in a while?'

She looked suitably abashed. 'Just been caught up in things, Grams. I'm sorry, I'll be more regular henceforth.'

Nina scampered to her room to settle in, and we had tea a little while later. Sumit didn't join us for tea. Nor did he join me in the drawing room a little later for our customary early evening chatter about this and that and nothing in particular. This was a little uncharacteristic for him, but I put it down to him not wanting to intrude while Nina was around. A while later, I heard the front door close softly as I was reading the newspaper and saw him walking down the path towards the main gate, with his bright orange windcheater on, the hoodie up to beat the light drizzle.

The same windcheater he had on the day he had knocked at my door in the middle of the night and asked for a place to stay till the morning. Strange, the boy never stepped out without popping his head in and letting me know he was going to be out a while. This was a first of sorts.

My writing had hit a rough patch, after having flown along peacefully in the right chronological order for so many chapters. Now when I looked at it, it seemed more like a rambling diary, one that patched together bits and pieces of my life in some sort of coherence. Perhaps my daughter and my granddaughter would not want to read it. Maybe they shouldn't, perhaps that would be for the good of all of us. There were secrets in there that didn't need to be aired to the world, secrets that were best safe with me, that I could take with me to the grave rather than unsettle everyone I loved, and shatter their sense of self, cause them to seek out their ancestry. And after all, what proof did I put forth except my word, and that too, a word that did not hold much value when considered what it was up against. Who would take the word of an illegitimate half-breed against the reputation of one of the noblest houses in the country, without proof? I had heard there was DNA testing these days, testing that proved genetic inheritance without a doubt, but would Millie want to take it that far? And then too, what would she get out of it, except shame and the stigma of being illegitimate? It was unlikely that she would be entitled to any of Ranvijay's estate. Would she want to contest for it if she knew, I wondered.

I thought back to the unanswered letter still languishing un-shredded in my drawer, camouflaged beneath sundry receipts and bills, and wondered if I should pick the phone and call the number printed carefully on it. Why had I not destroyed it yet, was there a smidgeon of a hope that I would call her, that I would dial the phone number with a trembling hand and ask for her, with a voice that was suddenly choked with the tumbling of memory and guilt from the past? What would I have to say to Garima, I wondered, after all these years. Our last phone call was the one that had changed everything for me, had me take myself into hiding for months only to learn, when I returned, that the person I was hiding from hadn't attempted to search me out because he'd gone away, too far to ever return.

Nina trotted down in a while, and peeped into the drawing room, 'Grams, I'm going out for a little walk, would you like to join me?'

'It looks a little overcast, I think I'll pass the offer,' I replied. Then calling out behind her as an afterthought, 'Take an umbrella and put a sweater on.' Practical advice that she of course disregarded, closing the main door behind her with a hurried thump and racing down the road with unseemly impatience. I looked out at her from my vantage point at the window and found myself suddenly worried about my little girl running around alone down roads where a young girl had been found, snarling like an animal with her arms and legs inexplicably scratched and bleeding. A young girl, barely a few years older than Nina, who had died in a few weeks from being eaten away from within by something that had taken over her the night she fell in that pit.

Nina would be fine, I told myself, with that insistence that comes from inexplicable panic. She was just going for a short stroll, probably till the end of the road, to dip her feet in the little stream that ran behind the cottages. She would go around to neighbours I had stopped visiting when the knee began troubling me a little too much – Colonel Pratap Rai Singh, who had built his cottage here as a retirement home and lived with his delicate wife, Usha, and faithful manservant, Bilaas. Or she might go to the bungalow a little further off, with old Mrs Foster, who lived there with her daughter Myra, a sturdy lady in her fifties, and spend some time there nattering with them over tea and sandwiches. She was a friendly soul, Nina. It had been a while since I had met my neighbours, I realised. I resolved to step out more now that the ankle was better.

I went back to the newspapers without really paying attention to the typeset words on the pages telling me about political rallies and power outages, lovers being hacked to death, children being abandoned, acid being flung, women being raped, politicians embroiled in multi-crore scams, ministers being asked to resign. It seemed to have been a packed day for the nation. Nothing changed. Ever. Things went on in the same cyclical loop, spinning on towards a great cataclysm that would sweep things up into the dustbin of time, whether through an atomic war of our creation or a meteoroid coming in from space and slamming into our planet. Our civilisations and destinies and stories would be wiped out, leaving us as pure, etheric souls, rising into another level of consciousness, another existence. Was there an afterlife? I didn't know, but the recent events had me believe in the vacuum of it, a plane of existence where souls lingered with no hope of moving on wherever it was that deceased souls moved on to, released from the bonds of their earthly existence. Or was this earth the purgatory that we were taught in our childhood, a limbo land where we exist despite ourselves, propelled onward through time by forces beyond our control.

The telephone rang, Bimla answered it, and shuffled to announce with an uncharacteristically grim expression, 'Daktar saab ka phone hai.'

I went slowly to the instrument, took the receiver and sat heavily on the little footstool I had got placed there only recently. 'Hello, Dr Sanyal, good afternoon,' I said, 'How are you? It has been a while since we saw you. Does one have to fall ill to get you to drop by these days?'

He laughed heartily. 'My apologies. Have just been tied up with things. I was thinking of coming across tomorrow in the morning if you are at home and not busy.'

'For you, dear doctor, I will un-busy myself even if I was,' I replied, a smile coming unbidden to my face. He always made me smile, this young man. I then added, for good measure, not knowing what made me add it, 'Nina and Sumit would be glad to meet you too.'

There was a sudden long silence on the line. 'Nina is down from school? It feels like yesterday that I dropped her back. It would be good to meet both of them, yes.'

I detected a certain wariness in his tone, a wariness that was absent at the start of the conversation. 'I'll see you around eleven tomorrow morning then. Is there anything you'd like me to get for you from the market when I come up? Any marmalade, fresh baked bread, anything at all?'

'No, nothing. Just bring yourself over and do stay for lunch,' I replied, knowing that he would arrive with some little things to stock my larder – cold cuts, sausages, jam bottles from the farmer's cooperative that retailed from a tiny store at the end of the main mall road.

'I will, thank you so much,' he replied. 'Goodbye, see you tomorrow.'

'Goodbye.' I replaced the receiver in its cradle, wondering why I had a sudden sense of foreboding.

The shadows had darkened across the grass outside, the lawn needed trimming I noted, as did the flower beds. Hari Singh had been unwell for a few days and Manikji had been doing the indifferent watering that one with no love for flowering things does when compelled to take over the duty of tending to plants from one who loves them as flesh and blood offspring. Not that the mountains needed water to make plants grow, there was enough water in the soil to make any errant floating seed take root and flourish. There is a perceptible difference between caring for plants and just ensuring they were watered, and the lawn and gardens right now were evidence of this. The plants seemed to sense Hari Singh's absence and wilted under Manikji's lackadaisical care.

I looked out of the window, hoping to see Nina tripping up the path towards home. Manikji had taken his cycle out sometime ago and was cycling around the estate hoping to spot Nina and hurry her home before it became dark, given that it was already gloomy with the November eeriness of fog and mist curling around the corners of the road like menacing presences by themselves. Despite myself I began worrying, the heartbeat accelerating into an awry thudding within the chest cavity. Why had she not returned yet, where had she gone? A short walk she had said... had Manikji found her and informed her that she needed to come home now, or not? The uncertainty between knowing and not knowing, waiting and imagining the worst things ever is what sucks away at the soul. I stood up, exhausted by the monstrous situations I had built up in my head and moved out to the porch to be able to see her coming up the path next to the cottage or the road up ahead. Apart from the women walking back to their homes after a day's work at the factory, their faces tanned by the high-altitude sun into a grim leathery brown with wrinkles that aged them prematurely, I could see no one. No Manikji cycling slow enough to win the slow cycle race at the local Gymkhana, no Nina tripping down the path to the cottage, some odd flower she had plucked off the path in her hand, her face damp with excitement, exertion and tinged with the wet caress of the mist.

After around ten minutes of wringing myself out with anxiety, I saw Sumit trudge up the path, bearing a packet of something wrapped in newspaper in one hand and a huge plastic bag in the other. His hoodie was still up, a sprinkling of drops on them to indicate that there was a slight drizzle. Nina hadn't even worn a sweater or taken an umbrella.

Sumit approached the porch and stomped his feet on the mat kept near the first step. He spotted me sitting in the cane chairs and grinned at me. He was a good-looking boy, this one. The kind of beauty that didn't hit you at first glance but one that gradually grew on you, the kind of beauty that made you comfortable with it, before gradually taking your breath away when you spotted him in

certain light. I wondered if he had a lady love in his life. He was
so closed about his life back in Delhi, I knew nothing except that
he had parents living there and a grandmother who was rather ill.
He worried about her; he said sometimes that I reminded him of
her. In what way, he never specified.

'Just had to check if there was any mail for me at the post
office,' he said by way of explanation, and went inside to deposit
the bag and the package in his room.

Sumit had, given the uncertainty of the duration of his stay
here, opted to receive his physical correspondence via a post box
number rather than have it dropped here at the cottage. He made
a regular weekly trip into town to check out his mail and to
stock up on little things he might need, shaving foam, toiletries
and some beer, some gin or brandy for me, and odd things for
the house, like biscuits, toast, tea or whatever it was he noticed
us running short on. I had no clue how he kept an eye on the
resources within the jars and tins in the kitchen, but I realised
this was his discreet way of contributing to the household over
and above the amount he handed across to me as rent for his
room, and I appreciated it.

The frugal pension I received from Datham Hall kept body
and soul together. And the rent from the small flat I still owned
in Calcutta kept my daily expenses out of the red. And there was
Windermere or Cottage Number Two as I had to mention in all
correspondence, a cottage I had partly funded with the amount
bequeathed to me by Ranvijay on his death. A father Millie didn't
know about. She considered herself a McNally. I had never had the
courage to tell her the truth. Not yet. She would get the cottage
when I died. It was only fair.

Nina wasn't back yet. The beginnings of a migraine began
their delicate insertion of phantom needles into my eyeballs. The
heart began pounding once again, having been distracted by Sumit's
arrival. He emerged from the recesses of the cottage, after divesting

himself of the wet windcheater and having towel-dried his hair, emphasising their shagginess that went way beyond his collar in a riot of curls which would have looked oddly feminine on someone with less angular features.

'Why are you looking so worried?' he asked, as he lowered himself into the cane sofa and flipped through the newspapers he had brought from the drawing room. It was almost too dark to read, the sun having disappeared behind a bank of cloud and mountain horizon.

'Nina has been gone for over an hour and a half and hasn't returned. She'd said she's going out for a short walk, and after what happened with Basanti, frankly I'm a little concerned.'

'Don't be,' he replied, 'I'm sure she will be back soon, safe and sound. It is getting rather dark though. Would you like me to go down the lane and look around for her? Which way did she go, down the road or the path?'

For a moment I blanked out; I could remember her running down the gravel path leading to the gate without a sweater or umbrella and then nothing. Blank. I was losing my mind.

At that precise moment, Manikji turned the corner and cycled up slowly, resentment seeping through in every turn of the pedal. He turned up the path, looked at me reproachfully and parked the cycle at its usual spot where it continued to be an eyesore to all who approached the cottage, his entire manner dripping disapproval, which was voiced a second later, after he readjusted the small topi that never left his head.

'Nina Baby aa rahin hai, in ten minutes. She's playing with some children near the centre,' he informed me in carrying tones. Then added as he moved off, in an undertone that he thought my ears wouldn't catch, 'I've been feeling unwell all day but what does anyone care about me, a poor landless man...' and disappeared into the recesses of the cottage, switching on the lights as he went in.

'Where does your daughter live?' Sumit asked me, strangely. We had barely spoken about each other's families in all the months that he had stayed here with me, except in passing.

'She's in London. She works for a women's organisation in the UK,' I replied, suddenly uncertain about discussing Millie. She was a stranger to me, even though she was my flesh and blood. I felt I barely knew her, and all the years we had known each other post her return to the convent hadn't changed the wariness between us. Me consumed by the guilt of abandoning her in her childhood and she, resentful and bristly at being so obviously unwanted and thrown from foster home to foster home until she took charge of her own life.

'And her husband?' he asked.

'He passed away when Nina was a little girl, in a road accident, down this very road,' I replied. The words sounded so bare when they were said in a matter-of-fact manner. Nothing could come close to encompassing the horror of the moment – Millie's screams as she saw the body, mangled, unrecognisable, only the ring on the finger and the watch on the hand identifiable as belonging to him, this crumpled mass of flesh and broken bones, he who had been a living, breathing human being just a few hours ago. And me rushing to hold her, to comfort her and her pushing me away in barely concealed loathing.

'Did your daughter always live in London then, or did she move to London after he passed away?'

She had always been a bright student, Millie. She had managed, on her own initiative, to get into college in Delhi, take care of her expenses by working part-time and moved to London for further studies after completing her graduation in Delhi, managing to get a part-paid scholarship at a little-known university for a degree in social work. She stayed on when she met and married Nina's father. I could barely remember his face, but he was a good man, if very young. Their car crashed on the way back from the boarding school where Millie had just enrolled Nina. Millie survived, with merely a deep gash on her arm that was sutured together roughly by the resident doctor at the civil hospital they had been rushed to. She still had the scar, an ugly jagged keloid, one that she kept covered most times, rather than open to curious questions from insensitive observers. Her husband had bled from his ears and collapsed on the spot from the impact, when his head hit the windscreen and crumpled in on itself. I realised I couldn't remember his name anymore... They had been married for eight years when he died. Millie had settled down to a life in London and decided to continue living there. 'My daughter decided to continue living in London and Nina had already been enrolled at boarding school here, so she was sent here. It was easier for Millie, I guess, to have her daughter taken care of at a boarding school while she worked,' I replied. A sigh was welling up within me and despite my best efforts, it escaped. He looked at me curiously.

'That's rather sad. You came to India from the UK, did you?' he asked.

'No, actually, I was born and brought up in Calcutta. I lived there till I was around fifteen and then I lived on a tea estate near Darjeeling. I lived there for a few years, then we had to move back to Calcutta. I lived in Calcutta again for a few years, and then got a teaching position in a boarding school not far from here, Datham Hall, you must have heard of it. I lived there for almost thirty years, at the school. I moved here after I retired.'

It seemed a simple enough life, one that would withstand the prodding of a curious mind. But he had more questions. This was the day, it would seem, when he needed his questions answered. 'I've heard of Datham Hall, my mother studied there for a couple of years when she was very young. And what about your husband?'

I looked down at my hands, the worn out plain gold band Mrs Dutta had forcibly put on my finger as she put me on the train to Datham Hall and a new life. I had no papers to support being Mrs McNally, but it was a lie I had lived all my life. The ring had never left my finger, and I wore it below the brilliant Columbian emerald circled with diamonds Ranvijay had given me, his mother's ring, he'd told me. I had no way of checking whether it was true and no desire to do so. I had no other jewellery. I had never made myself any jewellery in all my life. It felt superfluous to adorn myself when I had no one to adorn myself for. 'He died a few months into our marriage, it was a head-on collision with a truck. I was pregnant with Millie at the time.' The trajectory of my life was interjected with deaths. And at each point, my life changed. I kept changing the details to suit the story I was telling, to adapt it to whoever I was telling it to.

There was an awkward silence as he searched for words to take the conversation forward from the uncomfortable junction it had reached. Thankfully, I could see Nina rushing in from the distance, holding in her hands, as I had expected, a bunch of wild flowers she had picked from the side of the path, a riot of orange and yellow that spilled over from her arms. Wild flowers charmed the girl more than the careful cultivated ones in hothouses or in flower-beds.

She rushed in and hugged me, smiling shyly at Sumit. 'Let me put these in water, Grams, and be back.'

I smiled at her and changed the conversation swiftly to Sumit's family. 'So, since today seems to be the day to talk about families, tell me a little more about yours.'

He laughed. 'What's to tell? I was born in Delhi, I grew up with my grandmother since my parents were posted in remote locations most times. I went to study journalism in Boston, came back only a couple of years ago. I worked for a bit with a news magazine and decided to take a sabbatical to write a book. That's about it.' He looked at his hands awkwardly, almost like he was seeing them for the first time. In the distance, the moon rose slowly over the low hills and faraway mountains, in what seemed to be sudden, jerky movements, almost like an unseen hand was pulling it into place in the star-dappled, velvety night, tinged with a few clouds.

'What is your book about?' I asked.

He looked out into the distance, a curtain coming over his eyes. 'It is historical. Part-fiction, part-fact. About my maternal grandfather.' His eyes were shuttered and he changed the topic. 'So Nina will join her mother in London after she passes out this year, or will she continue her studies here in India?'

'I really have no idea,' I replied. 'She doesn't seem to have given much thought to it yet, and her mother hasn't discussed it with me.'

It was my turn to ask about him, I was curious. 'No girlfriend or wife? A handsome, young boy like you?' I asked, using the advantage of being old enough to risk being impolite and intrusive. After all, I'd just answered a slew of questions from him and surely I was entitled to ask him a few of my own.

'No. No one at the moment,' he replied, looking even more studiedly at his hands, which now that I noticed, were slender and tapered, and very obviously hands that had seen no physical labour.

Nina emerged, having added a light cardigan to her ensemble, since it had become a little chilly. She sat next to me, a trifle ill at ease and reluctant to step into the conversation. 'Grams, you should come inside, it is chilly,' she said. 'Let's go in and harass Bimla to get dinner on the table early, I'm starving.'

As I rose, I noted a shadow reflected in the glass, behind Nina's shoulder. I turned to see nothing there that could cast a reflection, just the evening spreading out dark and silent as the birdsong died down. I looked again at the glass, blinking my eyes furiously, to force the tear film to activate and provide some clarity. She was there, coming slowly into focus, her glare as baleful as ever, her eyes red pinpricks in a sunken face and she was right behind Nina. She was back, she hadn't gone away with Basanti.

Nina looked at me and smiled. A chill ran down my spine. It was a smile I'd seen before, a smile that the girl found scratched in a pit behind the house had on her face when I'd looked at her.

'Nina,' I cried, sharply, looking at her face, searching for the child I knew.

'What is it, Grams?' she replied, rushing to me, her voice worried. 'Are you alright?' I grabbed her hand and looked at her face, my hands trembling at what I might see. It was her, my grandchild. I was imagining things. The moment passed and she was back again, my Nina, her face open, puzzled.

Sumit knelt in front of me, holding my other hand. 'Mrs McNally, why are you shivering, what is it?'

'Come inside, quick. Close the door,' I whispered, holding onto Nina's hand and his, pulling them with a strength I did not know I possessed into the house, in a misplaced hope that we would be safe within, despite knowing that there was no safety in the house. It was everywhere, beyond windowpanes, and in rocking chairs, lurking behind doors, tapping at the walls. As I held their hands and shut my eyes, feeling an unnamed fear crawl into my body, working its way up from my toes right up to my scalp, setting every nerve, every ganglion on edge. I said the only words that rose to my lips, the Lord's Prayer, dragging the words out from my core, words that comforted me, words I hoped would keep whatever evil was trying to enter my home out of it.

'Where did you go, Nina?' I asked her, conscious that my voice was sharper than it should have been. 'Tell me, where is it that you went?'

'What's the matter, Grams, why are you so upset? I just went for a walk down the back, around the cottages, down the path to where Bimla told me Basanti lived. I looked into her cottage, there was no one there, so I came away.'

'Did you bring anything from there?' I asked.

She looked shamefaced. 'How did you know, Grams? It was nothing important but I thought she wouldn't need it now that she was gone. I picked this up.' She pulled out a small brooch from her pocket. It was Nina's, one of those things a young girl discards when she decides she doesn't like it anymore and gives away. In this case she had given it to Basanti. She'd decided to take it back. I took the brooch in my hand, it singed my skin with a blazing heat, I dropped it with a soft scream, then picked it up carefully with my handkerchief. Nina had brought her back. The brooch was an ivory-engraved cameo of a woman in profile. Nina had found it in a drawer a very long time ago. I had never thought of how it had come there, who had owned it. Now I knew.

Sumit started and took the brooch from my hand, turning it over curiously. 'Wasn't this the same brooch that the lady in the photographs was wearing at her neck?'

Outside the window, through the glass panes, I could see a strange mist rising from behind the rolling expanse of the hills, swirling into the grounds where the cottages were, bringing with it a chill that crept through the flesh and pinched the bones. It poured into the body through the ears, through the nostrils, bringing with it a strange sense of dread that knotted my intestines with a twisting pain. Something was going to change irrevocably, I didn't know what it was and I was powerless to stop it.

Chapter 12

THAT NIGHT, I took a while falling asleep and when I did, I had a strange dream. She was sitting in my rocking chair and rocking herself, her dead eyes fixed on me. I lay on my bed, paralysed with fear, unable to move, unable to scream, my limbs refusing to move on my command. The room was suddenly freezing cold, the heater had probably stopped working in the night because the electricity supply had been cut and the inverter too had run out. At one point I was uncertain whether I was dreaming or awake, or in that strange space between dreaming and wakefulness, where the soul wanders out of the body and explores other dimensions. What I knew was that I was chilled to the bone, chilled in a way that made it impossible for me to move myself, to lever myself to a sitting position in order to switch the bedside lamp on and check whether this was really happening.

I could hear her in my head. Her voice was faint, feathery, and sibilant, as if she was whispering through a curtain of rain. Her words were indistinct, she called my name, she said words that pierced through my ears, words that meshed into ice slivers in my brain and when I thought finally that I would freeze to death, an ice-cold tiny body climbed under the quilt with me, putting frigidly chilly arms around me, and whispered, 'Mother, I'm cold.'

Icicles shot up my spine, and I sat bolt upright in my bed, feeling the covers fall from me and a small indent in the mattress where something had been a moment ago. There was a sudden click, the red light of the heater lit up, the bed and blanket warmer began radiating life-giving heat again and I felt myself thaw out, emerge from the scary limbo which marks one's descent into another dimension, and the shadow faded out from the rocking chair right in front of me into complete transparency and the icy presence in the bed faded away to nothingness.

I felt the world swim around just a bit with the rush of freshly warmed-up blood rushing through my veins. I switched the bedside light on and its golden light bathed the room in familiarity, far from the shadowed zone where something unearthly had sat in the rocking chair opposite the bed and whispered to me about a life unfulfilled.

Pouring myself a glass of water, I got out of the bed hesitantly and walked towards the rocking chair. It was empty. And yet, there was a menacing stillness that indicated something restraining itself. What that something was, I neither knew nor cared to know. I put my hand on the seat of the chair, the space was empty. I pulled on my wrap and sat down in the rocking chair, feeling the freezing chill of the chair seep through the layers of my wrap, my nightgown and my thermal wear. And I tried to rock myself back to sleep, wondering why she was haunting my home or whether I was imagining a spectre where none existed.

Was it time to call the local cab driver and ask to be taken to the local church? I did this occasionally, once in a few years, when I felt the need to connect with some form of spirituality, when I needed to grasp at straws. We had a church in the small town I lived on the fringes of, a lovely old, grey stone construction that had survived earthquakes and independence and stood in the midst of deodar trees, on the outskirts of the main town. It was a local tourist attraction, run over with indifferent visitors who clicked photographs of themselves standing on the weathered stone slabs, engraved with the details of those who were laid to rest below it. The tombstones, carved with inscriptions, were in a state of neglect and run-down; some of them were from the previous century, stories of lives lived and untimely deaths carved into their tombstones.

As I closed my eyes, trying to will myself back to sleep despite the fear that had my limbs shaking involuntarily, I thought of the only time in my life when I was happy, at Chaudharipore, when I was young, where the sun was crisp as the air, and the green of the tea estate dazzled the eyes for as far as one could see. When the first flush was harvested, just as spring set in – my favourite part of the year – after the long and often cruel, winter. I could be found skipping around the estate, with a book in hand, looking for a grassy spot to spread myself on and read undisturbed, or with my water colours and board, or tailing my grandfather on his rounds of the estate in his open jeep, his sola topee jammed firmly on his head, his expression grim, his manner kindly and his eyes tired.

Painting had kept me occupied during my days in Chaudharipore: painting and reading. I had painted the tall, still Himalayas in the distance, looking upon at us, sentinels of the icy, severe, unforgiving realm they guarded, beyond our ken, their snow-capped peaks flushed pink at dawn and a fiery orange at dusk. The soft roll of the green slopes with the tea bushes, dappled with the occasional tree planted to shade the tender bushes from the sun, the local women, their faces placid and sturdy, their voices ringing out across the slopes as they chatted with each other or sang songs in a language I was not familiar with, their foreheads furrowed as they worked. I painted them all, in as much detail as I could. Painting was a form of meditation for me, as plucking of tea leaves was a form of meditation for these deft-fingered women. I wondered why I had stopped painting and turned to writing. It was a turning inwards, a reluctance to step out, closing of the self to the outside and digging the psyche towards the soul, hoping to ferret out something of value, something beyond the dross and the everyday that made the bulk of me.

I spent most of my day walking around the estate, during harvest time. I went to the brooks running down its side and spent the mornings sitting on a rock, dipping my feet in the water, watching the fish dart around my feet nibbling at my toes. I wandered through the paths between the pines that stood guard over the periphery of the estate, slippery with moss. Occasionally though a wizened tea-picker would come up to me as I sat in a shaded nook, and talk to me, in the awkward language that was midway between what I understood and what they could communicate in. The mirror from those days showed me a pasty-faced, awkward, spotty girl, with eyes too big for her face and hair that hung limply to her shoulders with no pretence at even a single wave. When I was alone in my room, I dampened my hair and rolled it around old cardboard rolls that had once held thread and bob and pinned them optimistically to my scalp. I slept with them in my hair because that is what I read would put a wave in my hair in one of the many magazines that my grandmother subscribed to. They came to her, delayed by months, via post from across the oceans and then by train and cycle and finally put into the letter box at the start of the lane leading to the estate bungalow where we lived. My job by default became that of being the one who ran down to check if the mail had arrived and if there was anything in it for me or my grandmother apart from the letters and correspondence that regularly arrived from my grandfather's Calcutta office for him – auctions, orders, shipments. It was indicative of life at Chaudharipore, a place where time fell out of joint, where days segued into each other, where only the change of season told me that the years were passing, and with them, I was growing up, growing older and becoming an adult.

I began to learn the rhythm of the tea estate, the first flush or the springtime teas, harvested from late February to mid-April, and the tea it produced – light, delicate and almost floral. The banghi period, after the norwesters with their crackling thunderstorms and quick clouds. Summer storms, greens, then the second flush from April to June, where my grandfather looked for the aphids to feed on the leaves to give it that slight muscatel flavour. The monsoon, with its unceasing rains, months of continuous damp, followed by the autumnal from September to November, just before the winter rolled in with its initial crisp chill. The sheets of white snow and frost that set in thereafter confined us to the bungalow, shivering, putting logs on the fire and me refusing to bathe for days on end, until the sun emerged and thawed the estate and the people in it.

Through the dank winter months, the entire estate stayed grim and shuttered against the cold, and log fires and hot water bottles kept body and soul together along with the clickety-clack of my grandmother's needles, a pattern book kept by her side, creating sweaters for me, for my grandfather, in brilliant patterns that he hid beneath his overcoat and jacket, if ever compelled to go out of the house wearing them.

It was in my fifth year at Chaudharipore that illness struck my grandfather. A cough, ignored, neglected, grew into full-scale pneumonia in the thick of winter. And then morphed into something worse than we could have ever imagined. All I remember of those days now is the damp of the bungalow seeping in through the walls, the rebelling of the workers on the estate, the advice of my grandfather's peers to flee to the relative safety of Calcutta, his refusal to do so, and the embargo they placed us under, decrying our privileged existence. There was also the darkness of winter and the lack of supplies in the house. Dolma took trips to procure rations from the black market pretending they were for her family and then returned by a long circuitous route via a steep ravine to bring them to the bungalow. I also remember the light of the lamps casting eerie shadows on the walls, the silence in the house, the strained look on my grandmother's face, the nights spent waiting for what seemed like the inevitable and the grim faces of the doctors called, first from Darjeeling, then from Calcutta, potions administered, injections given, and dosages debated. Any earnest discussion about whether to transfer him to the nearest hospital would be silenced by my grandfather resolutely refusing to move out of his bed and his room, with its wooden flooring, old polished wood furniture and four-poster bed, with the mosquito curtains that gave it a quaint feminine touch and the framed botanical prints on the walls.

'This is my home, I was born here. If I have to die, I will die here,' he would say through his racking cough, in a tone that brooked no argument.

One evening I heard the doctor speak in hushed whispers to my grandmother. 'We detected it too late, there is nothing we can do now, but pray that it isn't painful for him.'

All those pipes he smoked, they said, the tar had steeped into his lungs and rotted them to sludge. My grandfather was synonymous with the comforting fragrance of tobacco that surrounded him, the paraphernalia of the pipe cleaners and tobacco pouches and matches that always lay strewn carelessly on his study table and by his bedside, the careful cleaning and polishing of his favourite pipes entrusted only to an old, trusted hand who could do it to the level of perfection he demanded. The tobacco from the pipes had taken over his lungs, congealed them into black tar, eroded away the cells into a raw oozing mass that came up as fresh red blood every time he coughed into his hand towels.

'I know I have no time left. My son has come for me. He's waiting by the window, every night. There he is, can't you see him, standing there? He's smiling at you.'

My grandmother's eyes would fly to the window, torn between
the longing to catch a glimpse of her dead son, and a horror-struck
understanding of the implication of what her husband was telling
her. 'There's no one there, you're imagining things, now just calm
down.'

And she would think it was the effect of all the medication
playing on his brain and confess to me, with her hand gentle on
his chest to check his breathing, 'My greatest fear whenever he goes
off to sleep is that he won't wake up again.' And outside, breathing
heavily at the gates, was the snowballing discontent of a generation
of tea estate workers who were hungry for revenge for what they
called decades of exploitation.

Adding to this was a movement that had been growing in the
hills, that would grow into a demand for a new state, a movement
that would take the youth out of their homes, lead to rallies and
blockades and curfews and hushed lynchings that would not be
mentioned in the national newspapers.

There is a stench to death. It crawls into your nostrils and
hollows out your insides, it follows you wherever you go. You can
smell it on your fingers, smell it on your clothes. When you are
in a house that has just hosted death, you feel death all around
you. For days after you have cremated or interred the person death
came for, death's miasmal presence lingers, like a malevolent curse
on the premises.

The funeral was a hurried affair. My aunt came down from
Delhi on the day of the funeral and stayed a while with us. Karuna
bua, as I was asked to call her, was a cold woman with a pinched
face, lines etched in before her time. She looked at me warily.
In retrospect, I think she resented me because my presence now
implied that there was one more piece of the pie to be carved out
of the estate's proceeds. It was the first time I was meeting her. In
the five years I had spent at Chaudharipore, she had never visited
the place. I would learn later that she had told her parents she

refused to come while 'that bastard child' was on the premises, but was compelled to come face to face with me during the funeral.

It didn't take much to convince my grandmother to sell the estate. Karuna bua had no interest in it, except for the proceeds of the sale. I opted to go back to the only city I was familiar with, Calcutta. My grandmother moved to Delhi, to live with Karuna bua.

She had also, unknown to her daughter, put in a fixed amount in bank deposits to my name, so I was ensured of a little amount to keep body and soul together every month, whether I earned a living or not. She hugged me and wept as we parted at Howrah station where she boarded a train. 'Take care of yourself, keep writing to me, call me when you can.' She pressed a scrap of paper with the phone number and address of her daughter's home into my palm. I crumpled it quietly in the palm of my hand and let it fall to the dirty platform as the train pulled out, lost in a melee of thousands of other crumpled bits and pieces, flotsam and jetsam of other lives. I would never meet my grandmother again. Three years later, Mr Ganguly would tell me she had passed away, a sudden stroke he said, she was found collapsed in the bathroom. She had been dead for a while and couldn't be revived. I had cried that day, huge gasping sobs. I was alone, completely alone, all over again.

Starting life afresh, alone at twenty-one, was a good thing. It taught me that nothing is permanent, and the moment you start taking a situation as permanent it is bound to change. Consequently, I spent the rest of my life in a state of flux, always packed, metaphorically speaking, ready to leave at a moment's notice. And now, at the fag end of my years, I was metaphorically packing myself up, day by day, closing the door on some memories, mothballing others, bubble-wrapping still others. Cleaning out the mind of all the accumulated junk, some memories that were too painful to go back to, some that were occupying mind-space because I had been too lazy to get rid of them. I was getting packed and ready to move on. Albeit to a different dimension.

As I drifted in and out of sleep, wondering whether I needed to talk to someone about what I was seeing, experiencing in my home, I felt the window snap open suddenly, and a gust of chilly wind blow through the room, making the curtains fly and the framed picture of an unknown Victorian beauty dash to the ground. I could feel myself swirling in a vortex that was not of my making. I gripped the arms of the rocking chair and squeezed my eyes shut, bracing myself for what I sensed would follow, until an instinct made me open them and look straight into the darkness outside. That face floated outside, in the blackness of the night, looking at me, mouthing something indistinct, inaudible and sibilant that stabbed through my ears into my brain. And then a hand reached out into the room and grabbed my neck, squeezing it, squeezing it with a force that threatened to snap my neck in two. I felt everything around me go completely dark and the next thing I knew, it was bright morning and I was in my bed. The window was fastened shut, and my neck was raw and tender, painful to the touch.

Chapter 13

NINA WAS LATE for breakfast the next morning. Sumit grabbed a couple of slices of toast, buttered them haphazardly, dunked them in his tea and was done with breakfast. He smiled apologetically and disappeared into his room shortly afterwards, while I continued to wait for Nina, finally sending Bimla up to wake her. She came down apologetically, still dishevelled from sleep and grumpy from adolescence. Her skin, which usually had that enviable patina of youth and freshness, was suddenly tinged with a pallid sallowness that disturbed me, and there were dark rings under her eyes.

'Morning, Grams.' Her voice was dull. She hugged me and kissed the top of my head, in a gesture that was oddly maternal. A gesture I had never experienced all my life but felt surprisingly familiar, like I was supposed to remember it from a distant past.

'Good morning, darling,' I replied. 'Would you like to have some breakfast? There are eggs which can be made the way you want, there's toast, there's fruit, jam, cheese, cornflakes. Or would you like Bimla to roll out some aloo parathas for you?'

I prided myself on a generous table at a meal, especially when the child was here. 'Nope, I'm good with toast and tea, thanks.' She picked up a slice of toast, spread some orange marmalade on it and sat with one leg up on the chair, munching it thoughtfully, still wearing her night clothes. It was something I had never been able to do, wear what I had worn through the night to breakfast, nor sit with my leg up on the chair. Perhaps it was the years spent in the convent in my childhood and the five a.m. baths that had done this to me, but I had to be bathed before I had my breakfast. I raised a brow at her leg; she guiltily put it down and straightened her posture. Ah, the teacher in one never relaxed its vigil, even for a beloved grandchild.

'Slept well?' I asked her, noticing her eyes were ringed blue, and her face was rather drawn down, weighed down by something I didn't understand. I thought of the shadow I had seen reflected behind her shoulder in the glass pane the previous evening. I remembered the split second her eyes flashed red before returning to their normal blue, blue sapphires set in dusky skin.

'No, actually,' she replied. 'I didn't. I kept dreaming of this horrible woman sitting in my room, glaring at me and at one point I didn't know whether I was dreaming or whether she was really sitting there, it was such an eerie feeling.'

I started with fright and almost spilt the tea I was sipping. 'What did she look like, this horrible woman and how dare she glare at you while I'm around?' I asked her, quickly mopping up the few drops that had fallen onto the white-and-red checkered tablecloth, before they stained it.

She frowned, putting the last bite of toast into her mouth and pouring out the cornflakes into a small bowl, topping it with some milk and spooning on the sugar generously before shovelling it all ungraciously into her mouth and not slowing down her conversation while eating. What was with children these days, weren't they being taught to never speak with their mouths full of food? Manners and simple graciousness were fast becoming something that belonged to another generation.

'Couldn't see her too well, she was transparent-ish, if you know what I mean. Like she was there and not there. And she kept saying something to me, I don't know what it was.'

'What do you think – was she a figment of your imagination, were you reading anything last night, before dropping off that could have brought this on?' I asked, knowing that the answer would be in the negative.

She shook her head, while simultaneously shoving down cornflakes and milk into her gullet, without, it would seem, the need to chew the spoonful before swallowing it. Her lopsided fringe, which I suspected she cut on her own, fell into her eyes, covering the expression in them from view. I suspected they were already shuttered to begin with, shuttered with secrets I would never know.

'Nope, I was reading some comics last night, nothing with sad-looking women in it. And then I surfed the net for a while on the laptop before turning in.'

The stomach wrenched itself a bit. I decided that the topic could be changed before it got grimmer. 'Dr Sanyal is dropping by for lunch,' I said, looking at her face for any change of expression and it happened on cue.

Her voice was careful, guarded. 'Any special reason?'

'To meet us, I would presume, it has been a while since he visited. In fact, I haven't seen him since a little after you left the last time,' I replied.

She looked thoughtful and ate her cornflakes without pause or comment, emptying the bowl in two minutes flat. 'Grams, I'll see you later, I need to bathe and get dressed. It's ten in the morning and here I am still in my night clothes like a street urchin.'

I wondered what could be the solution to this other-worldly infestation, now that the rest of the household was seeing her too.

Not that anyone had been harmed yet. But that wasn't a chance I would like to take. An alternative could be selling the cottage and moving to another home closer to the middle of town, with easy access to the stores and the hospitals, rather than being out here on the fringes, with no available transportation in case of an emergency, something Millie had been vociferously advocating for a while, but which I had been resisting.

I needed help to deal with this, perhaps I could speak with Dr Sanyal about it, he might understand. I was losing the little courage I had, the marks around my neck were real and tangible enough to stop me from continuing with the self-delusional explanations I kept giving myself that I was hallucinating. I instructed Bimla to have a wider spread at the lunch table than she normally did, given we had an additional person joining us for the meal.

I decided to take a little stroll in the garden, soaking in a little sunshine before Dr Sanyal arrived. The old bones could do with a little warmth. There seemed to be a chill that had steeped into me, from that icy grip around my neck the previous night. The marks remained prominent, covered by a stole wrapped carefully around the wrinkled skin. The pink rose bushes Hari Singh had planted the previous year along the skirting of the verandah were in full bloom. The glorious, brazen pinkness of the blooms against the emerald green of the grass stood out against the grey-stoned façade, hitting the eye with their arrogance of colour and filling the air with a strong, full-bodied fragrance. Hari Singh was back from his break, pottering around by the bushes at the back of the cottage, wrestling with some unpleasant-looking weeds that seemed to have sprung up uninvited, cursing and grumbling as he did so. 'Salaam, Masterniji, yeh dekho. Two weeks ago I cleared this area of all the weeds and now they've sprung up again.' He cursed Manikji roundly for having treated his beloved plants in a step-fatherly manner, allowing them to be invaded by these social pariahs of the plant world.

I clucked my tongue in commiseration. While it pleased me to have a garden that was neat and kempt, I had no special interest in tending to it or getting overly involved in its upkeep. 'You're doing a great job, Hari Singh, I wouldn't know what I would do without you,' I told him, and moved away before I could get roped into discussions on fertilizer and rain, and the quality of top soil and such things which would glaze my eyes and cause me to keel over and fall asleep on my feet.

'There's some hungama happening down the path, behind chaar number. The workers digging to change the water pipes have found something, human bones,' he shouted behind me. Bones. Human bones. Kurnal had told me about the diggings, Basanti had fallen into one of the little pits that were being dug. I turned towards the path leading to where he said the human remains had been discovered. It was towards the rear of my own cottage and veered steeply round a bend. I noticed the back of my cottage looking rather shabby. Repairs and renovations were long overdue, the roof needed looking at, the woodwork needed a fresh coat of paint, and there were patches of moss caused by the damp which needed to be cleaned up before it accelerated and took over the entire wall. I realised I hadn't been this way in months. In fact I barely emerged from the house these days. I was content to have the days pass by doing absolutely nothing.

A channel was being dug to lay out additional pipes, given the old ones had been in existence since the days of the Raj and needed changing. The men digging seemed to have hit something, something that had people flocking to it like the proverbial flies to sweet, sticky stuff. But the expression on the faces surrounding the pit were uniformly grim. As I made my way up to the gathering, they parted graciously to allow me through. Two scrawny men, sweating despite the rather pleasant weather, stood in a pit, where clearly there seemed to be human remains, a human skeleton. I gasped in shock, and held onto the shoulder of the little boy who stood in front of me, his home-knitted sweater a patchwork of repaired and frayed edges. He looked back at me and smiled cheerily, his face a maze of freckles and chapped skin and snot; it was my own Kurnal. 'Masterniji,' he said, 'dekho, neechey... it's a skeleton.' I peered in, holding on to him. The wind whistled through the deodars fringing the path, an eerie whistling quite at odds with the bright sunshine of the day.

It was not a pleasant sight. The blood rushed to my head, and I was vaguely aware of the voices around me, talking to each other in an animated buzz, seniors being summoned, the police being called, women gathering their small children to their sides and forbidding them to look inside. Bones, muddy, rib cage, a grinning skull, exposed. A fetid smell, rose rank and foul, into the air, making me want to hurl up whatever breakfast I had consumed.

'Did anyone go missing in these parts and was never found?' I asked one of the men standing at the side.

He shook his head, scratching his neck in a vague manner. 'No, Masterniji, the police will have to figure that out.'

On cue, the sound of a jeep pulling up came from behind us. The crowd parted again, and two uniformed men came through asking questions. I moved back to allow them access to the pit, which, interestingly was pretty deep. Not something that had been dug in a hurry. Nor someone who had been interred in a hurry either. The police inspectors got the crowd to fall back and examined what they could from the surface without going down the ladder carefully placed along the edge of the pit.

The news had spread and I could see more people gathering from around the estate and from the homes outside too, I was sure. Some were clicking pictures with their mobile phones. One more jeep drew up. Some more khaki-clad men jumped out officiously, and pushed the now-surging crowd back. Such gruesome news spreads faster than any happy news could. Women were hurrying from their homes on the estate, wiping their hands on their aprons, tucking their little ones on the hips, to catch a glimpse of the skeleton. I decided to get back home before I got jostled into the pit myself. I was not sure my bones would survive such a fall. I turned around to go back home. A kind man noticed me struggling to make a path for myself and urged the crowd to let the Masterni through. The crowd graciously parted to let me pass and I spotted Hari Singh and Manikji hovering ineffectively on the fringes trying to get a peep.

'What did you see, Masterniji?' Hari Singh asked me, with his customary lack of reticence, as I emerged from the throng.

'Some bones,' I replied. 'Of someone who has been dead a long, long time.' A shiver ran down my spine. The pipeline digging had commenced a couple of months ago. Almost at the same time as the sightings began. Perhaps, at the exact same time I first saw the face at the window.

Kurnal came up to me from the crowd, and took my hand, for strength or support, I did not know. I held onto his hand as he led me back to my home, my knees suddenly wobbly, unable to bear my weight.

Rounding my corner of the pathway, I could see Dr Sanyal walking up, his little red car parked a distance away at a part where the road was a little wider than usual, in deference to the police vehicle which must have undoubtedly passed him on its way to the place where the bones had been found.

He smiled and waved as he came closer. 'What is happening? There seems to be much activity going on here today, two police jeeps passed me as I was driving up.'

'They seem to have found some human remains just behind my cottage,' I replied. 'And while I am curious to know who they belong to, I refuse to be pushed into the pit by the jostling crowds and end up a corpse myself.'

He laughed and looked curiously in the direction I had mentioned. 'I think I should go and take a look for myself or I would never be able to forgive myself for missing out on the only brush with dead human bones I've had outside of medical school.'

'Please go right ahead,' I replied, gesturing towards where the brouhaha was taking place. At the same time I noticed Nina emerge from the house behind him, dressed in a pair of light blue jeans and a red pullover that made her suddenly seem more woman than child, her breasts high and rounded under the tight-fitting pullover, her legs long and slim, her manner womanly wise and self-aware. Her skin was clear and unlined, and her hair, tied back loosely with a thick black scrunchie, fell straight to her waist, sparkling in the sun. She was taller than I had been at her age, and she stood straight, her limbs encased in the fitted denim, lithe and a testament to the plethora of outdoor activities she occupied herself with at school.

'Here's Nina,' I said, smiling at her, wondering what the world would offer my child-woman with the blue eyes and the black hair and the chin that seemed too fragile to take any knocks. Dr Sanyal turned around and for a moment they looked at each other, their expressions guarded.

'Good morning, doctor,' Nina said, her voice catching.

'Good morning,' he replied, his voice polite. 'It is good to see you again. Are you down for a while?' I picked up undercurrents in their conversation that puzzled me. It felt like they were talking in a code I could not crack, a conversation that excluded me, private to the two of them, even though I stood right there.

She nodded, smiling her half-smile, the expression in her eyes, womanly and knowing and suddenly older than her age. 'Yes, I'm here for a week, and then I'll be back for the winter break. Perhaps. My mother is still undecided about her plans for the winter break.'

Dr Sanyal turned back to check the voices coming from where the crowd had gathered, buzzing like a confederation of drones. 'I'm going to check out what has happened,' he said. 'Would you like to come along?'

Her face lit up like she had stuck her finger into an electric socket, and she nodded her head. 'I was just on my way to see the excitement. It isn't everyday that we get not one but two police jeeps whizzing past our front door. In fact, most days we don't get any vehicle except the pick-up trucks or the two-wheelers and cycles of the estate workers.'

I moved back towards the house, trying to get the sequence of events clear in my head, from the time the digging commenced to the appearance of the face at my window for the first time ever. 'I will get back to the house then, will see you both in a bit. I shall be in my study.'

The good doctor waved at me and waited graciously for Nina to fall in step with him before setting out down the path. I turned around and looked at their retreating backs engaged in what seemed to be animated conversation from the distance. The words floated over the breeze back at me. 'I've told you time and again, this is ridiculous, you need to stop…' Dr Sanyal was saying.

'Why not? This isn't some silly school girl infatuation…' Nina replied sharply, the rest of her words blown away by a wind that changed direction. I stood, rooted to the spot, breathing heavily, knowing now the reason why Nina was so keen to visit me at any given opportunity, the reason she wandered off down the pathways sometimes and returned home having encountered Dr Sanyal on the path by chance, and having hitched a ride with him or so she would tell me. And I had believed her with the intrinsic trust one has in those one loves, because one doesn't want to believe otherwise, one doesn't dare let the construct of goodness one has about the person shatter.

Could this be love yet? Was she grown enough to know of the love that tore you apart and patched you together so you were never quite yourself again, to know that hearts got broken and mended and broken again, to feel the gaps between successive loves rattle with the hollowness that comes from pieces of the heart being scooped out. I took myself with heavy feet into the house and made my way slowly back to my study, feeling the twinge in the knees intensify, a sure warning that indicated winter was closing in on us.

The pain, in my heart and my knees, was intense.

I tried to do without painkillers as much as possible. But the crunching pain in my stomach these days was scaring me, as was the sudden growing incidents of retching up bright red blood. I decided I would mention it to Dr Sanyal only if the pain intensified. Hopefully it would subside without needing medication or any surgical intervention. It might be an ulcer or the beginnings of one. It might be worse. I didn't want to know. I was content being ostrich like and not wanting to investigate it further. I could feel the days slipping away, and this would hurry it, I knew, the spattering of red that occasionally heaved itself up from my gut.

Dr Sanyal was one of the rare doctors who believed that the body must be given an opportunity to heal itself, before stepping in with medication. He applied that philosophy to his life as well. He lived spartanly, with the bare minimum of belongings. His house, the only time I had visited it, on his insistence, in the days when I still went down to the main town, had minimum furniture, no decorations, and a wall full of books.

'I live light,' he had told me once. 'I have barely five sets of clothes at any point, I can pack and move out in five minutes. The only thing that I do collect are music CDs and books, but I'm slowly moving to a digital library of everything I own, so even the need to physically carry those around will become redundant.' And he explained to me the concept of the Kindle and how he could download movies and music from his computer and I wondered about how curling up with a little device could compare with the joy of holding a book one couldn't put down... the crisp spine of the fresh-off-the-shelf book, the thrill of the unturned page crackling as one turned them, the pleasure of underlining something that pleased one, or made one ponder, with whatever was close at hand, a pen, a pencil, a marker, the returning to the book after some years and seeing the page yellow, curled at the edges, the ink a bit faded, revisiting the markings on the pages, remembering where one was when one read it and go back to that moment.

I would speak with Dr Sanyal, I decided, when Nina would be back at school. I would ask him about the snatches of conversation I had overheard, what they meant and did they mean what I had imagined them to mean. From my vantage point in what I called my eyrie, I saw Sumit emerge from the front door and wander off towards where Nina and Dr Sanyal had headed. I saw one of the police jeeps roar past my cottage. People were dispersing now, going back to where they had left their work half-done, guard posts, positions at the machines in the tea factory at the estate, and children squalling at home and whatever worries of the day they had laid to the side before coming here to view the remains of the unknown human, interred unceremoniously.

I sat back in my chair, pondering over the unfinished conversation I'd overheard, wondering what to make of it. Voices coming from downstairs told me that Dr Sanyal, Sumit and Nina had returned. There was much loud discussion on about skeletons and cadavers and medical school and bone age.

'So, you can tell the age of a person at the time of death from the bone?' Nina was asking (I assumed) Dr Sanyal, as the voices came up the stairs. The voices died down and there was a knock on the door, and Nina poked her head in.

'Grams, it was so exciting, my first skeleton,' she said, her face flushed and happy. 'It was so gruesome, it was fabulous.' The generation these days is more delighted by the macabre than they should rightfully be. There was no sign of any uneasiness from the discussion I'd overheard as they had walked away from me. In its place was an easy camaraderie that was frighteningly normal.

They spilled into the room and seated themselves on the sofa and armchair. I put aside my glasses, covering the typewriter with the little plastic cover to keep dust from settling on its keys and turned around to face the trio which had now seated itself amicably.

As Dr Sanyal spoke, Sumit looked at him, his face clear as a mirror, an expression I recognised and which made me catch my breath. Suddenly, many pieces of the jigsaw puzzle I was trying to fit in place regarding Dr Sanyal, his almost hermit-like life, his lack of a family of his own, all fell together. And I looked at Nina, staring at Dr Sanyal with an adoring look, a look that had the stars shining out of her eyes from the other side of the room. I closed my eyes. I knew that expression. The expression of someone devouring another person's face with their eyes. And I knew such expressions could only lead to pain.

Chapter 14

CALCUTTA, LIKE MOST cities, was not kind to a young girl living alone. No one in the area took kindly to me, save Mrs Dutta, an Anglo-Indian nurse married to a doctor. She kept an eye out for me, brought me cakes and pies she had baked, food she had cooked and ensured I ate enough to keep myself healthy. She and the Ganguly family were the ones that helped me survive alone in the city.

'You're the daughter I never had,' she would tell me, in rare moments of sentimentality that pierced the gruffness she normally drew on as a carapace every morning after she had bathed and before she had dressed in the voluminous floral dresses that were her preferred choice of clothing for home-wear. And I told her about the mother who would not accept me. It was a bond that suited us both; I needed a mother figure and she needed someone to care for.

She was light-skinned enough to pass for a European, with liver spots beginning to take over her hands and her face. I now saw the same spots on my own arms and hands, and some creeping along the sides of my face. She possessed an expansive girth which gave her trouble when wheezing her way up the steep flight of stairs that connected our flats. Doctor Dutta was a benevolent presence who returned home from his clinic at seven-thirty p.m. sharp, at which time he would settle in his armchair, put the gramophone player with their LP records on and listen to some jazz, sipping his glass of single malt, with the one ice cube he was fanatical about. On days punctured by power outages when there was no ice in the fridge, the entire neighbourhood would hear him bellowing his displeasure in no uncertain terms. Mrs Dutta was inured to these outbursts and would calmly continue with her work in the kitchen as he fumed and slammed things around.

Occasionally, they had guests over, raucous gatherings with Mrs Dutta's relatives coming over for dinner or a Sunday lunch. The entire neighbourhood would know that they were in high spirits. Dr Dutta's relatives didn't drop in too often. He went across during festivals to his sister's home, dressed carefully in a white dhoti and kurta, his demeanour hesitant and skulking. When Mrs Dutta's family came over for one of her big dinners, which happened around Easter or Christmas or her birthday or the good doctor's birthday or their marriage anniversary, I helped her with the cooking and the cleaning and generally stayed back a bit for the dancing and singing, which inevitably were a part of the evening. I enjoyed the merriment and felt like a member of a family for a change. Sometimes her cousins took me dancing to one of the clubs, always careful to be acutely proper lest I complain to her. A new world was slowly opening up to me, a world radically different from the enforced piety of the cloistered convent I had grown up in, or the splendid isolation of my years at Chaudharipore.

It was at one such dinner, which also happened to be Mrs Dutta's birthday, that I met John McNally. I didn't notice him at first. He was standing quietly in a corner, looking at a shelf packed mainly with Dr Dutta's medical books, a few travel books and a couple of concessions to popular fiction that Dr Dutta allowed in the bookshelf because Mrs Dutta read them. He was dressed differently from the other men in the room – wide lapelled jacket, trousers that flared out a bit. His hair was longer than that of the other men in the room, and curiously tousled in a way that suggested someone had run their fingers through it and he'd resisted settling them again with a comb. Maybe he had run his own fingers through them. Maybe I should have run my fingers through them. He inspired such thoughts in me, thoughts that I hadn't had for any man so far. He was loose-limbed and languid, and looked around like he would rather be anywhere but where he was right now.

I stuck my not-too-impressive chest out and walked up to him with the tray of wafers I was circulating. The loudspeakers were blasting music that had Dr Dutta retreat to the inner recesses of the house, nursing his whisky and soda in a bad mood. I had to shout to make myself heard. John McNally bent closer to me to hear what I was trying to tell him. I caught a whiff of a fragrance I didn't recognise but would learn later was Old Spice, a fragrance I would forever associate with him.

'Want some?' I asked, putting on my most charming smile. He smiled slightly, picked one wafer and turned his attention back to the book shelf.

For a moment, this disconcerted me. I was not used to men turning their backs on me, for whatever it was worth. I was at an age when men stopped whatever they were doing to look at me as I passed. At the firm I worked at, the male staff made periodic random trips to the part of the steno pool where I sat to catch glimpses of me. I ignored most of them because none of them made my heart flutter in the way it should. The upcoming young partner at the firm, with his soft-spoken nature and trousers held up with suspenders, was gentle with my typing errors, whereas the other stenographer typists would have their eardrums punctured by the yelling which often ensued. He often extended unwelcome invitations to lunch and dinner that I turned down with the utmost politeness.

I looked at John McNally, puzzled, waiting for him to turn back and continue the conversation, but he didn't. It was a first for me.

'Who's he?' I asked Mrs Dutta when I got back into the kitchen. 'Distant cousin. From Bombay. Spends his time travelling the country, doing all sorts of photography and has never held down a job for long. He's,' she paused meaningfully, 'not dependable. Just packs up and goes wherever he wants to. Suddenly surfaces after years. Doesn't keep in touch with family.' She then looked at me, her eyes keen and knowing with the wisdom that age brings. 'He's bad news. What you need is a good man, in a solid job, dependable, reliable. Trust me, girl, don't fall for him.'

Of course, I proceeded to do just that.

I made sure I remained in his line of sight all evening. I laughed when I was spoken to, I played off the only three eligible men in the room against each other. I looked slyly at him to check if he had noticed. He looked bored.

I noticed how his eyes were a curious colour – not brown, not black but an indistinct tawny shade. How his hair curled around his ears and down his collar and how he smelt different from all the other men in the room. A clean, fresh, smell. And how he stood a little apart from everyone, like he was wrapped in some bubble that kept him from being contaminated by their forced jollity.

He wasn't interested in the singing or dancing, and he barely sipped at the whisky pressed into his hands by Milton, Mrs Dutta's rather rambunctious and genial brother. He stood in a corner through most of the evening, looking most disinterested in the proceedings and I finally found him sitting alone in the balcony, after a particularly energetic jiving session with Mrs Dutta's eighteen-year-old nephew who was quick and light on his feet and played the drums at a famous nightclub in the city.

'What are you doing here all alone?' I asked him, feeling my heart quicken its beat as I spotted him, dragging on a cigarette in the semi-dark.

'Waiting for you to find me.'

I felt my stomach lurch to my throat. It was the first time I'd ever felt the rush of the hormones in this way. He put his arm around me and drew me to him. I didn't resist. It seemed a waste of time to do so. The kiss, when it happened, was like it was something waiting to happen since the moment we had both set eyes on each other, four hours ago.

We were getting some curious stares from the rest of the gathering within the house, and only the thought of Dr Dutta, who unnerved me a bit, made me disengage myself and walk back shakily into the house, guiltily patting my hair back into place and wondering if my lipstick was smudged all over my face.

After dinner was done, the table cleared, goodnights said and the crowds dispersed, I went back up to my home. And waited for the soft knock I knew in my shivering gut, would come. There is a deliciousness in waiting that transcends the uncertainty of not knowing. I waited. And waited. And finally, it came. Soft, insistent. Confident in the knowledge that the door would be opened to it. Thirty minutes after the lights in the Dutta house were switched off, and the sounds of the partying lot had died down as they stepped drunkenly through the street and reached the turning from where they would find themselves some transport to reach their homes. I opened the door without a moment's hesitation, with no caution and without ascertaining who it was.

For a moment, as he quietly stepped in, there was an awkward silence. I didn't know what was expected of me, and yet there was this churning within me, which could only be the result of years of not giving into what I had branded as sinful lust. The next few hours were a whir of body, and sweat, and touch and arching and sharp pain, a release that I could never imagine and a clinging sleep, that was broken before dawn. I realised he was getting dressed silently, readying to leave. He came to me and kissed me, lingeringly. 'So beautiful. And all mine.'

I was. All his. In my head there was absolutely no dispute about that, even though I had met him for the first time that evening and even though I had been warned by Mrs Dutta to stay away from him.

'When will I see you again?' I asked him.

He ran his hand again all over my body, and I felt myself quivering in response. 'Tomorrow,' he replied.

'Where?' I asked, rising up from the bed and clinging to him, unwilling to let him go. He gently disengaged me.

'I'll come to you.'

He was my vampire lover, one who came to me in the dark, after the lights in the neighbourhood were shut down, when the stray dogs roamed the streets in packs.

The next night he came again. Knocking softly at the door, after all the lights in the windows of the small, squat neighbourhood we lived in had died down and the only sound was that of the street dogs barking their heads off at the intruder who moved swiftly inside.

We made love, again and again and again. I knew nothing of protection, of keeping safe, I didn't think of the possible consequences. And we talked through the night. 'Whenever I get restless, I run away. I travel.' His skin was that slightly bronzed version of a faded tan that was reluctant to go away.

'This time I'm going to spend some months in Darjeeling, before I return to Bombay. Come with me.' I was powerless to refuse him.

He was thirty. I was twenty-three. It had all the makings of a relationship that would redefine my life into a before and after. And I jumped headlong into it with the recklessness of not caring where it was headed, where I was headed and whether he was the one for me.

A week later, I put in a request for a month's leave and went with him to Darjeeling. I had long stopped going to church or confession and my immortal soul was damned to hell anyway, so a little more sin wouldn't matter, I told myself. Darjeeling was like being back in Chaudharipore; the mists, the greenery, the clear cerulean expanse of sky, the mountains rising pink in the mornings, the curving narrow roads, the aromas of the market. Darjeeling, the land of the thunderbolt, the glimpse of Kanchenjunga from Tiger Hill, endless mugs of hot chocolate and walking through the mall, and sitting down for a hearty breakfast of freshly baked bread and thick soup. And being in love made everything sharper, more focused, like I was seeing it all through a clearer lens. At times, sitting by the bedroom window, sipping on mugs of hot chocolate on a clear morning, we could see the sunlight kiss the clouds a delicate pink. It was a life I could get used to, but there was this niggling sense of unease beneath everything that this would end, we would need to get back to our regular lives. Marriage was never discussed. The here and now was all that mattered. It was convenient to be Mrs McNally, it didn't raise eyebrows, faces stayed friendly and didn't freeze into unwelcome hostility. It made things simpler, did away with unnecessary explanations. Those were trusting times, people were trusting, welcoming.

'I could live here forever,' he said, one night, tracing his finger down my arm to my hips. 'With you.' I clung to him with a sudden chill that told me this would soon get over, with the hope that it would never end, these moments we were stealing from our lives elsewhere, moments we would have to return to the box when we were done with them.

It was natural that something so beautiful would have to end. And so it did. Abruptly, without the gradual fading away that ebbs the beauty of most long-term relationships where love disappears into the bitter grunge of day to day living, of words bitten back and epithets swallowed. We had been in Darjeeling for four months, when he stepped out to buy some bread and vegetables one morning. Around ten minutes later there was the sickening sound of a crash and voices raised in the street outside the rooms we had rented in a genteel lodging house. It was a truck, a narrow turn and a misjudgement on the truck driver's part. I was asked to identify the body. I threw up all over the floor of the room in the local police station where he was laid out, like a piece of meat on the butcher's block, a bloodied dent in his skull the only indication that he'd been fatally hurt, the jacket he had been wearing stiff with the dried blood, his eyes closed, like he was in deep sleep, dreaming wistfully.

I called Mrs Dutta for the first time since I had fled to Darjeeling without informing her. She made arrangements for the body to be despatched to his home city for the burial.

I spent the next three days after his death lying in a daze, without eating a morsel of the food left behind by the kind neighbour in the lodge.

I hadn't slept for two days, the tears had been flowing out of me, almost like they were being wrenched out by a giant hand from deep within my gut. I returned to Calcutta, nauseous with the lack of food and grief. The house was musty from having been locked up for weeks, but the absence of cobwebs told me Mrs Dutta had been coming in, with the spare key I had given her in case of an emergency, and cleaning it up in my absence.

She had noticed my sickly pallor, which told her more than I had the courage to.

'Well...' she asked, looking up at me, censure in her eyes. 'What are you going to do now?' she asked me, confirming to me what I had suspected but hadn't dared confirm with a visit to the doctor. 'How many weeks overdue?'

'Two. Three. I don't know,' I replied.

'Are you sure?' I nodded. 'He didn't know about it, did he?' she asked. I shook my head, to indicate a negative, the image of him laid up on the floor in the police station like a piece of meat refusing to quit my mind's eye.

The words went through me surely, piercing what could have been my heart, but was a space that was now hollowed out and echoing. Some more tears spilled down my face. My hands went to my stomach automatically. 'I warned you,' she said, simply. 'I warned you. Why didn't you stay away from him?'

'Because I couldn't,' I replied. She sat on the bed and cradled my head in her arms and patted my head as more tears spilled out from my eyes.

'I'll ask the husband if we can get something done. You can't have it, you know.' I did. She was a practicing Catholic. Abortion was anathema to her. And to me.

I shook my head. 'No. I'm having this baby.'

She shook her head discouragingly, the jowls of her cheeks shaking of their own accord. 'It isn't that easy, darling child. You are alone, you have your life ahead of you. You can't be bringing a child into this world when you yourself have no support. You need to get married and have a husband, and then have a child. No, have as many children as you wish, then. But now, you cannot have a child.'

'I'm not going to get an abortion,' I told her, turning my head away. It could be a little boy in my stomach. A little boy with the dark brown-black eyes and the curls of his father. Or a girl, with the serious expression and determined chin of her father. The sky outside the window was grey, it was early October. The slight chill of winter had begun to set in here in Calcutta. In Darjeeling, we had already begun wearing sweaters and layers, and had lit logs in the fireplace every night. I winced at the memory.

'I will have this baby, Mrs Dutta. Can you help me?' I asked her. If she said no, I would have it nonetheless. She smiled at me, her eyes were sad with the memories of all the babies she had carried within her and which had never survived either within the womb or outside it. And nodded.

'We have to have a story for you, you know. We have to tell everyone you were married to John. You can't be unmarried and pregnant. Doctor would be terribly angry,' she replied. 'Doctor' being the term she used to refer to her husband, a carryover from the days when she was a nurse at his clinic.

I became Mrs McNally, a name I took on and added in all official documentation, with the help of a forged marriage certificate Mrs Dutta managed to procure through some insidious bribing at the local registrar's office. She bought a plain gold band from the local goldsmith and put it on the third finger of my left hand. 'There,' she said. 'No one will dare say anything to a young widow in a delicate state now.'

Chapter 15

D R SANYAL LEFT after lunch during which the discussion veered from life in Delhi to the rapid construction coming up in town, converting all the pretty, ivy-covered cottages and bungalows into triple- and four-storeyed housing complexes, with small patches of green that masqueraded as gardens. It eventually encompassed getting a good deal on rentals and life at boarding schools as well as the bones exhumed that morning. Sumit asked him for a ride into town; he needed to check for mail in his post-box, he said, and get some supplies he had run out of.

'I hope we will be seeing you soon, Doctor?' I asked, as he rose to leave after the bowl of custard which was Bimla's valiant effort at dessert today. 'Or will a couple of months need to pass before you honour us with your presence again?'

'I will try to drop by more often, it's just that the past couple of months have suddenly become very stressful,' he replied.

'What happened?' Nina piped up. 'Why stressful?'

He smiled at her. 'The practice is growing, I shouldn't be complaining. It barely gives me time for anything else.' She pouted and in a second, a flash of the woman she would be in a few years came through.

'Then you must cut down on your work, what is the point of working so hard when you don't get the time to enjoy yourself?' she said, with an implied coquetry that was much older than her years. I wondered if I had been as coquettish when I was sixteen. I would have had no opportunity to practice it if I had, either at the convent, or at Chaudharipore.

He laughed and shook his head. 'I'm better off being busy, I wouldn't know how to enjoy myself,' he said gently, knowing that he was letting her down in some way, and moved towards the main door, after giving me a brief and uncharacteristic hug. I went to the door, too, to wave him off.

Nina followed them to the car, looking awkward, even intrusive, between the two of them. Maybe she did not realise what I just had. My eyes had seen more of the world than hers had, even though the light in them had dimmed a bit, and spectacles determined how crisply I could see the world, especially with the beginnings of a cataract. But I could see what Nina couldn't and I could put together the pieces of the puzzle bit by bit. It was surprising how things didn't shock me anymore, things which would have done so some years earlier.

I went up to my room for a little lie-down. The leg, the one which had twisted awkwardly, was throbbing a bit, worrying me about whether there was something that the good doctor had missed and whether it needed an X-ray to rule out any lasting damage. I could barely eat or digest anything these days, there was an all-pervasive nausea that began in the morning as I woke and lingered through the day. Sometimes a searing pain would twist my stomach, and I would bring up fresh red blood. I could feel my appetite shrinking, and with it the flesh falling off my bones, till the skin hung loose, shrivelled. My body had been firm and strong, it was used to walking through miles of tea estate trails without tiring. This wasn't me. This was a stranger inhabiting me. A succubus, sucking out the vital force from my body, leaving a vacant shell behind.

The house was quiet and settled into its afternoon stupor with some assorted creaking of the doors and windows instigated by a sharp wind that was starting to build up from the east. By the evening, the wind would be howling and hurtling itself against the door-frame and the window panes, threatening to break them and render us helpless against its wrath.

I slipped into a dream, one where I was climbing up the steep paths of the estate at Chaudharipore, when the skies suddenly darkened over me and began pelting hailstones the size of little tennis balls down at me, pounding me on my head. One struck me hard, almost making me pass out. The path beneath me was getting slippery and turning into a river of slush, making my feet lose grip and slide, the canvas soles getting soggy and mucky, forcing me to hold on to stray bushes in the hope that I could climb my way back to safety and the house that awaited me. It was sure to be dry and cosy, with a warm fire burning. Dolma would fuss over me with a mug of hot chocolate and my grandmother, her eyes crinkled with worry, would insist on me getting out of my wet clothes into something dry and warm.

'Never stays inside the house, this girl,' she would chide me, gently, 'even after I warned her it looked rainy and a storm would come up.' But now the path was closing in on me, above me, and behind me and the brambles began overgrowing the tree bushes, reaching out to me, entangling me, scratching at my hands, my legs, tearing the cloth of my simple white shirt and the beige trousers that had become my de facto uniform for the days I would live on the tea estate and wander around the place, looking for people to chat with, and children to play with and teach the basics of the English alphabet and numbers. Rain was crashing down on me. The forest had invaded the tea bushes and was closing in on me;

the skies had gotten pitch dark and thunder was rolling through the skies, punctuated by jagged-edge lightning bursting out between the clouds. The acrid smell of something burning spiked the air, and then suddenly the sensation of being wrapped in a tight blanket of something thick, foggy and overwhelming came over me. Which is when I realised something was sitting on my chest, weighing me down, blocking me from breathing, and I opened my eyes to look into a pale, wan face, with two mournful eyes boring into mine. I gasped and struggled to sit up, but no sound emerged from my throat, which felt sore, as though great pressure had been applied to it.

I opened my eyes with a start – I was back in my bedroom in the cottage with the cabbage rose-printed curtains with their hand-tatted lace edgings, and the cupboard with the walnut wood and stained-glass detailing. The weight on my chest had gone, but the pressure remained, I felt suffocated. I sat up, trying to get my orientation back, the acrid smell of the burning forest still hung in my nostrils, my feet felt sticky as if they had been in mud, and my clothes felt a little damp, like I'd been caught in a quick shower.

Nina knocked at the door and entered. 'Are you alright? I thought I heard a shout.'

'Just a bad dream, will teach me not to snooze off in the afternoons, rather than doing something constructive with my time,' I replied with a smile and gestured for a glass of water. My sleeve had some mud on it, that I was sure wasn't there when I had come into the room for my nap. I could feel my hair in the kind of disarray that comes from brambles pulling at one's hair, clothes and skin, I could feel the sting on the scratches on my arms, my legs. I looked at my arms to find thin gashes with a trace of blood on them.

'My goodness!' Nina exclaimed, suddenly noticing the gashes on my arms as I looked at them. 'How did this happen? Let me get some cotton and Savlon.'

She jumped up and rushed off towards the bathroom, the floor echoing with the dull thud of her footsteps. The sound of a door opening, and some muffled sounds and then she returned, bearing a small bottle and a little roll of cotton. She gently daubed at the scratches on my arms. My legs were thankfully covered with my trousers, but the trousers seemed muddied as did my socks. Muddied and wet.

'Why are your clothes damp and dirty, Grams? You came in for a nap directly after lunch, and you weren't out at all today except for the morning. Why are you sweating, are you unwell again?' she asked.

'Probably just a sudden spike in body temperature, Nina,' I replied, not thinking it necessary to alarm her with a dream that now seemed real, a slipping through some vortex into a hellish version of my past, which seemed tangled up with my present, with the here and now. Having attacked all the visible scratches on the arms with gusto, she daubed a bit on my face, which apparently had some scratches too. 'Come on, Grams, you're done with those hot flashes years ago—you shouldn't be having them now.'

She laughed at my shocked expression. 'For real, Grams, I know my biology and reproduction.'

I rolled my eyes. 'I'm sure you do, my love, but I'd rather you weren't in too much of a hurry.' She laughed again. There was a woman of the world tone to that laugh that wasn't there the last time she had visited; the girl was growing up. Or perhaps, she had grown up while I wasn't looking.

I took my damp socks off and decided to change into fresh, dry clothes. 'What is the time, darling?' I asked her, wondering how long I had been asleep and in that place which was clearly not my bed.

'It's almost six in the evening. This sweating in your sleep and these scratches are worrying me,' Nina said. 'Maybe I should just call Dr Sanyal back. He really needs to get a complete checkup done for you.' Her tone was peevish. 'You aren't looking well at all, you've lost so much weight, your coordination is just that bit off, your skin is looking positively vile and I don't think your ankle has really healed completely.' She began dialling the phone at the bedside.

'There's really no need to bother Dr Sanyal with an old lady's sleep disturbances,' I replied, plucking the phone out of her hand and disconnecting the line mid-dial. She shook her head like the roles were reversed – she was the grandparent and I the grandchild. Maybe that is the way nature ordains it to be, after a particular point in the relationship, the grandparent needs the grandchild to take charge, to put oneself in the hands of the younger generation, to derive one's strength from knowing that they are around and they will handle things. Perhaps, it was too much of a burden on the shoulders of a sixteen-year-old to expect her to take care of me if I fell ill.

It was probably time to tell Nina why I didn't want her to visit anymore. It would keep her away from harm in more ways than one. 'There have been some unprecedented events over the past few months. It all started that night I fell down at the window and twisted my ankle.'

She sat down at the foot of the bed. 'What happened that night, Grams? I always thought there was more to it than you let on. What actually happened? Did you see a ghost?'

I took a deep, long breath to push the oxygen into my bloodstream, to get the brain functional again; it still felt clouded and murky, like it hadn't quite emerged from the dreamland I had entered for a couple of hours, a dreamland that felt so real that I had emerged from it with physical marks of what I had experienced while in it.

'I don't know what it was, or whether I was imagining things. Anyway, I saw a lady. At the window. I've been seeing her around the house for a while. And I suspect she is the same lady you saw last night. Transparent-ish was the word you used, if I am not mistaken.'

'Cool,' she whistled. 'A real ghost. Who could it be?'

There was a knock at the door. Bimla entered, carrying a tray with a pot of tea and some cookies. 'Aap uth gaye, Masterniji. The last time I came into the room, you were in such deep sleep, you just didn't respond to my asking you if I should leave the tea tray.' She set it down on the little table by the window. 'I even told my husband that this is the first time in so many years that Masterniji didn't wake up at a single call.' She looked at my face, 'Hei bhagwan, how did all these scratches come on your face. Did you fall down again?'

'I don't know, Bimla,' I replied, feeling weary in a way that was completely at odds for someone who had just slept for the better part of three hours.

I got up from the bed, and shuffled slowly towards my wardrobe to get myself a change of clothes. The light had gone dim outside, the sun had already dipped over a rolling slope of the estate, ready to go down to the other side of the earth, places where the morning was yet to come, where people were sleeping, having their own dreams and their own nightmares, living their fears and being dragged through dark forests by sleep monsters.

Perhaps I should seriously look at moving out of the cottage, to another place, but my options were limited. I didn't have the kind of funds to renegotiate another permanent residence here, given the way property prices were spiralling up with the boom in tourism. This was no longer the sleepy little hill town I'd moved into all those years ago. The sector had opened up and it was now a bustling centre for tourist arrivals with every home being turned into a home stay, the roar of cars driving through the town, stopping over, en route to various other tourist hotspots in the vicinity.

I would ask around, I would move out. I had perhaps a few years left to live, and it would be nice to pass them without being terrorised by something I couldn't quite explain.

Nina helped me to the bathroom; my limbs weren't feeling steady at all. I held her and the wall as I made my way, feeling inexplicably embarrassed at the sudden decline in my ability to navigate my own house on my own. I changed out of my clothes awkwardly, with the arms refusing to lift, weighed down by some injury or exertion that made them sore, probably battling away the bramble-bearing branches closing in on me in my sleep. It was also the first time I looked at my situation the way Millie did and suddenly I wasn't sure whether living on my own in an isolated cottage on the outskirts of a tea estate with only two middle-aged retainers to rely on and no transport was such a good idea after all.

Tea was a subdued affair. Sumit wasn't back as yet from his trip into town. It was Diwali, he might have stayed behind to watch the fireworks scheduled at the Governor's House later. Nina was on her laptop and grabbed some bites of the chutney sandwiches Bimla had put together with the distracted air of someone who had too much on her mind to be able to devote her entire attention to the spread before her.

'I really wish you would concentrate on the meal, Nina, you can always get back to the laptop once you're done. There could be bread crumbs falling on your keyboard,' I said, in as mild a manner as I could, but the school marm peeked out from behind the grandmom. She shut the laptop without a murmur and continued munching on her sandwich and sipping on her tea, which she insisted on getting from the kitchen rather than pouring what was there in the pot, because she liked it stronger and sweeter.

'I wonder if they've managed to figure out who that person was, before he or she became all dried bones,' I wondered.

'I think that will take some time, they'll have to run tests, I don't know if they have a forensics expert here or someone will have to come down from Chandigarh or Delhi,' Nina said. 'I was just checking up the procedure to identify bones on the net, it's pretty complicated and interesting. I think I should opt for forensic psychology as a major, I find it most fascinating. The motives behind murders, how people plan one... Did you know you can poison a person over time, and so ingeniously with little doses that no one can suspect a thing?'

'That would be an interesting career path, Nina,' I laughed. 'Right now, just focus on getting your grades for class ten. We can think about what you need to take up as a specialisation later,' I replied.

Sumit returned just in time for supper. 'Want to know what I've found out about the lady in the photograph, Missybaba?' he asked.

'Who's that?' Nina asked.

'What did you find out?' I asked, curiosity over-riding my determination not to speak about the woman at the window in front of Nina.

'The diary ends abruptly after she mentions giving birth to a child. A girl. And no one knows if the child survived or died. Nor whose child it was.' The room fell silent and still. Chilly tendrils of air that felt like a cold clammy touch crept up my spine, touched the back of my neck teasingly, like that of a phantom lover.

'Who is she? What are you talking about?' Nina piped up, her voice shriller and more insistent. She did not like being ignored and her queries going unanswered.

'How did you find out?' I asked.

He looked at me, his golden brown eyes flickering with excitement, 'It was rather simple, actually. I wasn't even looking for it. I found a diary. It was stacked among some odd books and papers in a file titled 'personal belongings' in the library at the Bungalow... No one stopped me from leafing through them.' He paused. 'It was her diary. But I don't have a name for her. Look, her photograph is right here, on the first page. She hasn't even written her name, isn't that strange?'

I reached out and took the hardbound book in my hand. As I touched it my fingers felt they were singed by an open flame. I looked at my fingers expecting blisters to rise but saw nothing on the skin. I opened the book to see her photograph, a head and shoulder studio shot pasted carefully on the first page. Written below, in a girlish, fussy script, was 'My Diary'. There was no name.

The phantom fist clenched my heart again in its python grip, crushing it with a pain that made me close my eyes and gasp. Digging up those bones had brought her out of the shadow world of the un-dead, it had released her out into the world, and to me. I looked out at the window, to see my face reflected in the glass pane. And something shadowy reflected behind it, a shadow that could have been a figment of my imagination or the real, tangible reflection of something that was long dead and buried, and still walking the earth in search of something she was denied while alive. I blinked. The shadow was gone.

From somewhere in the distance, I could hear Nina's voice repeating, 'But will someone tell me who this diary belongs to and what this is all about?'

I read the first page and knew why she was here. This is where she had lived. Windermere.

> '*I have been brought here to this distant place, this cottage in the middle of nowhere and will be here I'm told until I bear this child and can end my shame. They have kept me well cared for, the humble governess to their daughters. If the child is a boy, they might want it. Both his wives have only given him daughters, he needs a male heir. The keepers here tell me they might adopt the boy if it isn't too Caucasian looking. If the baby is a girl, she will be cast out like I was, far away, so far that she can never intrude on his glory. When the baby is born, this story will end. I will never be able to go back to him. I have to find another position, another employment. I have to disappear from my old life and find myself a new one...*'

Her story could have been mine. I threw my shoulders back and steadied myself to face the fact that my house was perhaps now inhabited by the spirit of a woman who had been kept there against her will, many, many decades ago, a woman with an illegitimate baby in her womb. A woman and her child who disappeared as swiftly as they arrived, leaving no trace of themselves.

Chapter 16

ISPENT MOST of the next day reading the entries in the frayed diary. Sumit had found it among the old papers on display in the main bungalow at the tea estate, locked beneath a glass case that was easily forced open by an enterprising hand and a straightened hairpin.

The entries weren't detailed enough, but they spread over a period of many months, seven months to be precise. The exact number of months I had been sent away from Datham Hall.

There was anger in her words, a sense of being let down, and fear. A real tangible fear.

'I fear for myself. I might not be allowed out from here again. My child will be taken from me and sent far away from me. It is unbearable, this waiting for it to be born not knowing what lies ahead...'

'Just a few days more, my child, just a few days more. You will emerge into this world. Will you be robust like your father or delicate and slight like me? Will you have the

swarthy handsomeness of your father or will you be pale like I am? I long to see you, to hold you in my arms, to suckle you, to hear your voice.'

And the final entry.

'She is beautiful. Perhaps they will let her survive, there is nothing of her father in her. As for me, I don't know. I bear too much of a secret to be allowed back into the world.'

There were no entries after that one. The year was familiar. It was the year I was delivered to the Convent in Calcutta. I wondered what had happened to her daughter if she had survived. What had happened to the lady who had been hidden away for all her confinement, who was she? Why had she been kept in such captivity? What did she fear? Why had she emerged, after all these years, to haunt this house? What terrible secret had she taken to her grave, what retribution was she demanding from me?

My knees were aching with the piercing pain that signified I needed to take painkillers in order to function with some semblance of normalcy. I moved to my bedroom after an early supper that night. Nina was keeping herself entertained with the laptop her mother had gifted her on her last trip, despite the very dodgy internet connection available in these remote parts. Occasionally I would hear a whiff of tinny music emerge from behind her closed door, and sneak through the house, infusing it with a momentary levity that it had long discarded. The wind continued to howl outside, setting the bushes outside rustling, making the curtains swirl around menacingly, dropping a small figurine of a young lady kept on the bedside table onto the floor, from where it rolled under the bed. I bent down clumsily, and reached out to retrieve it from the gap under the bed. The figurine rolled back towards me, almost as though an unseen hand had pushed it back from the dark space under the overhanging bedcovers. I picked it up, with a puzzled frown and looked under the bed. A low moan emerged, an indistinct sound that could have been the wind, could have been a person or perhaps even a stray kitten mewling around outside the window. The figurine was un-shattered, despite the impact, and covered with muddy finger prints.

I slept that night in the rocking chair, terrified to climb into my bed, terrified of whatever it was that was under the bed, terrified of being dragged again through whatever parallel universe I had been taken into that afternoon. I knew now that this bed was the bed where she had lain in her confinement, where she had given birth and this was where she emerged from, constantly, over and over again. The next morning, my bones were aching from sleeping in an impossible position, and my head was weary with the maze of dreams I had navigated, dreams in which I fell into a pit and emerged into a world populated with faceless people, who went about their daily business without looking at me, cloaking me with a patina of invisibility with their deliberately unseeing eyes.

Our part of the town was in the newspapers the next day, with photographs of the pit from which the remains had been taken out along with a brief write-up. The cottage was subdued, as was the air outside. There were secrets floating in the air that couldn't be whispered aloud, secrets between the trees and the bushes, the wind and the mountains, secrets between the stones and the brooks babbling through, hushed, hesitant, but insidious, ready to rear themselves up when they were done with staying secret and emerge to swallow whatever stood in their path.

'I might need to look for a new home,' I told Nina, as we sat on the verandah, enjoying the bright morning, in what could be the last of the bright days for a while now, before winter set in. 'I'm getting older and I have been thinking it is not such a good idea to live so cut off from the rest of civilisation. And what is happening here is scaring me.'

'It's scaring me too, Grams,' she said. 'Mom has been saying that she would be more comfortable if we were both with her, but she knows you don't want to leave India. And perhaps that is the only reason Mom is still keeping me here, in India, to be near you.'

That I didn't believe. Millie had kept Nina here for her own convenience, not mine. I sighed deeply. I didn't want to leave the country, yes. I didn't want to leave this town. I had set down roots, finally, after all my life was done with. It was too late now to relocate myself on this earth when it was time to move on to whatever the afterlife held. If there was one. 'I don't even have a passport,' I said weakly. 'And London is too far a move at this stage in my life. I haven't yet thought this through, I'm still toying with the idea, maybe move into a colony with neighbours and a hospital a short distance away.'

'Come on, Grams,' she laughed. 'A passport is easily made. I don't know why you've resisted getting one made all these years. Quite ridiculous this fear of air travel you have. You know that once you have a passport made, you will have no excuse to not go visit Mom.'

It wasn't just that, I wanted to tell her. I had no documentation to prove I existed by the name I called myself today. The name on my certificates was completely different. That girl was another person, someone I had left behind in Calcutta. The girl with that name no longer existed. I knew all it would take was an affidavit, easily made, to make this identity officially mine, an identity I had usurped off a man who had died and could never contest my word, but I still resisted it.

Would I have enough to buy a new home, could I move out of this one, could I borrow some amount from Millie, or should I just brazen it out and continue living here, in this house that had been mine for so many years? The options battled out with each other in my head, and I could feel the beginnings of a migraine. 'I feel a headache coming on, I should take a pill before it worsens,' I said.

Nina frowned. 'I'm going to call Mom either way and tell her about this, she needs to know too, and have some say in whatever you decide to do.' She went into the house, asking Bimla loudly for where the medicine box was kept. Manikji cycled up to the house with our weekly rations of vegetables, grain, flour, butter, jam and all that which made it possible to get by on a full stomach. He parked the cycle with the air of one bearing important news, took the parcels from the handles of the cycle and came up the stone stairs as briskly as he could manage, given his knees and his weight.

'Masterniji, we should also call the tantrik. The priest at the Devi temple told me this morning that it could be a chudail that has taken up residence in our home. That we must do a puja and make her go away or else she will demand blood. You saw what happened to Basanti, the chudail took her life. What is the harm in seeing if he can make it go away?'

I put my head in my hands.

'Manikji, Basanti's father sacrificed a goat, didn't he? But his daughter died anyway.'

'Because he didn't do a puja, he called the ojha. Sometimes black magic doesn't work, but a puja always works.' His face, rosy-cheeked at the best of times, was positively radiating certainty that this solution would work.

Then a shadow crossed his face. 'I forgot to tell the priest that this is an Angrez chudail. She might not be frightened away by a Hindu puja.' I couldn't help but laugh aloud.

'Yes, you should get this point clarified, it wouldn't do if the priest does an entire puja in our house and the spirit sits peacefully waiting for it to get done and get back to its business of scaring the bejesus out of me.' He looked confused, his expression signifying that the machinery in his brain was still sorting out all the implications of this inter-religious haunting and exorcism.

'Why don't we call a priest from the church?' he said, thinking most logically. 'The bhootni will get scared of the prayers from the Bible.'

I shook my head. 'I have a Bible in the house, Manikji. It hasn't scared anything yet.'

Nina emerged with a box and a glass of water. I indicated to Manikji that he should take himself into the house. The headache had intensified and flashing lights were popping behind my eyeballs in a magnificent display of internal *son et lumiere* in my eye sockets. I downed the headache-relieving medication before the migraine morphed into something evil with hammer and tongs attacking the middle portion of the cranium.

Sumit had been holed up in his room all morning and would emerge sooner if not later. I would ask him for his opinion on what I could do. And Dr Sanyal. I could count on his help. And of course, Colonel Dayal. I could call him now.

'Colonel,' I said into the phone, as he came on the line, sounding a little disgruntled from what I presumed was being woken up from his afternoon nap. 'How are you?'

'Good afternoon, madam, what a pleasant surprise to hear from you. Trust you are doing fine now, I heard you had a fall and were unwell sometime ago.'

'Thank you, sir,' I replied. 'Perfectly hale and hearty now, and needed a few minutes of your time. Now that I'm getting older, and frailer, it seems increasingly difficult to live so isolated. I was wondering if you know of any suitable options closer to the main town I could move to. I need help in identifying a possible house, and then selling this one and wondered if I could impose on your kindness.'

He harrumphed gently. 'I would be honoured to help you, madam. Consider it guru dakshina for Anupama.'

I had taught his daughter at Datham Hall – she passed away after a botched up Caesarean delivery. Her child hadn't survived either.

'She was a lovely girl. It must be painful to think about her even after all these years.'

There was a silence on the other end of the line. 'It is. When you have a child, you imagine the child growing up, getting married, giving you grandchildren, being by your deathbed. The most painful thing in the world is to cremate your child ...' His voice choked a bit. I was quiet, the wound was still raw. Did such wounds ever heal, could they ever heal? Death, no matter how unexpected or how prepared one was for it, sliced the soul open, revealing the bare nakedness of desolation. Death did not take away the loved person as much as it took away all the emotions one had invested in that person, leaving behind a barren wasteland we stumble through, trying to make sense of what was left behind.

'I think one never gets over losing a child,' he replied. 'It is against the order of nature.'

One never did. One remembered the child, like a phantom limb. It always existed on the periphery of one's existence, I should know. I'd had a child who passed away too. John McNally's daughter. The one who died before she was baptized. If she had still been alive, she would have been five years older than Millie. She would have had children of her own, I will have had more grandchildren to dote on. In my head she would always be Shirley. I had named her Shirley, as she came fighting out through my body, tearing me up in ways I never thought would have been possible, physically and emotionally. Physically, Dr Dutta had sutured me up. Emotionally, the wounds she caused still occasionally bled.

She was born at home. Dr Dutta was at hand to deliver the baby and Mrs Dutta assisted him, as she had many years ago, when she was still working with him as a nurse. 'One doesn't forget nursing,' she told me, 'I've birthed enough babies without the doctor being around, and I'll birth yours.'

I was only too glad to let her take charge of me and my

pregnancy. She brought me meals when I couldn't bear the smell of cooking, and found it impossible to get into the kitchen to even rustle up an egg. As the baby grew, I got more and more sluggish, my feet swelled up to sizes that made it impossible for me to walk for more than ten minutes without collapsing. The blood pressure stayed high, and the sugar levels were elevated. It was, as Mrs Dutta said, one of the most difficult pregnancies she had seen in all her years. By the time I reached my seventh month, Dr Dutta placed me on bed-rest. He said there were too many issues to worry my head about, all I needed to do was to stay calm and wait for the child to be born.

I could feel the baby in my womb, unconcerned by all the fussing, the worries in my head, her fatherlessness, the uncertainty of life ahead that stared at me as a single parent. She was cocooned, floating in the amniotic fluid, shifting to comfortable positions, occasionally kicking hard and strong, hiccupping, shifting position, bumping uncomfortably against my diaphragm, making my food burn through my windpipe. By the ninth month, I was in an agony of waiting for it to get over. The due date came and went, and no labour began. I was tossing and turning in the March heat, with the humidity pouring buckets of sweat down my body. The electricity came and went in spurts and the promise of rain hung over the city, making the heat even more unbearable. I tossed and turned, unable to sleep, plagued by horrific dreams that had characterised my pregnancy, dreams of monsters, demon children emerging from my womb, of the child inside being born dead, or being born deformed, with a misshapen skull, no features, no lips, just dark pools of questioning eyes. I would wake from these dreams with a start, and a heart that refused to calm down. I would pour myself a glass of water, drink it, and go to open the windows in a vain bid to get some breeze into the house, never mind the mosquitoes that sucked my blood. Standing there, mopping my face with a towel, I breathed deeply, every night, looking up at the sky, wondering what was in store for me and the baby.

And then one night, as I tossed and turned, a pain ripped my body into two and had me screaming in despair. The next moment, there was a gush of water from between my legs, completely soaking the sheets. I waited for the wave to pass and stood up, shakily, making my way to the door. All I could do was stand on the landing and call down for Mrs Dutta, my voice shaky, before collapsing on the floor. The immediate neighbour, a worried-looking lady called Mrs Banerjee, who in normal circumstances made it a point to politely ignore me, came out of her door, and helped me back into the house and barked at her thoroughly henpecked husband to go downstairs and get the doctor up, which he did. My eyes glazed over in a red flash of pain that seemed to come down as a curtain over them and colour everything I looked at in a haze of red.

The labour went on for over twelve hours, twelve hours of untold agony. Dr Dutta came up at regular intervals to check how I had progressed. He would palpate my belly and check the baby, and command me to push with the next contraction, and I pushed or tried to. It was exhausting work, pushing. And finally, after what seemed like a lifetime of pushing and pain that climbed arches I couldn't even begin to imagine, I felt my body ripping into two and something sliding out of it. I slid in and out of consciousness, the doctor administered an injection and began suturing me up and discussed the next meal calmly with Mrs Dutta, who was drifting around, with a bundle in her arms that I suddenly realised was the baby. Had the baby cried? Was everything normal, were there two arms, two legs, ten digits, a nose, two eyes, two ears? Was everything perfect? I drifted out of consciousness.

When I came to, it was dark outside, and a dim bulb lit up the room. The crib, borrowed from a relative of Mrs Dutta whose baby had outgrown it, was being rocked gently by Mrs Dutta, who seemed to have aged ten years overnight. I tried to sit up. She noticed me, and picked up the baby and placed it in my arms. 'A girl. Beautiful. Look at her,' she said. Her expression softened into a smile, and she looked at me expectantly. I didn't know how I was supposed to feel. My stomach felt like a deflated balloon, and the raw pain in the lower half of the body was excruciating. The baby was red and crumpled, more monkey than human, and I fell completely in love with her, with a fierceness I didn't know I had in me, with an absoluteness that couldn't be denied. The baby sensed the movement and turned her neck from side to side, like she was searching for something, something essential, an instinct for survival that she had brought with her from the womb. And she mewled, like a kitten, not the full-blooded, robust cry I was expecting, but a soft, gentle, almost apologetic mewling.

'She's hungry,' Mrs Dutta said, 'You need to feed her.' My breasts had swollen painfully, Mrs Dutta checked them, uncaring of my abashedness. 'Your milk has come in, feed her.' She squeezed out the first milk and threw it away and then placed the baby in my arms.

Whoever said being a mother comes naturally had it wrong. I couldn't handle my own baby, this delicate little parcel of flesh. I needed Mrs Dutta to help me hold her, while I unfastened my gown and let my suddenly pendulous breast loose. I was terrified the baby would smother under it, but she suckled away contentedly, drawing out all she needed to keep herself going. I was responsible for this child, this new person I had created. The realisation shocked me. No longer could I think of myself in isolation, whatever I decided or planned for myself would have to put my child's needs first.

Nothing prepares you for the indignity of motherhood, the blood gushing from between your legs, the lack of sleep, the fear of doing something wrong, the pain whenever you needed to make a bathroom visit, the floppiness of the stomach, the stitches, the pain when you sat.

And then, when she was barely a couple of days old, she stopped breathing. Just like that. I fed her, swaddled her the way Mrs Dutta had taught me to, and placed her on the sheet next to where I slept, and dozed off next to her, when a sudden, inexplicable panic awoke me, and the feeling that something was not quite right. I switched the light on and saw the baby turned blue, not breathing, ice cold to the touch, not responding to me or my frantic voice. The screams I heard coming from somewhere in the distance were my own.

We buried her in the section of the graveyard set apart for the unbaptized, no headstone to mark where she lay. 'Pray for her soul,' Sister Julianne told me, as she held me up, with Mrs Dutta buffering me on the other side, while my knees refused to support me. I didn't believe in prayers anymore. I didn't believe in a God. I spent the next few months in a kind of grey stupor that swamped me, dragged me into a marshland, where I struggled with the urge to take a knife to my wrists and end it all, bleed all over the bedding and go to where my child was, to where John was. Sometimes, I would wake up in the night, with a soft mewling, hold my baby, feed her, and go back to sleep to find her gone the next morning, and the side of the bed where I'd placed her, cold and wet. I barely ate. Mrs Dutta sat with the plate by my bedside, force-feeding me with a spoon, determined to talk. 'Post-partum depression,' the doctor said. 'She needs a change of scene.'

Mrs Dutta conferred with the nuns. And one day, I was informed they had got me a teaching position at Datham Hall, a boarding school for girls, at the foothills of the Himalayas. The school was part of a small hill town where the fresh air, the mountain climate and the change of scene would do me good.

Sister Julianne had come to visit me. 'There is something I need to tell you,' she said, her breath heavy and wheezing. 'Something you need to know before you go away and I have this on my conscience. There were two babies that came to us at the same time that year. Of the first, we have no idea who her parents were, but we were told there was no one to raise the child. The other was born here of a local Anglo-Indian girl and died within a week. The first one is you. Both of you had similar colouring, you were both light skinned and with light hair. But I knew you both apart, your eyes were the deepest blue. The other baby had brown eyes. When the Chaudharis came looking for their grandchild, it seemed like a chance to give you a life other than that of being a ward of the convent for the rest of your life. I chose that for you. I don't know if I did right or wrong, and I've been carrying this guilt around all my life.'

She didn't know where I'd come from. She had no recollection of who had dropped me off at the convent, how I had arrived there as an infant. All she knew was that I was not the person she had told me I was.

After that visit, I'd stopped trying to figure out who I was. Mrs Dutta helped me pack, Mr Ganguly organised my train tickets to Delhi and from there on to Kathgodam, the last junction from where I was to take a bus to the hill station where the school was.

Mrs Dutta's face was weighed down with sudden wrinkles and sadness as she hugged me at the railway station, after she had helped me find my berth and settle my luggage. Perhaps she knew then what I hadn't realised, that she would never see me again. Then she sat with me on the berth, since there was some time for before the train would leave the station.

'Take care of yourself, eat properly and throw yourself into your work,' she said. 'The only thing that can help you feel better is to keep yourself busy. And being around little children might help you stop missing your baby.'

'Her name was Shirley,' I said. 'I'd named her Shirley.'

She wrapped me in an uncharacteristic embrace. 'Call me when you can. Come to Calcutta for your holidays, stay with me. Don't forget this old lady, okay?'

I hugged her back, feeling the tears start to pour down my cheeks and the feeling of being adrift and alone twisting my gut. I watched Mrs Dutta make her way slowly out of the train, watched her stand on the platform and wave at me as the train chugged out, and ignored the curious glances of the few people in the compartment. I must have looked peculiar to them, I knew.

The half-lowered window pane reflected a face I almost didn't recognise as my own – wan, with sunken eyes, the skin lustreless and the hair stringy and held back off the face with an awkwardly placed clip. My clothes hung on me, like they were made for someone twice my size. I looked and felt frail, like the stuffing had been taken out of me and all that remained was a shell where a person should have been.

It was now, I realised, I had to be done with my mourning. I had to start life afresh. I had spent close to five months in a limbo of black grief, grief for my child, grief for John, grief for everything I should have mourned for and didn't. I was going to a strange place, with a strange name and strangers awaiting me. Leaving the memories undisturbed, keeping my hands from creating ripples in the muddy waters of my mind in order to dredge them up again.

Chapter 17

COLONEL DAYAL BROUGHT across his family pandit one morning and insisted I let him do a havan and a shuddhi of the premises. I did not resist, anything was welcome if it cleared the place of the presence. I couldn't see it, but I knew it still existed here, waiting, lurking in hidden corners, for the right time at which to make its presence felt again.

Nina returned to school the next morning, her extended weekend over. Manikji and Kishan dropped her back. Dr Sanyal took me around the main town searching for a home I could move into. I called the local real estate dealer to put the cottage on the market but no offers came, despite me willing to cut the price down. Word had spread that the cottage was haunted, that a spirit lived there. The pit behind the cottage had been filled and an alternate path had been dug up post the exhumation of the skeleton. We never did find out who the unfortunate soul had been, so unceremoniously interred in a stray patch of ground, with no headstone to mark his or her remains. In my heart, I knew though who it was – I needed no forensic confirmation. These were the bones of someone who was interred the year I was born, someone who had written a diary I had read, someone who had given birth to a child that was taken away from her.

Nina's room stayed locked through the month, she would perhaps come to visit me for her winter break or she might not, given she had her board examinations in March and needed to be studying for them. She had been undecided about whether she would stay back in school for the extra coaching classes organised by the authorities or come spend the winter months with me when she left. I could feel her slipping away already from me. Kurnal came every other evening with his books and some odd collectible he'd found in the course of his wanderings around the place and carefully placed them in his box. 'I want to go to the shehar,' he told me one day, handing across a ten-rupee note, with great solemnity. 'I'm saving money for that.' I placed it in the box and added a hundred of my own towards his going-to-the-big-city fund.

The days rolled by in a grey blur. I did not see the face at the window again. I did not have any more of those terrifying dreams that blurred the membrane between dream and reality since the last time I was scratched and bloodied in my bed.

The days were single-sweater worthy, while the nights had now started needing a heated blanket and a pullover. I hadn't pulled out the thermals yet, or the heavy-duty woollens. I planned to get Bimla to take down the trunks they had been carefully mothballed and packed away in back in April, and air them out before the cold really set in. The carpets needed to be beaten out and aired before the severe cold and damp set in. It was a monthly ritual that was most amusing, given Manikji would inevitably trip over his feet and fall down a few stairs while transporting the carpets from upstairs to the outside. Bimla would then yell at him for being useless and declared her fate was ruined when she was given in marriage to him, and approximately fifteen minutes of recriminations from either end later, the carpets and rugs would all finally reach the verandah from where they would be draped on the railing on the sunny side and beaten to within an inch of their lives to unsettle all the dust nestling within. And of course, there was the taking out of the woollens and winter wear that belonged to Nina, most of which she would have inevitably outgrown, which would go into another trunk, the trunk of memories as I called it.

A simple tin trunk, a hark-back to those days when most households had a few of these, stacked carefully one on top of the other, stuffed with the things that went into building up a home – bed linen, curtains, crockery unused or too precious to bring into use, winter clothes and blankets, neatly aired and then packed away with mothballs carefully placed between the layers, not to be opened until the cold came calling again at the end of the year. And children's clothes, the clothes they outgrew, wedding saris or dresses, the embroidered table cloth the bride might have created for her trousseau to prove her creative skills, the delicate silks handed down through the generation, too delicate to wear, too precious to dispose of, like most memories.

At Datham Hall, I had bought myself another tin trunk, not a very big one, but one that would be comfortable for the overcoats and cardigans I'd got myself. The trunk soon became the repository of happiness – a flower picked on a school picnic, which I pressed between the pages of a favourite book to dry and then placed carefully in an envelope to go into the trunk, so I could take it out, years later, crumbling to powder in my fingers and recapture just how the sun shone on the grass, and the kids played, the clear blue sky and the dreaminess that made it a perfect day. Or the onesie I knitted for Millie while I was expecting her, which I couldn't put on her when she was a baby, but which stayed behind, the ghost outfit of a baby who survived, but was taken away. This was my memory trunk, the repository of infinite little moments of my life. It stayed in my bedroom, under my bed. Always.

Covered neatly with a little discarded table cloth, which was periodically washed and put right back in place, the trunk stayed under my bed most of the year. I needed to drag it out again, and sift through its contents. I would do so today. I would air out the warm clothes, have the carpets beaten and aired, go through the memory trunk. The morning was bright, unnaturally so. Sunlight streamed through the windows with the angst of being denied a path through the clouds and being compelled to burst through. The clock by the bedside, with its big digital numbers, showed 6 a.m. Bimla was still to lumber in with my morning bed tea. I pushed the covers back, put my sock-clad feet into my closed slippers and made my way to the window. The air seemed still, hushed, waiting in a predatory manner. Something about it made the hair on the nape of my neck stand up, the gooseflesh prick my arms. I shivered, pulled my wrap closer around me and made my way carefully to the bathroom.

My movements were a little uncertain, my coordination a little off, with a slight dizziness. Maybe I needed to get myself some vitamin shots and start on some tonics. 'Come on, old girl, you're almost in the grave now,' I told myself. 'Stop expecting to have the litheness of a teenager. Just be happy that you are walking around independently and have all your faculties intact and that you aren't a patron of adult diapers yet.' I brushed my teeth and splashed water on my face, water that was definitely chillier than I would prefer and would now need heating up with the wheezing geyser every morning until it got to tolerably warm levels. Then, some days later, as the cold waved its freezing arm around the hills, water will be boiled on the stove before one dared bathe in it. A stranger looked back at me, with a startling thatch of limp white hair, awry from not having been brushed back into neatness yet, eyes, a faded blue, the edges of the iris a faint rim of milky white, hooded over, skin that had crumpled and folded into itself, like a firm hand was crushing my face into submission. How many years before the hand would reach into my chest and crumple up my heart? Or was the heart already crumpled up beyond repair but still soldiering on bravely because it knew no better, and therefore must keep beating in order to be.

I could hear Bimla come wearily up the stairs, the thump and drag of her footsteps denoting that her knee had begun acting up again, like mine. I missed the quickness of Nina's footsteps running up the stairs. I missed Nina, in a way I had never missed her mother, Millie. I hadn't seen Millie grow up. She came to me a teenager, searching for her mother, piecing together fragments of her origins.

Millie adopted the McNally surname once she learnt that, indeed, I was her mother. I did not dispel her misunderstanding. It was kinder to let her think her father had died of a head-on collision with a truck before she was born, when I was pregnant with her, than to know she was the result of a clandestine liaison between her mother and an erstwhile playboy who had probably not given her existence a second thought, who had thought no more of her mother than an indulgence, private, furtive and shameful.

I sat for a while, looking out at the green slopes, the road curving down from the hills down to where the main gate of the estate was, beyond a few turns and curves. I wondered if my life meant going down that road again, back into civilisation, into the hurly-burly of people, noise, traffic, and dust swarming around me, eating into my mind. It sounded like a nightmare. This was no longer the quiet town I had moved to over a decade ago, it had more vehicles, more traffic, more shiny stores, and fast food joints and cafes and tourists, and exhaust fumes. Charming squat homes had made way for apartment blocks. Tourist lodges had sprung up round every corner and this once seriously sleepy town was a hive of activity around the tourist season, with families in gaggles turning up to roam about its nooks and crannies, stomping through the tea estates, living on the premises, going on tea-estate tours, fishing, picnicking and such like until the quiet life began to ooze out of their ears and they longed to get back to civilisation. After a point they all longed for the toxic air laden with more pollutants than permissible, and the honk of cars that provided the background against which they conducted their most meaningful conversations.

I bathed myself carefully, noting for the first time ever, that the tiling on the bathroom floor was a little uneven and could make me slip and break a bone. My mortality was suddenly becoming increasingly apparent to me. The hands weren't as steady as they were until just a month earlier, the steps were uncertain, the eyesight seemed to have blurred a bit, the memory was still clear but fuzzy around the edges, like the corners of a sepia print turning yellow and curling up into the photograph itself. I would close my eyes and forget who I was or where I was, it would take a couple of seconds before my memory would un-fog itself and the present would return in a blast of blazing colour.

I dressed myself hurriedly, in a pair of old grey trousers and a cotton shirt, and slipped a grey cardigan on top of it all. I slashed my lipstick on, force of habit acquired all those years back in Datham Hall, when Mrs Nair insisted I wear lipstick in order to look a little older and more intimidating to the girls, some of whom were barely a few years younger than me. She had bought me a tube of post-box-red lipstick from a brand called Gala of London that sadly was no longer available. But I had found the closest shades in other brands like Lakme and now Millie brought enough lipsticks to last me through the year every time she came down. That slash of red across my lips was an intrinsic part of my self-image. When it was washed off at the close of day I felt like I was shutting myself away, to emerge the next day, to be put back on display.

Even on days when no one visited, and I saw no other soul except for Manikji and Bimla, I still dressed formally, powdered my face and carefully applied my lipstick. The same shade I had stuck to all these years. A red. A burst of red spilling over my mouth and wiping away the paleness from my face, a paleness that was admired by many but detested by me. The girls laughed at my vanity. Grams and her lipstick, Nina would tease me, when I would go to my room after a meal to reapply it, but they accepted the lipstick as part of me, no matter how inappropriate the shade might seem at this age.

Bimla had emerged and was standing behind me, 'Masterniji,' she said softly, 'Breakfast is ready.'

I nodded and rose to my feet, holding onto the chair I had been sitting on with a grip that was suddenly uncertain. I made my way, hesitantly into the dining room. Sumit was seated at the table, and rose as I entered. Over tea, he announced that he was leaving for Delhi. 'It's my grandmother. She's turned critical and might not survive. I need to see her before she dies. I need to tell her something.'

'Oh, I'm sorry to hear that. I hope she recovers,' I replied.

His face darkened. 'She might not, we've been expecting it. She has been terminally ill for a few months now.'

There was a moment's silence while I debated about what I could say to a man who had been part of my home for a few months now.

'There's something I need to show you,' he said, drawing out a photograph from his pocket and placing it in front of me. A print of a studio photograph I had seen before, many decades ago. A man sitting in an ornate carved chair in a posed stance, dapper in a sherwani, his features aquiline and imposing, and a demure woman behind him, draped in a misleadingly simple sari, which was clearly French chiffon, with a long string of pearls around her neck. It was an informal portrait – there was no turban, no sarpech, no layers of necklaces as one saw in the formal photographs meant to be studies for portraits. A girl was seated in the man's lap, holding the lady's hand. Garima. Ranvijay. I thought back to a letter I had meant to reply to, a phone number I'd meant to call but hadn't worked up the courage to. I leant back in my chair and closed my eyes from the very physical pain that knived through my rib cage, into my heart.

'That's my mother when she was a young girl, with my grandparents. My mother was from Rajasthan, I did tell you that she was a pupil for a couple of years at Datham Hall before her parents moved her closer to home. Wasn't my grandmother pretty?' He looked at me and his eyes knew the secrets I had told no one.

'She was beautiful, your grandmother. And so is your mother.' I replied, feeling the lump in my throat thicken to obstruct all semblance of coherent speech. He came across and hugged me warmly, the first time he'd done so in all the months he'd lived with us, in the cottage.

'You know, I've said it before, you remind me a lot of my grandmother. You both have the same gentleness of spirit, the same innate elegance. They don't make ladies like you anymore.'

I hugged him back, this light-eyed boy with the genetic inheritance of a man I had loved once. 'And you remind me of your grandfather,' I said, realising that there was no reason to pretend anymore.

He looked at me, his eyes a mixture of empathy and kindness. I stood up, feeling my legs shake despite myself, and went up to my desk in the study to retrieve the envelope I'd put in there all those months ago. He followed me, his eyes unquestioning. He knew.

'I'd like you to read this,' I said, handing it across to him. He read it silently, his brow furrowed. And looked up at me, unperturbed.

'I knew it was you. The person my grandmother considered responsible for taking her husband away from her. She blamed you for his death, you know. She always said he was heartbroken after your relationship ended and he took his own life. I had to meet you in person, to know if you were really as terrible a person as she made you out to be.'

I drew in a deep breath and felt the hollowness within my chest. 'Am I a terrible person, Sumit?'

I thought back to the phone call I received, the pleading voice at the other end of the line begging me to break off all contact with Ranvijay, telling me that the scandal, if it became public, would make him lose all chances of winning the elections he was contesting from his constituency. The voice still echoed in my ears, 'Don't destroy my husband's political career, that's all we have left now.' I had never met him or corresponded with him after that.

'No. I don't think so. And I've told my grandmother that too. I think she would have liked to meet you, to speak with you... but alas, it isn't to be.'

I sat down again in my chair, it no longer creaked under my weight. I could feel myself dissolving in more ways than one. 'It isn't a part of my life I am proud of. But I can tell you this, I never did contact your grandfather, never... Then I received the letter that told me he was dead. Not even when I had....' I stopped.

He stared at me, with the eyes he'd inherited from his grandfather. 'Not even when you had his child. I know.' I started in shock. 'I know. He knew. My grandmother knew. Which is why she wanted to speak with you, to make her peace, to meet his daughter by you. She's lived with that guilt all her life. But now she is dying and does not have much time. Would you like to speak to her, would you like to meet her?'

I shook my head in the negative, taking back the letter. I slipped it into a drawer, knowing that it would soon be buried under the flotsam-jetsam of bills, correspondence and other mail that would relegate it to the past where it deserved to be. 'Let the past stay in the past, Sumit. There is nothing to be served by digging it up,' I said, acutely conscious of the thick pile of typewritten sheets in my study which laid my story down, without naming Ranvijay.

'Well, I guess then,' he said, 'There is nothing more to be said. Goodbye, Masterniji.'

'Goodbye,' I replied, not trusting myself to say more, feeling the world swim up in front of my eyes and dissolve into tears that were threatening dangerously to splash out and spill down my cheeks.

He hugged me again. 'I wish...' he began and then paused. 'Never mind. Perhaps it is best this way...'

I held him for the brief moment we hugged, feeling the energy of a man in his prime seeping into me through his skin, through his clothes, knowing that perhaps I would never see him again, like I had never seen his grandfather again. 'Come back,' I wanted to say. I dared myself to articulate the words and lost the moment as he went out of the door. I looked at him from the window, knowing within my heart, that perhaps this was my closure, the goodbye to Ranvijay that I hadn't had the opportunity to say, knowing that, apart from me, there were at least two others who knew about the ridiculous, passionate affair between an illegitimate school teacher and a man who was nobility, and the unwanted child that was born of it.

Chapter 18

THERE WAS JUST one relationship after John. It had happened quite by chance, as all illicit relationships do, a moment that if shifted in time would have changed everything. If I hadn't been late for class, if he hadn't decided to come up to the school to see his daughter on the off-chance of being able to spend time with her, things would have been very different. But there is some reason, beyond our ken, beyond our control, that throws people together and ensures their lives will never be the same again.

'Excuse me, I beg your pardon,' I gasped, as I dashed into him while rounding a corner in that long corridor leading to my class. I was running a little late, I had lingered at a window, looking at the view of the hills dropping down from the school walls, the mottled pink and green of the rose bushes fringing the lawns, the clouds passing solemnly overhead, dashing against the mountains in the far distance. The man I bumped into also seemed to be in a hurry, and was headed in the opposite direction. The books in my hand went flying down and the answer-papers

I had in my file scattered themselves all over the corridor like the proverbial confetti.

'A million apologies,' he'd said in a deep baritone and dropped to one knee, gathering up as many papers as he could as I stood there struck to a pillar of salt. It was a scene that one doesn't expect to happen in real life, but which has been hackneyed to death in the movies.

He looked up at me to hand the papers over and it was almost like time stood still and all that was playing out was this acute awareness of those hazel tawny specked eyes in a face that was cut so sharp that his cheekbones could cut open a hand that dared to slap his face. Not that I had the urge to slap it. Quite the contrary! Every impulse was to reach out and touch his face, caress it. I restrained myself with an effort so strong, it made me shiver. He stood up, holding all the sheets as I made no move to take them from him. We stood for a long moment looking at each other, reluctant to break the silence with words. 'I'm Ranvijay Singh.' He held out a hand.

I took it hesitantly and gave him the name I was known by at the school. 'Mrs McNally.' His brow furrowed slightly at the 'Mrs'.

It was a handshake that burnt the flesh off my palms and charred my bones, welding both our palms together. Thinking back, I think, if we hadn't shaken hands, if I had taken those sheets of paper, thanked him and gone my way, my life wouldn't have changed the way it did. But I didn't and we shook hands, and that moment of contact seared us together in the way only mad infatuations do. Our hands stayed clasped together for such a long, long moment, that I finally compelled myself to wrench away from him, for fear that someone might be watching us. Already, in the first few minutes that we had met, there was a hint of the forbidden between us.

'Delighted to meet you,' he said and I took the answer-sheets, thanked him for gathering them, smoothened down my skirt, and wondered if the thudding of my heart was audible as I walked away. I could feel his eyes on my back, and as I looked back, while turning the corridor, despite my misgivings, he was standing there, where I had left him, staring at me, almost as if he was willing me to look back at him. When I emerged from the last class of the day and moved towards the teacher's quarters, he was standing awkwardly, lounging against a stone wall across the quad, chatting with a little girl from the second grade. I didn't teach her, but I knew her – Saudamini, a delicately featured girl, so exquisite she could have been carved from white marble. I walked across the quad to them, knowing well that the sensible thing to do would have been to turn the other way and walk away. Sometimes you don't do what is sensible. You just do what you cannot stop yourself from doing, invisible skeins drag you towards a fate not of your choosing.

'Hello,' he said, looking straight at me, straightening up as I approached timidly.

'Hello,' I replied, feeling my breath catch in my throat, looking at the little girl, noticing instantly the resemblance, the features that made him so rugged and masculine transferring themselves so perfectly to a delicate beauty in her. Her skin was soft, unblemished by the years, a soft golden, while his was angrier, duskier, from the many years blazed by the sun and by life.

'This is Saudamini, or Sandy as we call her. My daughter. I believe you don't teach her.'

I shook my head with a wry smile. 'No, I don't, I'm afraid. She is a very pretty little girl,' I replied.

Sandy beamed up. 'And you are very pretty, Mrs McNally.'

'Thank you,' I said.

'You must be wondering why I'm here,' he said, looking down at his daughter with a beaming smile. She held on to his hand, with the kind of firm grip a daughter has on the hand of a father she adores, and doesn't have much time with. 'I was missing my daughter terribly, and decided on a whim to drop by to meet her. I've requested for permission to take her to tea and dinner before dropping her back to school.' He paused and looked down at the little girl. 'Why don't you go wait for me in the car, Sandy,' he said, nodding towards the vehicle parked in the driveway, a little distance away from where we stood. She nodded and skipped off, the joy in her steps spilling over.

'Would you like to join us for tea?'

I agreed. Like it was the most natural thing to do, to go out with a student and her father and spend the entire evening talking with a complete stranger. He told me he would be waiting outside the gate in the same car for me if I would like to freshen up. It took me a frenzied ten minutes to make myself presentable. The face that stared back at me from the mirror as I slapped on some face powder was startled and anxious, the lipstick I applied carefully went beyond the edge of my lips and had to be carefully wiped and reapplied. My hands were shaking as I did so. I finally gave up and wiped it all off and looked at myself, clear-faced, in the mirror. My hair was now cut short, at a chin-length bob, which had now become my de facto hair length ever since I discovered how convenient and time-saving it was. It hung straight, with the off-centre parting making my face look narrower than it already was. My eyes were two bright blue marbles, shining unnaturally back at me. I splashed some water on my face to cool myself down. And then reapplied the lipstick, a sharp slash of red, which instantly gave me courage.

My wardrobe was limited. When I came from Calcutta, I had barely brought a few clothes with me, and the ones I had got stitched from Bisht Tailors in the market were matter of fact and perfect for teaching in a class room, but nothing quite worthy of going out to tea. I threw all the clothes I owned into an untidy heap on my bed, I would settle the mess later I told myself, uncaring that it did not behove a teacher to keep her room so slovenly. I finally decided on a soft pink shirt over a navy skirt, which hugged my hips and cinched my waist. It left my legs bare, even though it wasn't quite the season for bare legs.

I grabbed my only handbag, its edges rough and peeling with wear and rushed to the main gate. The car was parked unobtrusively by the side of the narrow road. I moved towards it, noting the familiar face at the wheel and feeling my stomach knot up in a flutter of most unseemly excitement. He emerged lithely from within as I exited the school gate and held the passenger side door open for me. It was an Ambassador, the trusty war horse of that generation, the Morris Minors that went on to become emblematic of a way of life when the only two options we had were these or the sleeker Fiat Padmini. I had not much experience of sitting in cars, and to me this was a luxury of sorts. He was wearing a crisp white linen shirt and khaki trousers that were the kind of relaxed fit which went contrary to all current fashion norms. He made it look fashionable nonetheless.

'I'm glad you could make it,' he said. 'I was afraid you might change your mind.'

'I almost did,' I confessed, wondering why I was doing so. 'But here I am.'

I looked behind, there was no one in the backseat. 'Where is Sandy?' I asked.

'Sandy decided to spend time with her grandmother, my mother, at our hotel. I couldn't let you down now, could I, having promised to take you for tea. So I dropped her there and came back to pick you up.'

'Will we be joining them?'

'We won't. My mother would welcome the chance of indulging her grandchild in my absence.'

It was a charming lie, one that I swallowed willingly. The watchmen at the gate were watching us curiously. In a small-town school, everything was grist for gossip and I was providing it by the shovelfuls for them right now. But it didn't matter, nothing did, except this man next to me, his strong hands changing gear with the practiced ease of one who is comfortable driving on hilly terrain despite being from the desert.

'I hope you don't mind,' he asked, and slipped the car into gear, driving past questioning gazes, down the spiralling streets, past the mall road, which was the centre point of the small hill town, past the lake promenade where people were taking their daily constitutionals or sitting by the edge, skimming stones off the placid waters or taking rides in the boats that dotted its surface, past the fringes of the town, past the bakeries and the tea shops where you could get tea and buttered scones and freshly baked buns, further up, higher to more mountainous territory. Here the road began to climb steeply and narrow out a bit so that vehicles passed each other with caution and homes clung to the edge of the mountains.

'This is a long drive for a cup of tea.' I laughed a little nervously. 'Where are we going?'

He looked at me and smiled, before pulling up on a grassy patch a little off the road. 'I honestly don't know. But I didn't feel like stopping in town, because I don't know whether that would be comfortable for you with so many of your students wandering around, given it is a Saturday and many parents seem to be here for the weekend.'

I hadn't thought about this at all. All I had thought about was that I had wanted to spend time with this man I barely knew and trusted blindly enough to go out on a drive with. We sat in awkward silence for a while. I played nervously with my handbag. He stared at me with the expression of someone drinking in an image, of something that didn't exist.

'Would you believe me if I told you we've met?' he asked.

I shook my head. 'I would have remembered if we had, I don't remember meeting you.'

'We have. I had come to Calcutta to meet my aunt. I accompanied her to the school her daughter, my cousin, was boarding at for a couple of years. And there you were, sitting on a bench, in a corner of the playground, reading a book and completely disinterested in what was going around you,' he said.

I gasped.

'This must have been years ago. At least a decade ago. You have a wonderful memory. Who was your cousin?' I asked.

'She left the convent abruptly in the middle of the term. Actually, we had come to collect her. I think you might remember her. She pointed you out to us, you had quite a temper then I believe. She still recounts that incident with the dictionary,' his voice was soft.

I remembered an incident of me hitting a girl on the head with a hardbound dictionary when she'd called me a bastard child. She was a boarder, from a landed family in the East. I had been called into the principal's room and made to apologise. The girl's family had pulled her out of the school. My hands shivered unwittingly. It was an incident I wasn't particularly proud of, but had never been apologetic about.

I looked down at my hands. 'How did you recognise me, after all these years?'

'How could I ever forget you? I fell in love with you the moment I saw you,' he replied, his voice so soft, I had to strain to hear it.

I looked up at him with a start. His eyes, green-brown, were fixed on mine. His nostrils, cut sharp on his straight nose, flared gently through a breathing growing intensely rapid. He took my hand in his, lifted it to his lips and kissed it. And that was the beginning of my unravelling.

It was a relationship that had no future, a relationship that was snatched between impromptu visits to the hill town I lived in and furtive trips to Delhi. A relationship where all thoughts of the future and how long it would last were thrown to the wind and only the moment mattered, fierce, angry and demanding. Letters came through the post for me, letters which were unsigned, and undated, and written in a strong, masculine hand that left imprints on the sheets below on the letter pad, written quickly so that the ink had at times not blotted on the first sheet before it was folded over for the next sheet to be written on, so some words were smudged and smeared, much like the relationship itself. Phone calls, twice a week, after dinner, for which I stood at the common phone in the main office, while the watchman waited to lock up the office after me, peeping in occasionally to indicate he needed to leave. Conversations abruptly terminated, leaving behind the fragrance of all that was left unsaid, of the long pauses that had us drinking each other's presence at the opposite ends of the static-replete telephone line, where shouting the words were the only way to have them audible at the opposite end, so that silences made their way through the wires, more than words did.

There had been others before me, I gathered. I didn't ask him about them. While he was with me, he was mine and only mine. I stopped looking at Sandy in the eye when I came across her in school. Her eyes were uncritical; she was too young to know or to understand my guilt. I didn't think of his wife, the mother of his daughter. That was a guilt I wasn't ready to confront.

Sandy was the apple of his eye, he doted on her with no reservation, carrying her on his shoulders whenever he came to school much to her embarrassment now that she was growing older. Her mother, his wife, never came to visit; she couldn't handle road journeys on winding roads, being a desert girl, he claimed. I suspected he dissuaded her from making the trip and she would not go contrary to his command. I never met her. Ever. She stayed between us, a ghostly presence, a glimpse from a photograph he once showed me of Saudamini as a baby, being held by his wife, Garima, her head draped demurely in a chiffon saree, with a light dusting of flowers over its pale surface, her skin clear and sparkling, her only jewellery a strand of lustrous pearls around her slender neck. She was beautiful, the kind of beauty that would make grown men hold their breath around her for fear of disturbing her, the kind of beauty that had petulance simmering beneath the surface, just waiting for a thread to be yanked to display its ferocity. I resented her home, her husband, her family, her sense of belonging. I hated her with a fury that she had done nothing to deserve.

'You are my guilty little secret,' he said. 'You know it is acceptable for men in our position to have mistresses, but that is not what this relationship is about for me.'

Nor was it for me. I refused to take any money or jewellery from him, firmly handing back the exquisite velvet-lined boxes he initially surprised me with, containing sparkling diamonds, rubies, and sapphires which he claimed were 'as blue as your eyes', consenting finally to accept only one ring, an oval Columbian emerald, surrounded by diamonds. A ring made this relationship feel official. I still wore it, getting it tightened as the flesh fell away from my fingers and the knuckles got knobbly. I would loop string around it as it got even looser over the years, but it rested on the third finger of my left hand, above the slim gold band that Mrs Dutta had compelled me to wear before setting off to Datham Hall. Both those rings never came off my fingers and never would. Sometimes, I would still play with the ring absentmindedly and imagine him turning it around and marvelling at how slender my fingers were.

The school nurse informed the principal I was pregnant when I went to her, unthinkingly, for some medication for the constant nausea I was experiencing. I had known I was, but was in a state of denial, hoping against hope that it was just one of those months when dates went awry. I was soon called in by

Sister Janet to confirm the news, which I did, expecting fully to be asked to pack my bags and leave on the next bus. What I hadn't accounted for was kindness, unexpected kindness that brought tears to my eyes.

'Some might say this is sin, but I do know that I cannot let you go out and endanger this child or decide to not let this child be born. That would be a greater sin,' she said. 'This is to be a secret. No one should know of this.' She didn't ask me who the father was. I think back and am grateful that no questions were asked and no answers given.

Perhaps she knew, perhaps everyone did. I didn't volunteer any information, not after the phone call I had received, a phone call that had shaken me completely. A call during which a sobbing female voice at the other end accused me of having already destroyed her marriage and now destroying his political career. His political rivals had got wind of his Angrez mistress and were having a field day with that information. 'Stay away from my husband,' the voice had told me, the anguish seeping through the static. I told her I would and put the clunky black receiver back into the cradle. I realised I was pregnant some days later.

I was sent for the rest of my confinement to a safe house, which was a bus journey of a few winding hours away, of a drive higher and deeper into the mountains. I stayed there for the six months leading up to the birth of Millie, and returned to the school a couple of days after I had delivered her. I was not allowed to take her. She would be placed in a caring home which had been denied the pleasure of an offspring, I was told. Maybe it was for the best, I thought, while handing her over to my caretakers until they found a home to place her.

Strangely, I had no attachment to Millie. Millicent, I'd named her. After my mother. The name stayed. She took on the McNally when she was eighteen, when she tracked me down after a childhood of growing up in foster homes and came to live with me. All I noticed of her when she was born were her eyes, which were her father's, and her skin, which was mine. Her features were yet too unformed for me to figure out if she took after me or her father. I'd had no contact with him ever since I'd been shifted there. Six months of complete isolation. No mails. No phone calls. No contact with the outside world. Within a few days of giving birth to her I was on a bus back to Datham Hall.

A bunch of letters awaited me when I returned to my room. All written in the same slanting, pressured hand, the tone of each letter getting increasingly desperate and then angry, before finally turning sad and despondent. These letters hadn't been forwarded to me. I hadn't written to him either; it seemed pointless. It would put him in a situation where he would be obligated to take charge of me and the baby and I didn't want that from him. Love, when tempered with obligation, becomes a chore, a drag on the senses, evaporating the effervescence of the emotion. It seemed better to me to closet myself away, far away from it all, and return like nothing had changed, except a few additional silvery lines on my stomach, visible only if you looked very closely, and in bright light.

I didn't reply to those letters. I kept them in the same envelope I put Millie's photographs in. When school reopened, Saudamini didn't return. Gentle enquiries informed me that she had been withdrawn from the school and placed in a school closer to home, where her mother could visit her regularly, a school for girls from genteel families. For one insane moment I toyed with the idea of applying for a teaching position in that school, anything in order to risk catching a glimpse of him again, but restrained myself with great difficulty. The semesters passed, blending into each other, the senior students passed out, new students came into the lower classes, teachers retired, new ones joined and quit when they got married. I remained the only constant. I had nowhere to go, and no one to go to.

Some years later, I received a letter. A thick letter from a legal firm. It informed me in curt legal terms that Ranvijay had passed away in a tragic suicide, a single gunshot to the head, and I had been mentioned in his will. I had been left a lumpsum of what seemed to be enough funds to keep body and soul together till the end of my life. My hands shook as I read the letter. The cheque enclosed fluttered to the ground. The words 'passed away' and 'gunshot' spun around in my head. The bile rose to my throat. I jumped up and ran out to the verandah beyond the corridor and heaved out all I had eaten for lunch onto the neatly manicured hedge that fringed the open ground. I leant against the pillar to steady myself. The nurse was called for, I was led shaking towards the sick bay. Later, the ayah returned a rectangular leaf she said she had found on the floor of my room. The cheque. For a moment I contemplated tearing it up. But then I didn't. It was guilt money. And it belonged to Millie, whenever I could give it to her.

Chapter 19

THE DOOR TO Nina's room stayed locked all through December. No apparitions manifested. Winter set in swiftly, bitingly cold, with sheets of grey gloom draping the rolling hills, the wait for the snow to fall excruciating.

Sumit didn't return. He called once, to tell me his grandmother had passed away and he had taken up the job of a television journalist. I sometimes saw him when I switched the television on, reporting on political news from Delhi. His hair was no longer tumbling past his collar and the four-day stubble that had been his signature look was gone. He was a stranger in a suit on television, a familiar face but not the person I knew, the person who had lived in my home for a few months, who had become, in those few months, a part of my everyday. What I didn't tell him was that I had called his grandmother after he had left, and that she could barely speak, her voice was frail and shaky. We had spent most of the conversation in an awkward silence, the tears rolling down my cheeks, splashing down on to the front of the sweater I was wearing, darkening into little tell-tale spots. 'Tell your daughter

who her father was,' she told me. 'She deserves to know.' I had
kept silent, reluctant to promise something I would not, could not
fulfil to a woman on her deathbed.

Nina came home for Christmas. Manikji and Kishan had been
deputed to fetch her again, and Manikji swam into the house, eyes
rolling, cursing cars and roads and the trials his wretched body
had to be put through in this old age. Millie was to come down
to India, but was roped into a last-minute charity fund raiser and
had to cancel her travel plans.

I hadn't been keeping well, not since the fall. The ankle was
never the same, and the stomach was constantly complaining. 'Why
have you lost so much weight, Grams?' Nina said, when she saw
me. 'Aren't you eating well?'

'I don't really feel so hungry these days,' I replied, unwilling
to tell her what was really afflicting me. I didn't know what it was
myself, but I had a fair suspicion.

I could feel something within me rotting, a wracking pain
tearing me up, and the inability to keep anything down. Constant
retching up of blood had been supplemented with occasional blood
in my stool. I could feel my insides disintegrating with a malaise
that perhaps had a name, one that I dreaded to think of. I preferred
to let it take over and overpower me. The pain, when it came on
me, was unbearable – I would double over at the spasm, but it
would pass as swiftly as it came. I knew I needed to get it looked
into but I was reluctant at what I might find. Every time I threw
up in the bathroom, taking pains to disguise the sounds of my
retching with flowing water, I could feel bits of me disintegrating.
I would throw up and lean against the window adjoining the little
basin in the bathroom, looking through the slatted panes to the
grey white peaks of the mountains in the distance, impassive in
their calm acceptance of the mortality around them.

I had Manikji buy the required groceries and the meat from
the market, decrying the rise in the rates of every single item, and

supervised the preparations carefully, sitting in the kitchen while getting Nina and Bimla to do the actual cooking. The Tipsy pudding layered with sponge cake, custard, pieces of fruit and a liberal serving of wine that soaked it, the Christmas pulao with raisins, the cutlets, the chicken curry, the mulligatawny soup, recipes I remembered from years of helping in the convent kitchen, and lavish spreads at the long wooden table for the staff who stayed back during Christmas at Datham Hall.

The house was cold, parts of it colder than it was outside. I could see the mist caressing the window panes, fogging them up so that everything outside was cloaked in a grey veneer of indistinctness. The bare trees outside were blurred, the grey swept over them mercilessly, until they merged into the darkness beyond which the clouds did not allow the eye to see.

Next year, Nina might not be here to spend Christmas with me; she would have passed out of school and moved to college, where, I didn't know. Delhi, Mumbai, London. She would no longer be a few hours away from me. I could feel the energy drain out of me in skeins that swirled around me, raising the hair to static levels of dandelion fuzz, ripping through my fingers as nips of faint sparking, falling around me in the form of dried skin, flaking off as the fabric moved against it as I got dressed to receive our visitors. I pulled on thermal-wear under the trousers and wrapped myself in a soft cashmere shawl with an exquisite paisley pattern which had been a gift from an ex-student, over the only good sweater I had left. It was one of my most precious shawls, one I'd used to wrap my growing belly when I had been carrying Millie. The dampness outside seeped into the walls and despite the kindling crackling away in the fireplace in the living room, the rest of the house was encased in the sodden, overbearing damp chill that winter brings, breaking out the plastering in patches in odd corners.

Nina was bubbling over with excitement, checking the pathway every few minutes to see if Dr Sanyal had arrived. I noted her excitement with a frown. When the red car finally drew up on the road outside, an indistinct blur against the fogged-up window panes, she ran to the door, unmindful of the chilly draughts of wind she let in when she opened it wide. He bustled in, rubbing his hands against the chill and heading gratefully towards the heater that occupied prime position in the living room. 'My bones are frozen, this feels good.'

'So how are you, Nina. Down for the holidays?' he asked her. She smiled and told him she was well and indeed, she would be staying till the end of January. 'Good day, Mrs McNally,' he said, heartily, as I entered the room, 'I trust you have had no further, er, *incidents* since? No sudden falls, no surprise intruders in your bedroom?'

'None at all,' I assured him, 'It has been calm for a while, else there would have been no other option for me but to move out.'

'Hopefully, it won't come to that, and I trust whatever it was has gone back to wherever it came from.'

The bones in the pit behind the house had been removed, I realised, by the police and whether a coincidence or not, the strange dreams, the apparitions, the sounds in the house, had all stopped. Or was it just lurking, gathering strength, planning its next move?

'Can I offer you something to drink? A little early in the day, but it is Christmas, for whatever it is worth. I might not get into church, but I don't mind the festivities.'

He accepted a snifter of brandy.

He was entertaining company that day, Dr Sanyal, and it turned out he knew Colonel Dayal and his wife who joined us a little later, bringing with them some pot roast and dessert. The gathering turned out to be quite a jolly one, with much local gossip being shared, spirits going high as the bar was steadily depleted of its meagre resources despite Colonel Dayal having brought in a couple of bottles of the good stuff procured at the

Army canteen at prices that had most of the residents vying to be in his good offices.

Somehow, in the course of the afternoon, the conversation turned towards the strange events in the house over the past few months. 'Are you still looking at selling and moving out?' Colonel Dayal asked, his wife, listening in intently, nursing her third gin and tonic with the same kind of care she would have, in the distant past, lavished on an offspring.

'I don't think so,' I replied. 'It has been pretty calm for a few weeks.'

'And it will be difficult to find a buyer too, given that everyone around in these parts knows about the incidents now, thanks to your very loquacious Man Friday who has been telling all and sundry about them at the local tea stall and in the market,' he added. 'But as long as the activity has stopped, I guess we shouldn't complain.'

'Let's drink to that – a year of peace and no otherworldly manifestations and many more happy gatherings in this house.'

The doorbell rang. A car had driven up, unnoticed, on the grey, damp strip of road outside, bearing the ubiquitous yellow license plate of the tourist vehicle. Manikji emerged from the kitchen where he was helping Bimla sort out the crockery to be laid on the table and exclaimed in delight, 'Arey aap! Bibijee, Sumit saab aaye hai…'

I struggled to my feet, my hand searching automatically for the cane I had placed next to my chair when I'd lowered myself into it. Without me realising it, the cane had become an integral part of me. Dr Sanyal was swiftly out of the room before anyone could react and they hugged and pulled away, a palpable tension between the two of them, a tension that made onlookers feel like they were intruding on the moment. I broke the silence, which had suddenly turned awkward. 'What a pleasant surprise, Sumit!'

He hugged me warmly, 'So good to see you, Mrs McNally.' He drew away and looked at me. 'Why are you looking so thin? Have you been unwell? Doctor, haven't you been taking care of her?'

I laughed. 'I'm perfectly fine, just age catching up with me.'

Nina smiled awkwardly, wishing him a Merry Christmas with barely concealed antagonism, her gaze shifting between him and Dr Sanyal with a wary, dawning recognition of something I had seen a long while ago and acknowledged. 'How long are you here and I hope you're planning to stay with us?' I asked.

'Why should he stay with us?' Nina interjected, rather rudely, before he could reply.

'I'm here just for a couple of days, and I'll find myself a room in town, it is off-season now, it shouldn't be a problem at all,' Sumit replied. 'I'd just dropped by to meet you, Mrs McNally. I had something I needed to hand over to you.'

'Do join us for lunch, and I'm so sorry about your grandmother,' I added, hugging him tightly, knowing that the one tie that connected the two of us to a different era was no more. 'But let's chat after lunch.' I was reluctant to speak about the past in the presence of Colonel Dayal and his wife, who was now, frankly a little glassy-eyed and laughing inappropriately at just about everything, and being unnecessarily flirtatious with the two young men, neither of whom were stepping a line beyond the perfectly polite courtesy of a public situation. They left after lunch, walking down the grey, damp path with slow measured footsteps, conscious that their legs were uncoordinated with alcohol and the path was treacherously slippery.

I settled on the sofa, stretching my aching legs in front of me, discarding notions of propriety now that I had only my granddaughter and my doctor around, and a boy who could be my grandson, in some distant convoluted manner of connection. Dr Sanyal was just beginning to rise rather reluctantly from his comfortable position in the deep armchair to leave, when Sumit went to the passage in the lobby area and returned with an envelope from his duffel bag. 'This is for you. My grandmother wanted you to have it. She really wanted to meet you, you know.'

I took it silently from his hands. It was a bundle of letters. All mine. All written to his grandfather. 'What's that?' Nina asked, hovering around, 'And why did your grandmother want Grams to have it?'

I looked at Sumit, a silent plea in my eyes. 'His grandmother and I were friends, these are old letters of correspondence between the two of us.'

'How cool is that. May I read them?' she asked, reaching her hand out to take them, complacent in her assumption that she would not be denied.

I moved them away from her reaching hand with an instinctive gesture of self-preservation. 'No,' I replied, rather sharply, 'You may not. These are not letters I would like to share.'

'That's strange, Grams, why would you not want me to read these letters? Unless there's something in them that you don't want me to know.' Her brow creased.

I beckoned Manikji across, handed over the key to my desk and asked him to place them within, and return the key to me.

'All in good time,' I told her. 'You may read them when I'm dead and gone. It won't matter to me then, and frankly, I have the feeling it isn't going to be much of a wait.'

She looked at me, puzzled, and then at Sumit. Dr Sanyal had moved to the window, looking unseeingly at the grey afternoon outside, seemingly nonchalant but his body language tense and impatient, almost like he couldn't wait to get out of the house.

'I'll take your leave now, Mrs McNally,' Sumit uncurled himself from the sofa next to me, and towered above me, dropping down for a moment to hug me, in a stilted manner. I smiled, and said my goodbyes to him and then to Dr Sanyal, who had moved from the window to the main door, and now was waiting politely by the door to leave.

Something flashed in Nina's eyes, anger, frustration, rejection, I couldn't fathom what it was. There was something that was discussed between the two of them that I could never know, only guess.

She cleared the table in silence, thoughtful and sulky, her eyes refusing to meet mine, a sharp, petulant line unpleasantly furrowing her brow as she kept her thoughts to herself, her dismay cloaked under politeness. Dr Sanyal and Sumit left together, the yearning between the two of them tangible and real.

Nina watched them leave and I watched the emotions play themselves out across her mobile face. Bitterness had twisted her face into something ugly. Her eyes were sparkling with the rush of tears that she was carefully holding back until she went into her room. Unrequited love could be agonising, and debilitating. Was this love, or was this a mere crush that was morphing into a dangerous obsession?

That night there was a wary silence in the house, a silence that was tempered by the hissing of the wind and the howl of the owls that swooped around on the wind. I was awakened by a screaming voice that registered from a distance. I blinked my eyes open and realised it was Bimla screaming for me. I sat up in my bed, feeling the body react slowly, as if it was swimming through slush. The door of the bedroom burst open and Bimla rushed in, trembling, 'Bibijee, Bibijee…Nina bitiyaa….'

'What happened to Nina?' I pushed my unwilling limbs out of the bed as quickly as they would move. I pushed my leaden feet into the warm fluffy slippers I'd left at exactly the spot my feet would hit the ground again in the morning, feeling a sense of dread sinking into my intestines. A cold clamminess rose from the pit of my stomach and coiled itself around my heart and began a persistent squeezing and releasing that made me breathless.

'She's unconscious… I went in with her hot chocolate and she was unconscious on the bed…'

The froth had bubbled up at the edge of her mouth and hardened there, choked in her gullet, her own vomit. My feet moved at a speed I would have not suspected they had in them. Manikji was on the phone at the landing as I passed. 'Daktarsaab ko phone kiya…'

Everything began slowing down in the terrible manner that marks the presage of something ominous. I looked in at Nina, lying on the bed, her head hanging off the side, her hands limp by her sides. The brown bottle of the prescription sedatives I took occasionally when I couldn't sleep was on the side-table next to the bed, the cap placed carefully next to it. It is funny how the mind takes in all the little details while the world is collapsing around you, how vignettes stay frozen in your memories when the moments have long passed away into the compartments in the mind that keep them accessible when needed, readily or not.

This was the scene that would stay in my mind long after she had been taken away in the ambulance that had come screeching down the road, with Dr Sanyal jumping out and carrying her himself, not waiting for the attendants to bring the stretcher down the gravel pathway, of Sumit looking on with an expression of what could only be regret. Nina lying on the bed, her head dropping off the side, her hands hanging limply down her side, a faint froth at the edge of her lips and her eyes open and unseeing, her face tinged with the beginnings of a delicate blue, her nails darkening. And standing beside her, the shadow, the faintest shadow of a woman who stood there mocking me for my inability to protect my only grandchild, to know that she was on the verge of taking her life for a reason I could barely comprehend.

Millie flew down two days later, alone. Her face was ashen and grim, the cheekbones standing out sharply, her face suddenly thinner, leaner, more haunted. There were dark circles under her eyes, she wore dark glasses and a blank expression. There was an email she'd received from Nina she told me, sent moments before she'd emptied the bottle of pills into her mouth and swallowed them down with little or no water. She made me read it. It was an anguished email, disturbed, incoherent. It wasn't the Nina I knew, this was another person, a girl on the edge, tormented by an obsession with an older man who didn't want her. When her ashes came back from the crematorium in a single urn, Millie held them and sobbed, deep, gasping sobs.

When Dr Sanyal came by to offer his condolences, she slapped him across his face and spat at him. 'She was crazy about you,' she yelled in an uncharacteristic loss of self-control I had never seen in her. 'You led her on... she told me everything, I have her email telling me everything.'

Dr Sanyal stayed silent. The only sound in the room was my breathing, which was heavy and rasping now. 'That's not the truth, I did not lead her on. But this is not the time to discuss it,' he said in a shaky voice. He then turned around and left the room without saying a word. Millie turned to the wall and put her head to it. When she turned back, her face was wet with tears.

Millie left the next day, carrying the urn in her arms, swaddled in a soft baby blanket, almost as if she was carrying an infant in it. When she stepped into the hired tourist taxi to take her back to Delhi, from where she would get on a flight to London, she looked at me for a long moment. Perhaps it was then that I knew I would never see her again. That she would never come back to India.

'Wait, Millie,' I called, as the taxi went slowly down the road, out towards where it would wind down the mountain roads and join the main road taking her lower and lower towards flatter lands, 'I need to tell you something, I need to tell you who your father was.' My words blew away with the wind. She would never know. Perhaps it was for the best, I thought.

I was back to where I'd begun in my life. Alone. Bimla and Manikji were still with me, they were my guardians against slipping into a ferocious loneliness that would eat away my will to live. Death didn't frighten me, it was living on that did. Living through a retinue of days and nights which blended into each other, with no purpose other than chalking out the march of time. I deserved this, I told myself, this end of my days surrounded by nothing other than isolation.

Chapter 20

THE NEW YEAR came upon us silently, creeping upon me with the suddenness of the change in date on the cheque book when I sent Manikji into town to do my monthly withdrawals from the bank. Millie would transfer a certain amount into my bank account at the end of every month, and it supplemented the humble pension I received from Datham Hall. There was nothing transferred this month. I would have to tighten my purse strings. Or perhaps I could take in a boarder to supplement my funds. We could do without a few luxuries, the meals would be frugal and we could use things sparingly, I told myself. I did try calling Millie a couple of times, but she neither took my calls, nor called back. All I wanted to know was whether she was alright. I emailed, I received no reply. The days passed.

The house was surviving yet another winter and so was I, but my survival was fragile, like the house. An evil cough had lodged itself in my lungs and was digging demon shears into my chest. I felt the house settle down to another presence in it, a presence that hadn't made itself felt again visibly but was no less real.

Someone or something that lurked in dark corners in passages, at a spot behind the curtains where a sudden chill grabbed you and shut down your bones despite the heater in the room being set to high. I rarely stepped out all through January. I could feel myself welding into my bones, my body shrinking into rag and flesh, pitifully marionette-like in my jerky, uncoordinated movements. I took to sitting all day by the window, looking on at the grey sky outside, the clouds sifting shape, my tongue too leaden for appetite, my intake decreasing by the day while Manikji and Bimla worried about me, bringing in priests and the local vaid to take a look at me. I spent my days leafing through photo albums with pictures of Nina. Sometimes, when I woke in the morning, I imagined her still at school, a phone call away, a few hours away and then the fog in the mind would clear and I would remember, with a wrench, that she was too far to be reached. Not in this life.

Sometime at the end of February, the doorbell rang at noon. I was sitting in the parlour by the tiny fireplace, which was unlit right now, as the heater had been moved from the living room to this room, which was smaller and easier to heat. We were through with the worst of winter, and I hadn't stepped out beyond the front gate all through it. Sometimes, even coming to my front porch seemed like an effort. At least when I had the dogs, I forced myself to take them for a walk, but when they died a couple of years ago, I'd lost all motivation to step out. Manikji announced Dr Sanyal with an uncertain air. I asked him to be shown to the living room. I hadn't seen Dr Sanyal since that day at the hospital morgue. I'd often almost picked up the telephone myself to call him, but my hand had wavered and pulled itself back. There was nothing to be said anymore, there were questions I didn't want to ask because I didn't want the answers to them.

I was down with a slight fever that day since the morning, a cold and the beginnings of what seemed like a mild flu. I had taken a pill but knew the fever would return. My skin was itchy and paler than it normally was. My mouth was dry, making it difficult to move my tongue. He looked at me concerned, doing a quick pulse check, forgetting for the moment, the wary awkwardness with which we acknowledged each other.

'You have lost a lot of weight,' he said in the stern voice he reserved for admonishing patients who didn't follow his advice. 'Have you not been eating well? Have you had your sugar levels checked recently? I think we need to run some tests on you. Why didn't you call me?'

Indeed, why hadn't I, I asked myself. I wondered why I had been content to continue feeling increasingly unwell, watching my state of decline, almost from the outside, checking to see how long it would be before I finally went. The sugar levels had not been monitored for a while, the effort to trek to the diagnostic clinic had been too much and I had been lazy about calling for a house visit for samples. I felt like a blanket of darkness had been pulled over me. I had no urge, no desire to do anything, to go anywhere, to step out of the house. Within me, something knew that this was it. I was just waiting, counting the days, for the end to come upon me.

He had lost weight since I'd last seen him, his expression was decided. There was something he had come to talk with me about, he said. He made a few calls asking for the pathology lab in town to send someone across to take my blood and urine samples the next morning, and then settled back in the small armchair that had been built for fussy diminutive women. Dr Sanyal looked conspicuously ill at ease in it, his knees sticking out, his tall torso looming.

'For a while I had been debating about whether I should move out of this town and go to a more mainstream location to practice, Delhi perhaps or Kolkata. I have made up my mind now. I am moving to Delhi the earliest I can.' I kept silent, knowing that there was nothing I was expected to say, but there was something that I was meant to hear, something that would perhaps be even more painful than what I was expecting to hear.

'I'm here today, because there is something I needed to clarify before I leave. I don't know what you know or what Nina or your daughter has told you, but I need you to know my side of the story.'

I sighed and closed my eyes; the pricking of tears beginning to well up and slide down kept me from opening them.

'I did know Nina had a crush on me, and I very clearly told her that this was crazy and I would not encourage it. I knew I was the reason she kept coming down every chance she got. She would drop in at home, telling you she was going out for a walk. She thought she was in love with me. I must assure you that I did not encourage her at all. I know she is underage and secondly...' he paused awkwardly, '...I was not interested in her. I must assure you that at no point was there any inappropriate sexual contact between me and her.'

The story tumbled out. Of a man who was not drawn to women, who was adored by a will-ful girl, who treated him like a challenge, something that wasn't hers for the taking unlike the boys she came in contact with at school, boys who were battling each other to gain her favour. And a refusal to take a no, despite the fact that he had explained to her, patiently, that it couldn't be. That it wasn't just the age difference between the two of them that was the reason. Of her throwing herself at him on the drive to her school.

'I liked her as a person, but I was not attracted to her. But she refused to understand. I didn't want to spell out to her just why I was not attracted to her. I hate to tell you this, Mrs McNally, but Nina was not the innocent, young thing you thought her to be.'

And then, that day at Christmas lunch, the reason for her being rejected became obvious to her. It had been staring me in the face, but I somehow never quite acknowledged it. He rose slowly, with feet that seemed unwillingly leaden, came forward and took my hand in his gentlest manner, so gentle that it made me aware of how brittle I had become. 'So in case I don't get to see you again, goodbye, Mrs McNally. I'm sorry it had to come to this.'

The pain in my chest was almost physical, I winced at the suddenness of it. But I knew, within myself, that what he had told me was the truth. How much of it he had varnished over, and how much he had left unsaid I did not know or care to know.

'Goodbye, Dr Sanyal,' I said, steeling myself. 'I hope Delhi treats you well.' Conscience is such a malleable thing, we mould it to what is convenient to us, snipping off bits that don't quite suit us, and wrapping around the prickly parts. There are layers and layers to people, even if you think you know them through and through, even if they are connected to you by blood and flesh and the deep bonds of genetic coding, there would always remain some areas that are off-limits for you, some parts of their selves that remain buried deep within, coming out only when they have a limited audience, only when it suits them to reveal themselves. Hadn't I done the same with Millie and Nina, hadn't I fabricated my entire life to them?

He moved out quietly and shut the door behind him. The cup of tea by my side had gone ice-cold, rendering it undrinkable. I put my head down on the table and wept silently. The strength had ebbed out of my body. There was nothing to look forward to anymore, nothing worth fighting for, to live for, anymore. The manuscript lay incomplete on my table; I hadn't typed a word in the past few weeks. I could feel myself shutting in on myself, the hands trembling, the limbs shaky, the thinking suddenly disoriented and panicky at times, at others crystal clear and lucid.

Dr Sanyal left town soon after, I heard. I didn't hear from him again. Or from Sumit. The bundle of letters he had handed over to me was safely in my drawer, under lock and key. I never read them, I didn't want to go back to the crazy, infatuated fool I had been back then.

The door to Nina's room stayed resolutely shut. I dared not open it, I feared I would collapse with grief if I saw the things that belonged to her. I remembered the face at the window sometimes, staring into my eyes with its red, pupil-less eyes, the voice in my head, calling out to me, its voice sibilant, insistent, hypnotic, drawing me towards it despite every nerve of my body telling me to stay away, to block my mind to it. I had last seen it when we had found Nina, unconscious, her body limp and heavy, her eyes unseeing.

I was tired, just so tired. The body was giving up on me, the pain in the lower abdomen was increasing, the head felt heavy, disoriented. I could barely get out of bed to go to the bathroom and the need to go to the bathroom was stronger and more frequent than it had ever been. I found myself saying the Lord's Prayer in unguarded moments. I slept with the rosary under my pillow, and under the buttoned up sweaters I wore, which were beginning to hang on me. I found my hands curling around the Bible before I went to sleep. Was it a turning back to belief, I didn't know. What I did know is that as one grows older and feels the end drawing nearer, lurking around in the shadows behind cupboards, in the swish of the curtains on a breezy day, in the darkening of the shadows as the day ends and the night falls, one needs more to hold onto than the knowledge that this will be all there is... that there is nothing beyond the moment when life snuffs out of one, and what one knows as the self will be obliterated into a void.

It was a cruel winter, the nights were long and relentless. The rasping cough had grabbed hold of my lungs and squeezed them into agony through the night where I would wake from a dream of Chaudharipore or of Datham Hall, gasping for breath as the coughing fits shook my body into tremors. I could feel my bones protruding through my skin as I slept. The body was on its way out, I could feel the rasping of my voice as my breath got shakier. Was this how death came, the hushed presence in the room, the acknowledgement within oneself that it was just a matter of time before the self disengaged from the body and squirted out into a dimension I didn't know. The cough became ugly, it became a death rattle. I pulled the blanket closer over my head and drifted back to sleep, feeling the greyness outside seep into my head.

Then the unexpected happened. One evening, as I climbed up the stairs to reach my study, I had a sudden crazed desire to open Nina's room and bury my face in her baby clothes. I missed her with a fierceness that was almost visceral. The lock was stubborn, unyielding, it felt red hot in my hands, raising blisters on my palm as I held it for a while, before it suddenly gave way, falling open by itself, without a key, almost like it decided to give up the fight to stay locked. The door swung open. I stepped in hesitantly. I flicked the light switch on. The evening had passed into night, the bulb sputtered weakly and flickered a warning I did not heed. I walked to the bed, to the window – it was shut, latched from the inside. Everything was as we had left it the last time we were here, the dust had accumulated over things proprietarily, cobwebs hung from the corners of the room. It barely took a couple of months for a locked room to go to seed.

Her cupboard was neat and organised. Unlike many youngsters, and I'd seen enough of them at Datham Hall, she was finicky about her things. A small pile of T-shirts. A smaller pile of jeans. Another pile of sweaters and cardigans, some of which she had outgrown but still insisted on holding on to. I sat heavily on the bed, my legs giving way under me. I closed my eyes and leaned back against the headboard, the effort of standing for so long making my head swim. A sense of anticipation gripped me, there was something that should happen about now, I thought, and waited, feeling my breathing grow laboured. Nothing did. For a long, long while. Then, at the exact moment I decided to get up and go back to my room, cold, clammy hands grabbed my ankles from under the bed, a grip that was impossible to break free from, the stench of rotting flesh filled the room, swam into my nostrils, asphyxiating me. And then, with a quick sudden jerk, those hands pulled me down, through the bed, into a dark, dank tunnel, through the floorboards, through the earth. I felt like I was falling forever, until I landed, with a thud, in a cold damp patch of earth, with what felt like bones next to me, I felt, rather sensed, the slithering of masses of writhing, crawling creatures slowly making their way over my body. The face hovered in the air over me. I could feel her put her cold, slimy hands into my chest and rip out my heart while it was still beating. At that moment, I knew who she was and why she wanted me. She had spent all her afterlife waiting for me. And fate had taken me right there, to the house where she had given birth to me, to the bed where she had slit her wrists in after I was born, I; the offspring of sin.

When I opened my eyes, I was in my own bed. The sky outside was dark, night had fallen, the moon was blotted by clouds, nocturnal sounds from unseen creatures wafted in through the shuttered windows. The wind hissed through the leafless branches of the trees outside, the branches scraping each other, the scratching sounds ominous. My chest felt emptied, the rattle of the cough that was plaguing me now strangely still. I tried to call Bimla, no voice came to my lips. I tried to reach out to press the bell to call her, my arms wouldn't move. I was held down to the bed by some force that wouldn't allow me to move my body of my own accord. This was what paralysis felt like, a sense of being locked up in one's body, willing oneself to move only to realise that one is trapped in a straitjacket of one's own flesh. My ankles were still raw from the unseen hands that had grabbed them, the smell of the fetid pit I had been dragged into was still on my body. This would never end – this creature, whoever she was, was determined to drag me into her world, the slimy dark pit from where she had emerged after years of lying, restless and tormented by a horror I did not know.

I felt the rays of a winter moon sweep in through the window and gently pass over my body, releasing it from the state it had been locked in. I moved the covers down and gingerly swung my feet off the bed onto the floor, while gently raising myself to a seated position. It was difficult taking control of my body again. I had to learn to work it every time I returned from the pit hole to the purgatory I had been dragged off to. My fluffy slippers were placed in exactly the right position I liked them to be in order for me to put my feet into them without the chill seeping into my toes. I stood up and stretched my body, feeling its fragility, understanding that deterioration was the way now. The body, the mind, they were all going, slowly and steadily. I padded up to my study and took the sheets of paper I had been typing and went down slowly to the sitting room where the remnants of fire were still burning in the grate.

'Bibijee,' Bimla was at the door of the room. She must have heard me drag myself up and down the stairs. 'Aap theek toh ho?' Her voice was wary, hesitant. She stood at a distance, which was uncharacteristic of her. As I looked up at her, she flinched, and drew back a step, cowering behind the banister, looking with dread at my face. Was there something she had seen that had so terrified her, I wondered. Whatever it was, I decided, it would not triumph over me. How had they found me, how had they taken me to my bed, had they cleaned the muck of the pit off me before changing me into my nightclothes? The mind was blank, I knew nothing of what had happened.

I assured Bimla I was fine and told her to go sleep and that, I would call for her if I needed her. She stepped back, the uncertainty in her settling around her like a disgruntled cloud. I heard her steps as she walked down the passageway into the back of the house where she and Manikji had their quarters and the quiet shutting of the door that signalled she was no longer lurking behind the door. I waited for an additional few moments before doing what I had come down to do. Page by page, I fed them into the fire and watched the sudden flare of iridescence as each page flared into black embers, all the memories I had carefully keyed in on the pages dissipated into black carbon ash that floated down the grate.

Then I fed in the letters Sumit had handed me. Unopened. I had not wanted to read them, to relive the madness of a relationship that wasn't meant to be. And the bundle of letters I had kept all these years, wrapped in muslin, tied with a ribbon, a soft pink ribbon that had yellowed with the years, letters which were proof that Millie was not a McNally. And the letter I had received, the one emblazoned with the embossed crest, which asked me to call. The embers glowed and then faded into grey ash, my secrets were safe. There was no proof anymore that I was not who I pretended to be. That I wasn't Mrs McNally. I wasn't the Chaudhari girl. I had no idea who I was. And Millie would never know that she wasn't who I'd told her she was.

The house was silent, hushed in anticipation of something about to unfold. I knew what I had to do next, and could feel the muscles of my stomach tensing up in a primeval fight-or-flee response.

I returned to my room, and sat heavily on the bed, feeling the skin burning where the unseen hands had gripped my ankles. I pulled up the flannel gown I had been changed into by Bimla, who had most probably found me passed out on Nina's bed. The area where the skin felt as though it were on fire had ugly, blistered welts. I felt my heart thudding in a beat that was echoed in my ears, loud enough to drown all the soft night sounds of the owls flitting about, the breeze rustling fervently against the bare-branched trees, the sibilant sounds of unknown creatures trawling the darkness beyond the path outside. I took out the bottle of pills Dr Sanyal had prescribed a few months ago in order for me to get a deep night's sleep when I'd complained about the sleeplessness. I hadn't mentioned the hallucinations and the apparitions that had then begun appearing with frightful regularity. I shoved all the pills down my throat at once, quickly gulping them down with mouthfuls of water. I gagged and sputtered with the ferocity of the chemicals rushing down my oesophagus into my stomach where they would dissolve and quickly shut down this body. It would be faster than the prolonged horror of the every day, the body falling to pieces by the illness eating away at my insides, the loneliness that engulfed me, the hands dragging me through nightmares every day. I would go to hell, I knew. If there was a hell. Or perhaps, I had lived out my own private hell here on this earth already.

I lay down on top of the covers and waited. I felt my breathing slow down, the blood slow its rushing around in my veins, the thoughts deferentially leave my mind and render a blank void of myself I couldn't bear to see. I could feel myself gagging, the nausea rising to my throat while the body couldn't react enough for me to rise and prevent myself from gagging on it.

And the snow, when it fell from a navy blue sky outside with a full moon shining in the midst of it, was soft, gentle, hushed. As hushed as the room was as I felt the breath leave my body. I felt myself float out to the ceiling and hover there, looking down at myself, shrunken and wizened in my bed, covered with blankets, my hair, spread white and stringy on the pillow, my skin yellowed, wrinkled, the cheeks hollowed out, the eyes open and staring, looking back at me, my expression bewildered, the vomit that had surged up in my throat and blocked my breathing trickling out from my half-open lips, the hands, claw like, gnarled and skeletal, still clenching the now empty bottle of pills. The death rattle in my chest stilled for this lifetime. The blood in my body had stopped coursing its way round the veins and the arteries, with the heart slamming itself shut, the organs shutting down, one by one, from lack of oxygen, the brain flickering into stillness, a deep black omniscient stillness which was far removed from what any dreamscape could offer, from any sedative-induced sleep. So this was what death was like, a silence, a shifting of consciousness, a lack of gravity, of bondage to the earth, a floating into a timelessness where nothing mattered, not even the self. And then I noticed her.

She was sitting in the rocking chair she often sat in, staring at me through the night and looked up at me on the ceiling. Not at me, or the carcass of me, lying on the bed, my eyes open, my mouth open, the hands frozen like chicken claws. She smiled, twisting her face into an expression that was almost maternal, and rose towards me in the air, her arms stretched out before her in welcome.

Acknowledgements

My first thank you, from the bottom of my ever-grateful heart, to Rupa Gulab, for her kindness and encouragement, always.

Thank you to Rashmi Menon from Amaryllis, who took this manuscript on and believed in it. And to Smita Khanna Bajaj who patiently sifted through it.

Infinite gratitude to Shinie Antony for her invaluable inputs to the manuscript. And the lovely cover I owe to Mishta Roy, thank you!

A special thank you to Sumant Batra and his gracious hospitality at the magnificent Te Aroha in Dhanachuli, Uttarakhand. The few days I spent there, in the splendid isolation of the mountains, with the unfettered view of the mighty Himalayas before me from the window of my room, was the genesis of the story that eventually grew into this book.

Thank you to my mother and my mother-in-law, for all the pahadland stories they told me, especially the ones with ghosts in them.

And as always, to my long-suffering husband Kirit. For putting up with me when I am writing a book. I can be most insufferable to live with during that phase. And I'm always, always in the thick of writing a book.